AN IRISH MAN'S LUCK

AN IRISHMAN'S LUCK

E. A. WHARTON GILL

A TALE OF MANITOBA

WILDSIDE PRESS

Originally published in 1914.

Published by Wildside Press LLC.
Visit us online at wildsidepress.com

CHAPTER I

A MANITOBA SPRING

'What a beastly spring—if it is spring,' grumbled Daisy Enderby, as she flattened the tip of her nose against the window-pane of the 'living-room' at the Dingle, and looked disconsolately at the mingled snow and slush which lay around the verandah, and which was all of the outside world that a steady drizzle left visible at five o'clock of the afternoon in the end of April.

'Why do you say "if it is spring?" Of course it is spring—to-morrow is the Second Sunday after Easter—what would it be if it wasn't spring?—Easter and spring are the same thing—light the lamp, child, and help me to finish this mending;' and Marion Enderby pointed to a large heap of socks, stockings, and other garments which need not be particularised, with which the table was covered.

'Mother says,' she continued, 'they always had primroses and violets at home on Easter Day, and how could they have primroses if it wasn't spring?' with which quite conclusive argument she resumed her work.

'That's all very well, I daresay, in the "Old Country," Marion,' retorted Daisy, making a final moue of disgust at the weather outside before joining her sister at the table, 'that's all very well, for where "April showers bring forth May flowers," and "Hark! Hark! the lark," and so forth and so on—spring maybe spring, and come in some particular time with some particular herald—the cuckoo, for instance—in that "happy land." I wonder which end of this stocking is the hole and which the legitimate entrance? I'm sure there's no difference in the size of them—and I wonder which particular variety of the weather we have had for the last three weeks you would like me to glorify as "balmy spring"—balmy, indeed! The week before Easter was so hot that our Barnardo pet said when he came in from the chores that he was all in a "muck—" '

'Stop, Daisy—I insist—you shall not repeat the land of expressions that boy uses—you know how mother objects.'

5

'Well, you know what he said, Marion, and it was quite true, and I saw a mosquito myself almost as big as a dragon-fly——'

'Don't be so ridiculous, Daisy, I know it was very warm then——'

'Very warm!—and the next Sunday Mr. Jordan came up to take our service in a snowstorm, and it was a foot deep by night, and all this week we have had hot days—cold days—and drizzle days alternately—but if you cling to the name—like Barkis—"I'm willin'," and spring let it be.'

'But seriously, Daisy, if you can be serious, I do hope we shall have some dry weather soon—for Bert says it will be a week before they can get on the land, and you know how little ploughing they did last Fall owing to the early frost, and it will make them dreadfully busy when they are able to begin—besides, we must try and do some spring cleaning.'

'Why should we do spring cleaning—if we don't have any spring?' retorted Daisy teasingly. 'Why not pretend, when the fine weather comes, if it does come, that it's summer, and that the spring cleaning is all done—we pretend such a lot of things.'

'I think, Daisy Enderby, if you look at the curtains on the windows and the colour of the whitewash on the walls and the dust on the pictures and books, even you can't pretend the spring cleaning—wet or fine, we *must* begin on Monday, so that Bert can help with the whitewashing before the outside work begins.'

'Oh, I know it's "needs must when"—when you speak like that—I only hope Dad will be busy in the granary or some other where while we do it—because he's not quite restful when there's agricultural "duty to be done—to be done," and he cannot be doing it from "dewy morn" to milking the cows while we are waiting for our supper.'

'I don't like to hear you speak in that flippant tone of your father, Daisy; if you knew how long and hard he had to work when I was a little girl and you weren't born, or only little more than a baby, you would understand how anxious he gets even now, when we are rather better off, if there is any set back on the farm.'

'Come, Merry dear, don't be angry; you know I was only joking, and there is Dad coming in from the stables—and the dear man is as like a Manitoba spring as Santa Claus is to Christmas, for the drizzle is turning to snow and he's mud to the knees, and snow to his crown, and his face is as bright and rosy with it all as a midsummer pippin—and he will want his supper before we have time to boil the kettle and set the table, so we'd better "rustle" '—with which objectionable last word Daisy started to sweep the contents of the table into a large basket as a preliminary step to preparing the evening meal.

While the two sisters are so engaged, we will take a slight glance at the other members of the 'Dingle' household. Their father, the younger son of a Leicestershire squire, of old family but small estate, finding himself at three-and-twenty with a patrimony of a few thousand pounds, an optimistic disposition, and no particular calling in life so long as it be spent in the open air, took to himself a wife. The young couple had grown up together —he at the Hall and she at the Rectory—and if it was not very worldly wise the young folks had mutual love which, perhaps after all, is the highest wisdom—in any case, it seemed nobody's business to make difficulties. William Enderby was his own master; and so long as they did not forget to put the *Times* by his plate at breakfast, and did not touch the litter of papers on his study table, the old Rector was quite content for his motherless daughters to settle any smaller matters, such as matrimony, to suit themselves.

Being happily married—what next? The rumours of the boundless possibilities of the Great West penetrated even to the rural parts of Leicestershire at the right moment, and offered the ideal solution of the problem— an estate—a patrimony—where the old Enderby stock could take new root in a new land and develop a worthy branch of the old Leicestershire tree.

The promise to the imagination had not been very literally fulfilled in the reality, and Mr. and Mrs. Enderby had shared to the full all the hardships and disappointments inevitable to the sudden change from the settled material and social conditions of the old land to the conditions of life in a newly opened up settlement on the prairies of the West.

The small capital of money was rapidly diminished in the acquirement of that most costly commodity—experience—and then followed a long period of struggle against the early frosts, the dry seasons, and other visitations of nature which so often seem sent to test the endurance of the pioneers in a new land. As the ready money went there came, of course, all the ugly offspring of such seasons—land mortgages, chattel mortgages, lien notes—the costly price of continuing the struggle till better times came.

They came at last, not only in the shape of good crops and a higher price for wheat, but also in the form of a legacy of a thousand pounds from a maiden aunt of Mrs. Enderby's, which paid off all but a small mortgage on a quarter section of bush and meadow land which Mr. Enderby had bought in the name of their only son, Bert, the week after he was christened Bertram Babington Enderby.

Though the money capital slipped away so easily in the early days, happily the larger capital of mutual love and confidence in the future remained, and if his friends may have had misgivings as to its truth, they never doubted Mr. Enderby's sincerity in maintaining that the two wisest things he ever did were to marry his wife and to homestead the 'Dingle,' and as he shakes off the wet snow from his coat and takes off his muddy boots in the 'lean-to' to-night, he has no greater anxiety than as to whether it won't be better to sow oats instead of wheat in the north ten-acre field if the weather does not 'let up' by the beginning of the week.

In the West, as elsewhere, where life is largely a struggle for existence, the heavier portion of the primeval burden of life falls on the wife rather than on the husband. Perhaps the most that can be said of Mrs. Enderby's attitude to Western life is that she accepted it as a dispensation of Providence—of Providence with quite a sincere and genuine large P—but it was an acceptance that varied with the circumstances of the moment, between a cheerful resignation and a reminiscent regret of the material comforts and social advantages of her childhood. Though the loneliness and household drudgery of the earlier days had robbed her cheeks of their bloom and dulled the vivacity of her spirits, large compensations had come in the later years from her children. So narrow and conservative is the sphere in which the character of the wifely and motherly type of woman develops, that it is probable that in all essentials Mrs. Enderby would have been the same at fifty if she had married a curate on a hundred and twenty pounds a year in a big city, and had passed in middle age to the comparative luxury of a small country living. It should not have been a matter of offence to her Canadian neighbours that Mrs. Enderby remained so steadfastly 'English,' for it was not the expression of any conscious sense of superiority or of a desire to be unneighbourly—she was simply herself.

Of the children, Marion, the eldest, developed early a fair measure of the capacity to run the house which rarely comes adequately to any but the Western born; Bert, two years younger, was in reality now, what his father had used to call him as a little boy when he followed him about the farm, his 'right-hand man'—a little too serious, a little too quiet for six-and-twenty, but that was the price which the West exacts of most of her sons who take a farmer's life seriously. Daisy—the 'baby' of the family, now twenty, was Daisy—a secret joy to her mother from her liveliness and high spirits—but a joy tempered by regret that Daisy rarely thought before speaking, and rarely spoke without shocking her mother either by the irreverent aptness of her adaptation of her scriptural knowledge to very secular circumstances, or by the facility with which she picked up indiscriminately the colloquialisms of the West, the East-end drone of the Barnardo chore boy, or the public school slang of the moment from her father's farm pupils and the other young Englishmen who were 'making good' or otherwise on farms of their own in the settlement. Of course Daisy was spoilt—it is the privilege and penalty of the 'baby' in a good many families—but a spoiling which is the result of a mother's unselfishness and a too tender love, is not the worst kind of spoiling in a world where remain sufficient harsh realities to prevent even the spoilt children of Earth from finding a too satisfying happiness in the dulciest of *dulce do mums*.

CHAPTER II

A DISTURBING PROBLEM

'I wonder what is making Bert so late,' said Mrs. Enderby an hour and a half later as they still sat round the table after supper; 'I do hope nothing has happened to him; it was quite early when he went down to Dawson's for the mail, and it is nearly eight o'clock, and it is so dark and the roads are so bad—I do hope——'

'Why, mother,' interrupted Daisy, 'what could happen to him?—Perhaps the mail was late getting up, or, what is more likely, he has gone into Jim Hardie's, and he is stopping there for supper, and they are having a nice comfortable bewailment over the horrid weather, I guess——'

'Daisy, dear!'

'Well, then, mother, I think we may as well wash the dishes and tidy up a little for Sunday, and if he has not had his supper, we can easily get it for him when he does come—but there is Rover barking down the lane—that will be Bert for sure.'

'Get the lantern, Sam, and take it down to the gate,' went on Mrs. Enderby, 'and if it is Mr. Bert, you can take the pony up to the stable, and then if you will get a pail of water from the well and put some wood to dry under the stove, you can go to bed—and, Sam, as it's Sunday, you need not get up till your master calls you in the morning—and there's Mr. Bert calling for the lantern.'

The Barnardo chore boy hurried out willingly enough to do Mrs. Enderby's behest, for he had a good home and lighter work than most of his fellows who were scattered among the farm houses of the settlement—of course, he had a grievance or he would not have been a 'chore' boy, and Sam's was the polite insistence with which Mrs. Enderby required his using Mr. and Miss in speaking of the members of the family, 'but you bet I don't do it outside,' Sam confided to Frank, the chore boy at the Hardie's —'it's just Bert or Daisy, without any of your blooming Misters or Misses then.'

A few minutes later Bert entered from the lean-to, where he had left his overcoat and riding-boots, and carrying a big bundle of papers and letters strapped together.

'Now, Bert,' cried Daisy,' give an account of yourself—here's the "mater" imagining all kinds of catastrophes that might have happened to you between here and the post-office—perils by mudholes—perils by old Mrs. Dawson's tongue—perils by——'

'Well—there's no peril of you forgetting the sound of your own tongue, Daisy,' said Bert good-humoredly,—'Yes, I've had my supper, mother, I had it at Jim Hardie's—I took some letters in for them as I came by, and they were just sitting down—and you know his way——'

'Oh, yes, we know his way—"Sit in and make yourself to home," ' mimicked Daisy—'and you forgot all about your anxious parents—mother thinking you were lost, and Dad that the English mail had not come.'

'Well, the English mail did come, and that is what made me later than I should have been, for I stayed talking over with Jim a letter that he had from England——'

'Jim Hardie a letter from England—why, whoever does he know in England?'

'If you'll only keep quiet, Daisy, for two consecutive minutes,' went on Bert deliberately, 'you shall know. You remember hearing about Miss Raye, mother, that used to teach the school up in "Sweden"—Jim met her up at Ole Swanson's where she boarded—well, she went home about two years ago, and this last winter she wrote to Jim saying that her brother was coming out to work on a farm before homesteading, and that she wanted to get a school till he was able to make a home for her on the homestead. Two or three letters have passed between them—I've been doing the writing for Jim——'

('This is getting thrilling,' murmured Daisy aside.)

—'and the upshot is that they—that is Miss Raye and her brother— sailed ten days ago, and will be in Minnedosa some time the end of next week—and there is a little difficulty——'

'As to which of you shall meet her at the station—if Jim Hardie goes his wife will be jealous, and if you go the mater will see visions of a bash- ful young man and a designing schoolmarm.'

'Daisy, dear,' said Mrs. Enderby mildly, 'do please let your brother fin- ish his sentence—I'm sure Mr. Hardie and Bert are just thinking of being kind to these poor people and helping them——'

'Oh yes, of course, mother, it's just the milk of human kindness—but I remember seeing Miss Raye once when she was out before at the show in Minnedosa, and she was an awfully pretty girl then—and a pretty face adds a little cream, as it were——'

'The trouble, mother, is this—young Raye is to work for Jim Hardie, and Jim and the two other trustees have engaged Miss Raye for the year for the Lakeside School, but there is a difficulty in getting a boarding-place for Miss Raye.'

'Couldn't the Hardie's take her?' suggested Marion, 'they have quite a large house, and——'

'I know,' said Bert, 'but Jim has a regular hired man and the chore boy, and then there will be young Raye and the children—it would make too much work for his wife—Jim suggested it, and talked of getting a hired girl to help, but I could see Mrs. Hardie didn't like the idea.'

'That settles that, then, for Mrs. Hardie's ideas count for the whole pile ——'

'For more than my ideas of English do with Daisy Enderby,' said her mother, 'but there are a number of other places, surely, where Miss Raye could find a suitable home—there is Mrs. M'Culloch's, a most motherly old lady, and old Mr. M'Culloch is an elder, and——'

'Yes,' broke in Daisy, 'the Shorter Catechism in the daytime and—have you forgotten the night you—I won't say slept—there last July, Bert —"how the hosts of"——'

'No, that would never do,' said Bert quite decisively, 'we did think of Dawson's—but then—it's the post office, and there is only the one sitting-room where everybody goes for their mail. I fancy Mrs. Dawson and Mary Ann might be kind enough in a way—and of course Miss Raye has lived in "Sweden," and is used to things—but old Dawson—it would not be a nice place for——'

'A nice girl,' finished Daisy for him, 'not unless she is interested in William of Orange, the Pope o' Rome, and has a sympathy for the lavish use of tobacco—otherwise than by smoking it.'

'I wonder, mother,' said Marion, who had remained silent during the latter part of the discussion, 'I wonder, mother, whether we might not have Miss Raye here—that is of course if she is quite a nice kind of a girl. She would be near her brother, and it would not be too far to walk to the school.'

'Oh, I don't think there is any doubt of her being quite a lady from your English point of view,' said Bert, 'her father was a clergyman, and she sent testimonials and certificates from Cheltenham Ladies' College when she applied for the school—Jim says she was a great favourite up in "Sweden" both with the children and the settlers. Ole Swanson wanted her to go back to their school again when he heard she was coming out, but she wants to be near her brother.'

'Don't you see, mother, that Jim Hardie and Bert are two dark conspirators who have made their little plot before we innocents knew anything about it. But, really, mother, as Dad says he will take no more pupils, why,

11

a girl would be better than nothing to liven us up a little, and I should dearly love to see Bert smitten for once.'

'Well, children, I really do not know what to say—poor girl—life is very rough here—and there used to be quite the best kind of girls at Cheltenham College when I was a girl myself—and her father a clergyman—but then clergymen's daughters are often very pretty and attractive—so your father used to say—and what she paid for her board would enable us to have one of Mrs. Peterson's girls in to do the washing and scrubbing—really, I do not know what to say,'—and Mrs. Enderby was quite distressed by the many conflicting vistas that opened to her view. 'It would be very nice if—then again it would not be so nice if—really, Bert, suppose we leave it over till to-morrow before we decide, and I'll speak to your father —of course, it must be as he says.'

'Bert dear,' said Daisy as she lit her lamp and kissed her brother goodnight, 'Bert, dear, you are becoming altogether too clever—you had better settle with Jim Hardie to-morrow as to who is to meet the young lady at Minnedosa and bring her home to the Dingle—Joe Bagstock was a mere child in slyness—though I'll spare Marion's nerves as to his way of putting it.'

CHAPTER III

ITS SOLUTION

The observance of Sunday in Manitoba has hardly yet settled into anything which can be described by a general term, sufficient in itself, as when we speak of an 'old-fashioned English Sunday,' or a 'Scotch Sabbath.' The first homesteaders mostly settled in groups, linked by ties of nationality or former neighbouring in the older provinces of Canada, and they brought with them the customs and ideals of their old homes.

The Scandinavian settlement in the bush to the North, Sweden as it was usually called, had a little Lutheran church where they held a Sunday-school all the year round, and church service when they happened to have a regular minister. Their young people danced frankly and with a good conscience of a Sunday evening—though the rumour of it was rather a scandal in the English-speaking settlements. West of the Enderbys the greater number of the settlers were Scotch Canadians who had brought from Ontario the Scotch Sabbath, a tendency to vote Grit and a capacity for getting, only equalled by their tenacity in keeping, what they got. Here and there, even among them, there would be a backslider from strict orthodoxy—but the backsliding itself was typical—neglecting the stables, maybe, for a day or two at the end of the week at busy times, and then setting the hired man to clean them out on a Sabbath morning—for the comfort of the cattle—and regard for the well-being of one's cattle is quite biblical. The views of the hired man have not been preserved.

Eastward of the English settlement, Irish Canadians, mostly from the Ottawa country, predominated. For some reason they did not maintain their national characteristics to the same marked extent as their Scotch neighbours—possibly from a lack of the same uniformity in religious views. Not quite so regular in their church-going—a little more latitude in Sunday visiting—more thrifty than most of the Old Country English in their farming, but open-hearted and open-handed if a neighbour had ill-luck on his farm or sorrow in his home. A strain of Orangeism ran through most of them, though softened and modernised in the younger generation by the broadening influences of Western life—still, here and there you would run across an old-timer from some backwoods settlement who preserved all the rancour and bitterness of the feuds of his youth, when a twelfth of July free

13

fight with the Black Irish was a retrospect to New Year's and an anticipation to the next anniversary of the glorious victory of the Boyne.

Sunday at the Dingle followed the old Leicestershire Rectory pattern as far as Mrs. Enderby's influence and circumstances would allow—morning service every other Sunday at the little English church a mile or two away, to which everybody went, and from which they returned to a cold dinner. In the afternoon Mr. Enderby retired to the curtained-off end of the room, dignified by the name of his study—to read. As he read in a recumbent position on a comfortable home-made lounge, and as he was not naturally a reading man, possibly he dosed a little too, though he would not admit it. Mrs. Enderby retired to her room to write home letters with similar probabilities. Bert and his sisters sat round the stove and read if it were winter, in the summer they would take their books and magazines out on the verandah where there was a hammock (usually appropriated by Daisy), and two or three old deck chairs in various stages of dilapidation and insecurity. More often than not two or three young Englishmen who were 'baching' in the settlement, would be asked up for dinner on church Sunday, or ride over during the afternoons on the off Sunday—glad to get away from the discomforts and loneliness of their own 'shacks.' They always met with a kindly welcome at the Dingle, and soon learned to recognise the fine shade of additional warmth in Mrs. Enderby's greetings to those whose visit to the Dingle was prefaced by attendance at the church service. It was a quiet, wholesome day, and its home atmosphere did more to keep many a young Englishman straight than would have been effected by a more rigid Sabbatarian observance. Sometimes a newcomer would vote it rather slow to Daisy, and suggest a little tennis, but even Daisy, if secretly sympathetic, knew her limitations.

The morning after the conversation in the preceding chapter brought a welcome change in the weather in the shape of a westerly wind and a clear sky. It also brought the fulfilment of Daisy's prophecy, for when Mr. Enderby and Bert had gone to the stables after breakfast, Mrs. Enderby announced to the girls that their father was quite willing for Miss Raye to board there, 'at any rate till we see—' as she added cautiously.

'Till we see whether she falls in love with Bert or tries to cut out Marion with——'

'Don't be ridiculous, Daisy,' said Marion sharply; 'mother means, of course, till we see if she fits in to our life here, and if father likes her.'

'I wonder what the brother is like—if they both play, we shall be able to have all kinds of tennis this summer without Marion having to victimise herself to make a fourth for doubles——'

'Well, Daisy, I would not trust too much to that,' said Mrs. Enderby, 'for if he is to work for Mr. Hardie he will not have much leisure for tennis.'

'I expect not; still Jim Hardie is awfully good-natured, and if I ask off for the young man on a Saturday afternoon sometimes, I guess I shall get my way—that is if Mrs. Hardie does not put her spoke in.'

'You had better leave that to your brother, Daisy,' said Mrs. Enderby quietly. 'In the meantime, Miss Raye can have the little west room, and we will clean that first this week and get Bert to whitewash it, and put up some shelves for her books, and a few hooks, and whoever goes to town to bring up their luggage can get a nice wire stretcher and a little dressing-table, and ——'

'I foresee that Miss Raye is going to be a much favoured person,' interrupted Daisy; 'you see, Merry, what it means to be a parson's daughter and to go to Cheltenham——'

'And when Bert comes in,' went on Mrs. Enderby, 'you had better ask him to go down to Mr. Hardie's this afternoon and arrange about meeting them in Minnedosa, and who is to bring them up to the settlement—and now, girls, you must hurry, for there are Bert and Sam coming in with the morning's milk, and the pans are to be scalded.'

Though quite astray as regards the motives, Daisy was undoubtedly right in her surmise that Bert had suggested the solution that was now accepted of the boarding-place difficulty. As they talked it over at the Hardie's supper-table the evening before, Mrs. Hardie had made her views quite plain in reply to a hesitating interrogative remark of her husband's, 'I suppose, little woman, you couldn't be managing?'

'If you are going to ask me to take her, Jim Hardie, you can save your words; I don't mind the brother, he can share the hired man's room, and one man, more or less, about the place does not make much difference—he'll be working and out of my way—but to have a schoolmarm with her fine English——'

'Well, well, little woman, we'll let that go.'

'Besides,' went on Mrs. Hardie, 'there are lots of folks in the settlement with more room and less work than I've got to do—but you men never think of your own wives.'

'I'll tell you what, Jim,' said Bert, 'suppose we leave it to-night, and I'll talk it over with my people at home—of course, I don't know, but perhaps my mother might ask Miss Raye up to the Dingle for a time, anyway till we see what can be done.'

'Well, it would be fine if she would, Bert, and I'm sure she would be more to home with your sisters than with any of us other folks.'

'And she would have our children for company on the way to school,' added Mrs. Hardie, recovering her good humour, 'besides a few dollars is always handy on a farm, and I'm sure I'd be glad for her to come over and see her brother of a Sunday or any time when he was not at work,' and so the matter was left.

CHAPTER IV

THE VAGARIES OF JACK DENNIS

Rosebank, as the Hardie homestead was called, was only some half mile away from the Dingle, and thither Bert Enderby made his way through a good deal of mud and slush in the course of the afternoon to tell Jim Hardie of the success of his plan and to arrange for the meeting of the newcomers at Minnedosa.

So far he was not conscious of any particular personal interest in the matter, and had been moved entirely by his natural willingness to help others out of a difficulty. It would be nice for Evelyn Raye and her brother to be near each other, and he felt satisfied that she would be a pleasant companion for his mother and sisters. Daisy's sly innuendoes as regards himself were quite uncalled for, and based entirely on that young lady's imagination. The wholesome round of farm toil, in which he was too interested to find it monotonous, coupled with a steady purpose to win, if hard work could do it, a release for his father and mother from the money worries that had pressed so hardly upon them in the earlier years, had left him little time for day dreams of his own future; as a result the other young Englishmen in the settlement summed him up as 'an awfully decent chap but rather slow,' while the Canadian girls charitably put down his indifference to their charms to 'those stuck-up sisters of his, who thought nobody was good enough for him to take to a dance or a picnic.'

With the Hardies he was on the easiest of good terms and a great favourite. With Jim he often exchanged work at the busy seasons of seeding and harvest, and he alone, of the Enderbys, was entirely a *persona grata* to Mrs. Hardie as being quite clear of all suspicions of English exclusiveness.

As a privileged person he passed round the front of the house and entered the lean-to without knocking, and was busy cleaning the wet mud off his boots with an old broom, when the inner door opened, and Jim stood in the doorway.

'Ah, Bert, I thought it would be you, when the old dog here didn't bark when the latch lifted—come right in—it's no use minding a bit of mud these days, and the wife has put some old mats round to keep the worst of it off her clean floor. Here's Tom Dennis here, and I put a handful of fire in

17

the stove, and we were having a quiet pipe and a chat, and I was telling about our troubles with the schoolmarm and all.'

'Well, I think those troubles are over for the present, Jim; glad to see you, Tom, don't get up—just shift those long legs of yours so that I can put my wet boots on the mat—no, thanks, Jim, I've got some cut tobacco here —well, Tom, how's "Connemara Farm" these days, and where's Jack?'

Tom Dennis, who had made some show of rising from the lounge on which he was seated when the door opened, contented himself with holding out a hand of greeting when he saw who the newcomer was—at the same time making room for Bert's feet by the side of his own mud-splashed riding-boots.

'Where's Jack? Jack rode down to Minnedosa with a couple of plough points to get sharpened yesterday morning, and he came home, or providence and the old mare brought him home, without them, some time through the night, and whether he left the points behind or dropped them in Sanderson's Creek, I'm——'

'Well, well, it's too bad,' interrupted Jim hastily, 'but for the points, I could be letting you have a couple till you go to town.'

'Oh, it's not the bally points I'm vexed about—if only he were not such an ass—but I'm not the one to preach about that—but say, Bert, it's something fresh to find you interesting yourself in the new schoolmarm.'

'Oh, nonsense, Tom,' said Bert as he seated himself by Tom's side on the lounge and proceeded to fill his pipe, 'you see the brother is going to be with Jim here, and——' Bert broke off for a moment to strike a match —'and you can't let a girl of that kind just go anywhere—so, Jim, as I came to tell you, my mother will take Miss Raye, at any rate for a time, till we see how it suits.'

'Now, that's fine—just fine, I told the wife I was sure your Ma would help us out, and I guess it will suit alright—for they all say up in Sweden there is no one like Miss Raye for getting the children on and being friendly with everybody, and with her brother here and your sisters at the Dingle, she'll soon be right to home.'

'Oh, the girls seem quite taken with the idea, and Daisy is planning all kinds of tennis already——'

'I'll be bound she is,' said Jim, 'and Tom here and the rest of the boys will be wishing they were in your place, Bert——'

'Oh, I don't expect she will trouble me much, Jim; that kind of thing is not much in my line, but how shall we do about bringing her up from town?'

'Well, I was just talking to Tom about that when you came in—for I'd kind of got it in my mind that your Ma would not see us stuck—you see, there will be two of them, and they are sure to have a whole caboose of

18

boxes and such like. I'll have to take the wagon, and there'll be no room for a second seat, and even if it keeps fine overhead, the roads will be main heavy up at this end, and we'll be pretty long on the road.'

'That's so,' said Bert thoughtfully, 'I might take my own team and your democrat, if you'd let me have it, Jim, and I could bring both of them up comfortably and some of the smaller packages—but then—you see, Jim, we are awfully behind with our spring work, and it means losing a day on the seeder if my team is away.'

'Tell you what, Bert,' said Tom, 'why shouldn't I bring up the school-marm? I'll have to go down anyway at the end of the week for grub, and Saturday will suit as well as any other day—and I could bring Miss Raye up in the buckboard and let the brother come up with Jim. It's not a very swell outfit, but the old mare can travel, and we'd be up in half the time the wagon will take.'

'I wonder if that would be alright, Jim?' asked Bert rather dubiously, 'I don't doubt you'd travel—trust an Irishman for that—but you're not what I'd call a careful driver, Tom, still, if you get home safely she would never know the risks she'd run—I suppose it would be quite—proper—from my mother's point of view?'

'Now listen to that, Jim,' replied Tom in a most aggrieved tone of voice, 'listen to that—when I've not had a spill with the buckboard since I don't know when——'

'Not since you pitched old Dawson into Sanderson's Creek last Fall ——'

'Come, Bert, that's not fair to me and the old mare—that was only half accident—the old man had been celebrating with some cronies in town and had bored me so with his yarning about Ontario, that I let the mare take the bank where it was a bit steep, and he just rolled over the wheel into the creek—it was the funniest thing you ever saw, Jim,' and Tom laughed at the recollection—'but seriously, Bert, I'll just make myself as pretty as I can, and I'll not go within three inches of the edge of a culvert—tell you what, Jim, I believe he's beginning to want to go himself.'

'Well, if you'll promise to be careful, Tom, and my mother thinks it all right, I guess we had better settle it so.'

'Settled it is, then, and I'll walk back to the Dingle with you, Bert, and see your mother and get something to read, if you've any English papers, and then I'll come back here and tell Jim—will that suit you, Jim?'

'Sure, and you'll be back to have a bit of supper before you go home— I'll tell the wife you're coming, and we'll expect you.'

'That's the decentest little chap in the settlement,' said Tom, when the two young men had left Rosebank and were walking down the lane to the town line, 'he's as anxious to make Miss Raye comfortable and happy as if

19

he was paid for it. I've seen quite a lot of him this "break-up" and spring—drawing hay together from his place up north, and it's done me more good than going to church.'

'Perhaps you never gave the church quite a fair show,' put in Bert quietly.

'Well, perhaps not—anyway Jim has made me do a little quiet thinking for myself—and I wanted to have a chat with you, too, Bert—you see there are some things you can understand better than any one who is not used to our Old Country way of looking at things.'

'Of course, of course, Tom,' said Bert sympathetically, and impressed by his friend's evident earnestness, 'you know you can bank on me if I can help you out—what's the trouble?'

'Well, there's not exactly any trouble so far—but you see—confound it —it's hard to talk without seeming to cant—you see, Jack and I have made a deuce of a poor return for all our people have spent on us, and up to this spring we've never made a dollar or done what you or Jim would call a decent day's work since we went on our farm—it's a beastly shame,' and Tom gave an impatient flick to his riding-boots with his whip.

'Still, if you and Jack buck up now—you've got a good farm, and none of us will see you stuck if you want seed grain, or anything we've got——'

'I know, Bert, I know, and I'd ask you to lend us a hand just as readily as I know you would do it—but you see, it's not quite that—I could worry out of the work end by myself—it's Jack.'

'Jack?'

'Yes, you know we both of us got into the way of going to town pretty often last Fall, and we'd meet this one and that one, and it was a drink every time—it was just as much my fault as Jack's—more, for I'm older—you know how it goes when you get in with that crowd, they are pretty hard to shake off even if you want to—and Jack doesn't want.'

'Still, surely it has not gone so far but that you can both cut it out—you would have to stand a little chaff in town, but both there and in the settlement every one whose good opinion is worth having would be heartily glad.'

'Oh, I know that, and as far as I am concerned, I have cut it out; I never cared for the beastly stuff, and when it came out at young Neilson's trial that Jack and I took a bottle of rye to the Hardie's dance last Fall, I made up my mind never to touch it again. It seemed such a common, low-down sort of thing when the old Judge, in his polite, sarcastic kind of way, asked me if that was my idea of a gentleman's way of requiting a neighbour's hospitality—I felt like a cur, and when I tried to apologise to Jim he was awfully decent about it, and wouldn't let me say a word. I'm through with it for keeps, but it's different with Jack—he's been to town a good many times, off and on, during the winter, with the Burke boys—you know those Irish Canadian fellows who live north of us—they're a rowdy set—and every time there has been more or less drinking.'

'Oh, yes, I know them,' said Bert, 'and I've heard of Jack being with them, and was very sorry to hear it—they are not altogether bad fellows, they are rough and noisy, and I daresay get off on a drinking bout when they are in town in the slack season—but they'll settle down to work with the spring, and I daresay hardly go to town again all summer.'

'Very likely, Bert, but they've spoilt Jack—he's very miserable and disgusted with himself for a few days after one of his town trips—going to stay home and never touch whisky again—and then you know the comfortless, God-forsaken way we live—no regular meals—no decently cooked grub—not enough horses and cattle and so forth to make a regular day's work in winter—just the team to look after, and go to the bush once in a while for firewood, and then just lie around. It was bad enough the first winter, but the novelty helped it out, and Jack would go out more with me to the Dingle or to some of the neighbours. Now, nothing will get him off the place unless it is to go to town—he won't even have a shave and a clean up for Sunday.'

'I'm awfully sorry, Tom, still—now you've told me all about it, we must try and do something amongst us to help Jack out—of course, I needn't say anything to them at home, but I can give my mother a hint, and we must try and get him over here more and liven things up generally. There will be more of us with the Rayes for tennis, and we must try and get an afternoon a week and get up two or three picnics when the seeding is over—and Tom—I can tell you now—I've been awfully anxious about both of you all winter—the year you and Jack put in at my father's as farm pupils has made you almost like brothers of my own—it's bad enough with Jack, but now I know you're solid, I feel easier than I have done for a long time.'

'Thank you, Bert, I can't say what I feel about your kindness,' and there was a sharply suppressed quiver in Tom's voice, which he threw off with a laugh, 'it's just my lop-sided Irishman's ill-luck—when I was beginning to really feel like taking hold of the farm and trying to make things go to have Jack's vagaries upsetting my plans.'

'Well, Tom, we'll do our best, and here we are home—now just hear what a good character I'll give you as a careful and responsible Jehu for next Saturday.'

CHAPTER V

MEETING THE SCHOOLMA'AM

Though Tom Dennis was quite free from any thought of personal vanity when he told Bert that he would make himself as 'pretty' as he could for the trip to town, still the fact remains that he had taken very special pains for the occasion. The buckboard received a most unusual scrubbing and oiling, the old mare was groomed till her coat shone again, and Tom had not in reality half the reason he thought he had for being dissatisfied with his own personal appearance. The Stetson hat, buckskin jacket, breeches and long boots, though all showing a good many signs of wear and weather, were admirably suited to his tall, well-set-up figure, and quite free from the ridiculous results so often achieved when an Old Country town-bred youth strives to develop too suddenly into what he believes to be a typical Westerner.

The uninvited candour of numerous brothers and sisters had, at a very early age, robbed Tom of any native vanity in his looks, when one has been told so often and for so long a period that one's hair is red, one's mouth a perfect trap-door and one's face generally as plain as a pikestaff, it is difficult for the recipient of such brotherly and sisterly discipline to retain many illusions, though less prejudiced eyes would have admitted that had Tom been a girl, his hair would at the worst have been auburn, and that if his mouth was large it was full of expression. Even the home critics had to admit—among themselves though not to Tom—that he had splendid eyes—clear and steady in their gaze and swift to reflect the mirth, anger, or tenderness of his Celtic temperament.

The careless courage with which he had undertaken to meet Miss Raye and her brother began rather to slip away when he found himself, early on the Saturday afternoon, walking up and down the Minnedosa station platform with Jim Hardie, waiting for the train from Winnipeg.

'I say, Jim, you've met the schoolmarm before and will have to do the introducing and that sort of thing—then I'll drop into the background with the brother and look after the baggage while you tell her our plans for going up to the settlement—tell her I am a rather shy young man but a very careful driver—you know.'

'Now that's too bad—too bad for sure, Tom, for you to go back on me like that; I thought you would do all that with your easy English ways, and just keep me out of the fuss.'

'Still, Jim, you've seen her before—besides, you are a family man and look responsible—while, till you tell her different, she might think I was a kind of wild cowboy—there's Mr. Jordan coming up the platform—say, Jim, we'll get him to do the talking—a parson can speak to anybody—besides he's used to it. Good afternoon, Mr. Jordan, would you mind helping Mr. Hardie and myself out of a difficulty?'

'How are you, Tom? Glad to see you, Mr. Hardie,' and Mr. Jordan shook hands heartily with them both. 'Well, what's the trouble, Mr. Hardie, anything I can do for you?'

'Well, you see——' and Jim explained the situation.

'Oh, you need not worry about that, I'm not surprised at Mr. Hardie—but you, Tom—a too-diffident Irishman is something new—you remember the seven wonders of the world—and Tom Dennis, shy, makes the eighth.'

'You're as bad as Jim, sir, just because I try to carry my native modesty off with a bold face——'

'So you are not a "bould Irishman"—well, I've a good mind to take the young lady up to the Dingle myself, and then see how you'd be left—but seriously, I've come to meet the Rayes myself—I met the sister when she was out West before, and she sent me a line to say they were coming, and I did not know what plans had been made. There's the train whistling at the Summit; I'll do the introducing, and so forth, and then take them both over to the Rectory for lunch, and you and Mr. Hardie can come round for them when you are ready to start out.'

'Now, that's just what I call fine,' said Jim, greatly relieved to be free from taking the lead in anything that savoured of formality and fuss. 'And Tom wants you to tell the schoolmarm that he's a careful driver——'

'Oh, I'll leave her to discover that for herself—it's a mate for his modesty—here the train comes—now don't you run away on me.'

With a second whistle of warning for the crossings and the clanging of the engine bell, the train, which had come along at a good speed round the spur of the hill into the valley, slowed up as it approached the bridge over the little river and drew up to the long platform. Mr. Jordan stepped on board the first-class coach, almost before the train came to a standstill, while Mr. Hardie and Tom drew back among the crowd on the platform and watched the passengers alight. First came the commercial travellers and others bound for stations further west, who thronged from the train, jostling one another in their anxiety to get across the platform and to the nearby hotel, to make the most of the twenty minutes allowed at Minnedosa for dinner, then, more leisurely and with many parcels, came those whose journey was at an end—and last, when Mr. Hardie and Tom were beginning to think the expected ones had not come, Mr. Jordan stepped down from the rear of the coach, followed by a young lady in a navy blue serge suit and a sailor hat.

'They've come alright, Jim; that's the schoolmarm, and there's the brother behind—she's a pretty trim figure—but the brother is English, sure enough—Norfolk jacket, knickerbockers, the national boots—come along, Jim, let's get it over,' and Tom boldly shouldered his way through the throng to where Mr. Jordan and the newcomers were standing.

'Ah, here you are, Tom; this is Mr. Dennis, Miss Raye, who is to take you up to the settlement, and here is Mr. Hardie, who is to look after your brother; you've met him before, I think?'

'How do you do, Mr. Dennis, it's very good of you to take so much trouble for us,' and Evelyn gave Tom a frank and friendly smile as she shook hands, 'and you, too, Mr. Hardie. Do you remember coming to the Swansons for dinner one day when I was teaching up in Sweden?'

'Sure, I do, and when I saw Ole Swanson the other day and told him you were coming to our school this year, he was real vexed, and said the folks up in Sweden would feel like coming and stealing you back again.'

'Oh, they were always too good to me,' said Miss Raye laughing; 'I'm afraid they spoilt me—I hope you won't be disappointed when you find what a very ordinary young person I am.'

'Oh, I don't think they are afraid of that,' said Mr. Jordan; 'now, come, I'll take you two over to the Rectory for lunch, and we'll be looking for you, Tom, in an hour or so, and here, Mr. Hardie, are the checks for their things.'

'All right, sir, we'll be along; Jim and I will get the baggage sorted out now,' and lifting his cap, Tom strode off down the platform, very relieved to get the introductory scene safely over.

Tom's own business in town did not take him very long, and it was well within the time appointed when he drove smartly up the side street to the Rectory and jumped out on to the sidewalk by the Rectory gate. He had just finished tying the mare up to a post when a boy of thirteen or so, who had been working in the garden, came running up.

'Hello, Tad, how are you to-day? Say, will you run in and tell your father that I'm here—are they ready to start?'

'Good afternoon, Mr. Dennis, won't you come in? I don't think they've finished their lunch yet. Mother asked Dad why he didn't bring you and Mr. Hardie over with him, but Dad always gets rattled when any one comes from the Old Country.'

'Oh, that's alright, Tad, Jim and I had dinner over at the hotel before the train came in—no, I won't come in; I'll just wait round for a while.

24

How does the gardening go?'

'Oh, I guess it goes alright for those that are fond of it,' said Tad, quite without enthusiasm. 'I'm not struck on it myself—on a Saturday when it's supposed to be a holiday—it's not so bad on a school day. I never can think why Dad wants such a big garden—we always grow twice as much as we can eat, and then we kids have to go toting peas and beans and flowers and a whole lot of truck to all the old ladies in the parish—I think it's just foolishness.'

'You're a badly used boy, Tad,' said Tom laughing at the entire good humour with which Tad stated his grievances, 'you'll have to run away from your stony-hearted parent. How would you like to come up and keep "bach" with us at Connemara Farm for a while?'

'It would be just splendid,' said Tad eagerly, 'I'm to go and stay at the Enderbys in the Fall for the threshing if I pass my exam. This term—I haven't been working very hard in school this winter—you see there is skating and a whole lot of other things that must be done—but you bet I'm going to work now it's worth while.'

'Well, you are an immoral little beggar in the way you put it—but I'll ask your Dad to let you come over for a day's shooting while you are at the Dingle—how will that suit you? Can you handle a gun?'

'Well, I'm not exactly a dab at it,' said Tad modestly, 'you see, Rex is four years older than me, and when we go out he takes turns shooting with Dad, and I carry the game. Still, I was out with Dad alone a few times down among the willows by the river when the first snow came last Fall, and I've shot three rabbits—not running of course—still, I shot them.'

'Well, that's a bargain, Tad, there are all kinds of partridges and prairie chickens round our place, and we'll have a great time.'

'And when you ask Dad, Mr. Dennis, would you mind saying, in a kind of casual way, that you are very careful with a gun, and never carry it full cock or get through a wire fence without taking the shells out—just to make Dad easy, you know?'

'You're a wise boy, Tad, I see, and know how to bring up a father properly—now I guess you had better run in and tell Miss Raye I'm ready.'

'I'm just going, Mr. Dennis—but say, did you see the brother?—the schoolmarm is an awfully nice girl—I shouldn't mind having her for a teacher myself,' said Tad patronisingly, 'but he's some English. He came round the garden with me while mother was getting the lunch ready—he's been to some college in England where they are supposed to learn how to farm—and he's quite a learned guy—I was planting potatoes in hills with a hoe, and he asked me if we did not cut the "tubers"—tubers indeed! I told him we didn't grow tubers here, but just common potatoes; and then, you see that row of pinks Dad has put along the border—well, he got poking

25

amongst them, and said he was glad to see the Dianthus vulgaris grew here —vulgaris! I'll bet they are no more "vulgaris" than the flowers in the Old Country.'

'Well, Tad, you scoot now or he will be saying that I am an Irishman vulgaris to keep them waiting—I'll just turn the rig round and be ready— and there's Jim Hardie and the wagon just coming down the street.'

Tad hurried into the house and soon reappeared with his father, Miss Raye, and her brother, and in a few minutes a start was made—Tom and Miss Raye in the buckboard leading, followed more slowly by the wagon, which was well laden with numerous boxes and miscellaneous packages.

Many a time afterwards did Tom Dennis call back to his memory his first drive with Evelyn Raye, and try to reconstruct its details, but in some strange way the details seemed to elude him. When soon after dusk he turned into the lane at the Dingle it seemed to him as if he had known Evelyn a long, long time ago, and as if the drive up had been a kind of dream. He knew that he had told her all about his own life at home in Ireland as a boy, about his mother, about the aimless way in which he had lived in the West. He did not know how or why he had talked so freely and easily about many things that he never before had dreamt of allowing to pass beyond his lips—the real past was become the dream, and the only reality the future, and the only future Evelyn Raye.

CHAPTER VI

A SEASONAL SERMON

Evelyn Raye fell very easily and naturally into the family life at the Dingle, and within a very few days of her arrival even Mrs. Enderby dropped the apologetic tone in which at first she alluded to the necessity for her own daughters taking their part in the menial work of the household.

'I don't know, I'm sure, what their dear Grandpapa would feel if he could see Marion and Daisy doing the washing—and such washes as we have when their father and brother are doing the harrowing,' she remarked to Evelyn as she was cutting some sandwiches for the latter's lunch to take to school on the Monday morning following her arrival. 'You would hardly believe how vexed he, that's my father I mean, Miss Raye, used to be if even the faintest suggestion of boiling cabbages reached his study where he was writing his sermon, and you know how pervasive even Brussels sprouts will be if you leave the kitchen door open for a minute—and here when we are boiling the clothes, the steamy soapiness seems to get all over the house—and I've put in two hard-boiled eggs and a little pot of cranberry jelly, and I do hope you will have enough.'

'Oh, thank you, Mrs. Enderby, I'm sure that will be more than enough, even for the north-west appetite that I expect will soon come back to me, and,' went on Evelyn, half amused and half touched by Mrs. Enderby's evident, if rather confused thoughtfulness for her comfort, 'and I do hope you will let me be just at home and help in the house like one of your own girls; you know I'm quite used to the country, Mrs. Enderby, and I shall be ever so much happier if you will let me.'

'Well, my dear, I'm sure it is very good of you to say so, but I'm afraid you will be tired enough when you get home after having all those children round you all day, and they say some of the boys are dreadfully troublesome—and come to school without shoes and stockings—even the girls when they are quite big. I suppose it is quite harmless—though I could never let my girls do it when they went to school—though indeed, I know Daisy used to cry about it and say the other girls called her "proudie"—indeed, one whole week she went barefoot—hid her things in the bushes at the end of the lane and put them on again before she came home, and I

27

never discovered it till I bathed her on Saturday night, and found the soles of her feet as hard as leather and her poor little legs as red as an Indian's and covered with scratches and mosquito bites.'

'Oh, I'm not a bit afraid of the children, Mrs. Enderby, I'm used to all their little ways, and when I was up in "Sweden" I used to have some quite big boys in winter—ever so much bigger than myself—and they were much more polite in a funny foreign sort of way than many English boys I've met at home, who would consider themselves quite superior.'

'Well, I'm sure I hope you will find the children at Lakeside School quite nice too,' said Mrs. Enderby rather doubtfully, 'and here's Mr. Hardie coming down the lane with his buckboard—he's one of the trustees, and I know he told Bert on Saturday he would come and drive you over for your first visit to the school, and see that you had everything you wanted—so good-bye, my dear, and Daisy will come and meet you at four o'clock and see you do not get lost on your way home.'

Evelyn's first three weeks at the Dingle passed very quickly and un-eventfully. There was a small attendance at school, the bigger boys being kept at home to help in the seeding, and even some of the girls to drop potatoes or mind the younger children while their mothers were busy with their spring cleaning, which for Western wives often includes the white-washing of the whole interior walls of the house and the repainting of floors. It was usually dark and bedtime when Mr. Enderby and Bert came in from the field, and they were out again with their teams when Evelyn would come down to her breakfast in the morning.

At last the spring rush was over, the wheat and oats were all in, and the early-sown wheat already showing nicely above the ground, the house cleaning was an accomplished fact, and not at all the pretence which Daisy had pleaded for, and for some evenings the three girls had been busy with the flower garden and, with the pressed help of the chore boy, had rolled and marked out the tennis court.

The congregation at the church service, which had suffered severely from the break-up of the winter and the following rush of spring seeding, revived much in numbers if not in piety, and there was a general sense of relief from strain which expressed itself in different ways, and Daisy even averred that Mr. Jordan's theology was distinctly modified by the larger number present at church and the better state of the roads.

It was the Sunday afternoon—church Sunday—Mr. Jordan, who had come back to the Dingle for dinner, had started off for his nine-mile drive to his afternoon service, the boys—Bert, the two Dennises and Chris Raye —were smoking on the verandah, and Marion Enderby and Evelyn were washing up the dishes with the rather erratic help of Daisy.

'Wasn't that just a lovely sermon we had this morning, Evelyn; Mr. Jordan is a dear old man——'

'Daisy, you should not speak of Mr. Jordan like that,' rebuked Marion; 'he is not an old man.'

'Well—he's a dear anyway—and if I talked about a "dear young man," you would say it was not proper—do you know, Evelyn, I can tell just as soon as he gives out his text how his garden is looking at home. Now, as soon as he started this morning—"For lo, the winter is past, the rain is over and gone, the flowers appear on the earth; the time of the singing of birds is come, and the voice of the turtle is heard in our land"—aren't those just lovely words to hear in church—I knew just as well as if I saw them that his bedding plants had got a good start without wilting, and that he'd have the earliest green peas in town.'

'Daisy, you should not rattle on about such things—Evelyn will think you have no reverence for anything.'

'Oh, no, she won't, she will feel just like Mr. Jordan, for she knows the grubs haven't taken a single one of the stocks she put out last week—I'm sure when everything is looking lovely we were meant to be happy about it —only each one in our own way—Mr. Jordan's way is early spinach and green peas, Evelyn's way is double stocks and mignonette, and Bert's way is spring wheat and the last litter of little Berkshire pigs, and mother's way —I could see it in her face in church—was just a lovely sad happiness, and she was thinking of the old Rectory garden in Leicestershire and the path through the woods to the Hall—and the bluebells and lilies of the valley and the wood pigeons cooing in the tree-tops, and——'

'Now, Daisy dear, that will do for your imagination—and what was your way?'

'Why, my way was the tennis court; I felt sure there were not going to be any holes in the bottom corner for the water to stand in, and that Dad would get me a new racquet and that—and that——'

'And what else did the sermon promise you?' asked Evelyn, laughing heartily as Daisy stopped suddenly and blushed.

'Well—it's shocking, but I'm a regular little Washington sometimes—it promised that the boys should have lots of time to play, and that they should play mixed doubles as if that were just the kind of tennis they lived for.'

'Well, you and Evelyn had better go out on the verandah and talk it over with the boys and see if they will help you to realise your hopes—I don't know about Bert and Mr. Raye, but I expect the Dennis boys will fall in with anything which does not look too much like work.'

'And I'm sure Chris will be keen to play,' said Evelyn, 'he is a little short-sighted and not a very good player, but there weren't many of us to play in the village at home, and he's used to playing with girls.'

'That's a comfort,' said Daisy, emphatically, 'some of the English boys round here have got so high and mighty that they only play with Marion and me as a great piece of condescension—now, come along, Evelyn, and be sure you back me up if Bert begins to make any difficulties about not sparing the time or any foolishness of that kind—you know he won't snub you in the brotherly way he does me.'

The two girls passed from the lean-to where they had been washing the dishes into the living-room and thence on to the verandah, where, with un-expected good fortune, they found that the prospect of tennis was already the subject of conversation.

'You have come at just the right moment, Miss Raye,' cried Tom Dennis, jumping up from the old deck-chair in which he had been seated, and offering it to Evelyn, while Daisy, declining the offer of the hammock from Chris Raye, sat down on the verandah step—'of course, we haven't been having a tennis meeting exactly, but just suggesting what plans we would make for the summer if it wasn't Sunday.'

'Now, Tom Dennis, don't you dare to pretend that you have a Scotch conscience—for it's not a bit necessary—I have quite persuaded Miss Raye and Marion that Mr. Jordan was giving us a dispensation to talk tennis on Sunday when he preached this morning—though I don't suppose you know what the text was—you do! Well, don't try to repeat it, and we'll not expose your ignorance—now, what are you boys going to do about tennis?'

'Why, we thought,' said Bert, 'that we might settle to play every Satur-day afternoon, at any rate till haying begins, and then perhaps make up a little party to go down to Minnedosa and play in the Tournament there ——'

'Oh that would be great,' cried Daisy enthusiastically, 'you don't know what a swell time they have at the Tournament, Evelyn; they've got lovely courts down there, and everybody wears their prettiest frocks, and they have afternoon tea, and everybody that can play goes in for all the open events, and those that can't play go in for the handicaps and try to wiggle out with a prize in the end.'

'Well, Miss Raye, I don't think you had better trust too much to Daisy's ideas of the Tournament,' said Bert, 'I'm afraid just coming from England it may not strike you as such an altogether thrilling experience—but we may get some pleasure out of our quiet little games here at home, and we thought as next Thursday is the Queen's Birthday and really a kind of holi-day, we might have our first game then, and ask three or four of the other boys round, and mother and the girls would provide afternoon tea, and so forth.'

'Oh, we'll look after the tea,' cried Daisy, 'but what time can we begin —it's nearly five when you get home from school, Evelyn, and it would be too bad to begin without you.'

'Oh, you mustn't think I'm going to work when everybody else is playing,' said Evelyn laughing, 'we are going to have a holiday at school, at least the children are coming to school in the morning for what the Educational Department calls "patriotic exercises," but I shall be home again by the middle of the day.'

'Why, what are "patriotic exercises," Evelyn?' asked her brother. 'We used to do Latin and French exercises at school, but I never heard of patriotic exercises; do you teach patriotism out of a book like Latin Grammar, and conjugate the royal family like an irregular verb?'

'Of course not, you foolish boy,' replied Evelyn laughing, 'it just means that the children will keep the Queen's Birthday by saluting the Union Jack and singing patriotic songs, and I shall tell them a simple sort of story life of Queen Victoria, and there will be one or two speeches, and then we shall all sing "God save the Queen." '

'Well, I think that is awfully nice,' said Chris Raye seriously. 'I don't think we do enough of that kind of thing at home; half the people don't even know when the Queen's Birthday is.'

'Oh, you don't know the West yet,' said Daisy, 'we are pretty spectacular in our loyalty, and as for speeches, we just revel in them—but who is going to make your speeches for you, Evelyn?'

'Oh, the trustees will be there—Mr. Hardie and——'

'I hope you are not confiding in Jim Hardie for a speech, Evelyn, he's the dearest little man in the settlement, but he'd sink through the floor if you asked him to say a "few words," which is the usual prelude to half an hour's prosing—if it were his wife now——'

'Perhaps, if you give Miss Raye a chance, Daisy, you may hear who the speakers are,' said Bert.

'I think Mr. Jordan will be there, and Dr. Casey from town has promised to speak to the children.'

'Old Dr. Casey!' exclaimed Tom Dennis, 'Why, who would have thought such an old bachelor would give an address to a lot of little boys and girls?'

'He was in the school last week to see if all the children were vaccinated, and he's coming up to vaccinate four or five of the ones just starting school, and I asked him if he would come on Thursday and give a talk to the children afterwards. I knew him when I was up in Sweden, and he was always very nice to me—but why are you smiling, Mr. Dennis?'

'The doctor is an awfully fine man,' said Tom, 'and everybody respects him, and I know he can make a rattling good political speech, but I hope he won't warm up too much, Miss Raye, or——' and Tom hesitated.

'Or what, Mr. Dennis? Now you must tell me.'

'Well, you know, Miss Raye, though he is a very good speaker—if he gets roused a little on such things as patriotism and loyalty, and anybody checks him in the least—why, he sometimes uses words that are not in the vocabulary of good little boys, you know.'

'That's too bad of you, Tom; it's just jealousy—trying to prejudice you against our most eligible old bachelor, Evelyn. I'll go over to school with you and try and bring back the doctor for the afternoon—now, who'll go for a walk? I promised to show Miss Raye the view from the big spruce on the hill—will you come, Mr. Raye?—and you can come too, Tom, to talk crops to Mr. Raye while Evelyn and I admire the scenery.'

The four of them started out together. Whether Daisy was as entirely innocent as her words suggest, who can tell?—but long before they reached the big spruce the quartette was dissolved into two duets, and it is doubtful whether either scenery or crops was much in Tom Dennis' mind as he walked along by Evelyn's side.

CHAPTER VII

MARION'S CANUCK

The Queen's Birthday brought Queen's weather—a still, misty dawn—with the sunrise a gentle westerly wind before which the mist faded away into the fresh morning air, leaving a cloudless sky, the whole atmosphere redolent with the resinous odour of the budding leafage of black poplars mingled with the fragrance of the blossoming choke-cherry and saskatoons from the bluff behind the house—a perfect Manitoba morning—and the whole Dingle household early astir, and preparing in their different ways to do honour to the good Queen.

With Mr. Enderby and Bert it took the form of doing odd jobs round the farm which had been waiting for such a break in the rush of spring work. Mr. Enderby went off after breakfast, quite happy, with an axe, a hammer, and pocketful of staples to repair sundry breaches in the snake fence round the pasture, and to tighten the wire round the grain fields. Bert was busy keeping a deferred promise to his mother to build coops for certain broods of young chickens which were expected to come out during the next week or two, if the hens then sitting remained steadfast for their appointed time.

Indoors, Mrs. Enderby and Marion were preparing for the unusual luxury of doing a little cooking outside the monotony of the daily round—there were cakes to be made, and lemon pies—beloved of the boys, but with sufficient possibility of going wrong in the baking to make their preparation a delight tempered with anxiety—jellies, varying in name and colour but otherwise of indistinctive flavour, to be placed in moulds on a block of ice in the dairy after passing a test examination as to their capacity to set in saucers placed in the north window of the dining room. In the dairy, too, was a crock of sugar and water, to which later on is to be added the juice of the lemons which Marion is squeezing into a self-sealer—for the tennis players will be thirsty—all of which preparations make Mrs. Enderby reminiscent of long gone garden parties at the old Rectory, but with no stronger under-current of regret for the past than is compatible with a very real enjoyment of the present.

As for Daisy, she became quite irresponsible and useless for domestic purposes from the moment the fineness of the day was assured, for with the

33

exuberance of her spirits came a facility of varied expression for her emotions that promised ill for her mother's sense of propriety of speech if she remained at home for the morning.

She reached the limits of Marion's patience when she wound up a challenge to play her sister 'for the drinks,' with the further outrage of 'and if I don't lick you to a finish I'll eat my sh——'

'Daisy, have you no sense of common decency?'

'Well, I will, and you need not get wrathy—you know very well I would not have said that if the boys had been round. I say, Evelyn,' she added as the latter came into the lean-to, 'may I come to school with you and share in the patriotic exercises? My kind of loyalty is altogether too intense this morning for Marion and the mater.'

'Of course you may, dear,' said Evelyn readily, 'the more the merrier, and the children always like to have some grown-ups at their little functions.'

'Well, I'm sure it will be a relief to Marion to have me out of the way, and I'll promise to be as grown-up and prim and proper as I can, and I will talk English, as the Yankees say, "like your mother used to make." '

'I'm sure I hope you will,' replied Marion, accepting the sincerity of Daisy's last sentence rather than its form, 'and, Daisy, you might ask Dr. Casey to come back to dinner—I know father would enjoy having a quiet chat with him.'

'Sure—and is there any one else you would like me to ask—for a quiet chat with mother—or yourself, Marion, say—say——' and Daisy paused teasingly.

'You need not say—say, Daisy, but run away, and don't keep Evelyn waiting any longer with your nonsense.'

'I do delight in taking a rise out of Marion,' said Daisy, as the two girls went down the garden path to the lane, 'there is one weapon that never fails to cut off a scolding abruptly.'

'Why, what is that?' asked Evelyn.

'The slightest allusion to Marion's "Canuck"—I'll tell you a little secret—oh, it is quite innocent,' went on Daisy as Evelyn raised a deprecating hand, 'besides you would be sure to discover it for yourself. Marion's "Canuck" is my name for a certain neighbour of ours, Dugald M'Leod. He is a Scotch Canadian—quite middle-aged—he must be nearly forty. He has the next farm to old Dawson's at the post-office, and lives alone with a hired man and some funny kind of Englishwoman for a housekeeper. Her husband worked on the section at Minnedosa and got killed—run over by an engine or something horrible—and she had no friends, and Dugald, who is really awfully good, took pity on her and brought her up to keep house for him. She is very deaf and really a little "dotty," you know—but to come back to Dugald—he's very reserved and shy, but ever since a year ago last Fall, when he was at our threshing, he has taken to dropping in quite often at the Dingle.'

'But does he pay special attention to your sister?' asked Evelyn, 'for it seems to me that a good many young men drop in at the Dingle.'

'Oh, there would be nothing in it if he were an Englishman, because he hardly speaks to us girls, and talks most of the time to Dad and Bert, but with a Scotch Canadian it's different; the idea of matrimony slowly filters into his mind, and he's gone quite a long way in love before he discovers it himself—but really, I think Dugald is quite "serious" in his intentions, as they say, and I was sure by his nervous, jerky way last Monday that he had made up his mind to take the plunge. He came up in the middle of the afternoon when the men were sure to be in the fields, and he had on his Sunday clothes, and was generally spruced up, and I knew the moment I saw him coming up the lane what he had come for.'

'Why, Daisy,' said Evelyn laughing, 'you are quite learned in the ways of different lovers, where did you acquire all this Cupid's lore?'

'Natural talent, my dear, just natural talent,' replied Daisy sententiously, 'but really, it was as easy to see as rolling off a log—he walked very rapidly half way up the lane as if he were making a new record for a half-mile race, then he slowed up suddenly, and just dawdled till he got to the garden gate. He stood there a full minute and took out his handkerchief and took off his hat and "wiped his fevered brow," as the poet says, then he opened the garden gate and came up the path with a rush. I was peeping from the dining-room window, and waited for his knock. Well, I'm sure it was a full three minutes, then there were two nervous taps with an interval between, and then one big thump. It made me jump, and I'm sure must have hurt his knuckles. I ran out to the door, for I was not going to take any chances of Marion going and letting him fade away for the want of a little encouragement. Well, I opened the door—so suddenly I expect that it shattered what little nerve he had left—"Oh, how do you do, Mr. M'Leod; come in," said I.'

' "I just called round, Miss Daisy, to see if your father could lend me Bert—I mean, if your father or Bert could lend me an axe handle till I get a new one from town—you see, Miss Daisy, you see——"

' "Oh, yes, I see, Mr. M'Leod," said I, "but come in for a minute, I expect one of them is not very far away——" '

'Daisy—how could you?' interrupted Evelyn.

'Well, I could and I did—so in he came, and I piloted him safely into the dining-room and then called Marion at the foot of the stairs. Marion came running down quite innocently—"Oh, Marion," said I, "here's Mr. M'Leod, he came to see father or Bert—he wants to borrow an axe handle

—do you know where Dad or Bert is?" "Why, you know, Daisy, they said at dinner-time they were going to be cutting some fence rails on Bert's place all afternoon." "Oh, so they did, I'm so sorry, Mr. M'Leod, but perhaps, Marion, if you will entertain Mr. M'Leod for a few minutes I can find what he wants—I know where Bert keeps all those things, in a corner of the granary." Did a lover ever have such a chance? Will you believe it—he just jumped up and said it did not matter in the least, and he would not trouble me, and he had no time to wait—and he made his escape as if the Dingle was plague stricken.'

'The best laid plans of mice and men,' quoted Evelyn laughing. 'I honestly think you deserved your disappointment—but what does your sister think about it?'

'Oh, Marion scolded me for forgetting where Dad and Bert were, and when I remarked that Dugald would never get a handle for an axe or anything else he wanted to complete his happiness if he was so easily discouraged—why, Marion just looked at me as if my remark was absolutely unintelligible, and went off again upstairs. It's too bad—because with his slow fire it will take him a long time to get steam up again for another attempt.'

'Well, I hope he will have better fortune next time,' said Evelyn, 'that is, if seriously, Daisy, you think they really care for each other.'

'Oh, it's hard to tell with Marion, she's quiet—I have all the indiscretion in the family—but I know she has a great respect for Dugald, everybody has, and I think she really likes him—besides, he's very well off, and has a very good house and farm—not that Marion would marry him for that—still, they are good things to have, and any one who has been through hard times like Marion has—well—doesn't exactly despise them—and I've noticed lately that she speaks of the Presbyterian preacher as a "clergyman"—of course Dugald belongs to the "oatmeal" flock, and she didn't like it a bit the last time Dr. Casey was here—at the election time in the winter, when he said if the damned Grits had only one neck he would put a rope round it himself—and equally of course Dugald is a Grit—and I don't believe it was the big D that made Marion get up and leave the room.'

'Well, I'm sure I hope it will end happily for them both,' said Evelyn, 'but really, if I were you, Daisy, I would leave the course of true love—if it be so—to run its own way—and I'm going to try and forget all you told me about it, and there is the school and there is Dr. Casey tying his horse to the gate-post—I do hope he will not get too much worked up in his speech to the children—it would be dreadful if he were to——'

'To have a relapse into his election language? Oh, I don't think he will, and even if he did and the children repeated it at home nobody would mind. Dr. Casey is Dr. Casey with three-fourths of the people in the settlement, even at elections and with all people—Grits and Tories—for the rest of the time.'

CHAPTER VIII

WESTERN LOYALTY

Besides a crowd of boys and girls, a considerable number of grown-ups were already gathered round the old log school-house, four or five mothers of pupils who were to take a part in the patriotic exercises, and one or two nearby settlers who had heard that Doctor Casey was to address the children. There, too, was Jim Hardie, in his capacity as trustee, happy to be among a parcel of children, and secure under a promise from Evelyn that he should not be asked as chairman to do more than announce the 'pieces' on the programme.

After a few minutes spent by the 'grown-ups' in mutual greetings, a small boy, specially honoured for his clean hands and face and smoothly brushed hair, rang the school bell, and the children marched into school and quietly took their seats at their desks, while Doctor Casey and Jim Hardie were escorted to chairs placed on the little platform at the end of the room.

In spite of Mrs. Enderby's prophecies of the unruliness of the Lakeside children, Evelyn had them already under excellent control, though they were evidently looking forward keenly to their own part in the entertainment, for Manitoba children have a most unabashed love of taking part in any kind of a public 'show,' and would sing their school songs or say their 'pieces' before the assembled royalty of Europe with a perfect absence of self-consciousness and to their own entire satisfaction.

First on the programme came 'Rule, Britannia,' sung by the whole school, without any musical accompaniment of course, or copies of the words, and very well sung indeed. Some of the big boys' voices at the back were rather cracked, and the piping treble of the little girls rather shrill, but the immense enthusiasm with which they let themselves go at the chorus more than atoned for any musical defects. The fusion of races which is taking place in the West is producing a more demonstrative type of patriotism than used to be found in any of the old lands, and the same spirit was noticeable in the various 'pieces' and patriotic songs which followed—love to Manitoba, love to Canada, and above all and beyond these, love and loyalty to the Empire and to the Old Mother of Nations across the seas—this was the keynote of the whole.

At last, with much good-natured applause from the 'grown-ups' and honest appreciation by the children themselves of their own efforts, the climax of their anticipations was reached when Jim Hardie announced 'An address by our old friend, Dr. Casey. Now, boys and girls, mind what the doctor tells you.'

A general clapping of hands, in which the grown-ups' joined, was followed by a hush as Doctor Casey rose and came to the centre of the little platform facing the children. Doctor Casey was an Irishman with some thirty years or more of Eastern and Western Canada added to twenty-five of the 'Old Country,' and it did not require his name to tell you what 'Old Country' meant in his case. For twenty years or so he had shared the changing fortunes of Minnedosa and the Minnedosa country, and most of the sea of eager faces in front of him had been familiar to him from their earliest infancy. The stiffness of the medical man had been rubbed off in Manitoba country practice—he knew and loved children, and the children, in spite of a little awe inspired by his deep-set eyes and bushy eyebrows— the children knew it. He began his address in the offhand and casual way that will hold a Western audience, whether of children or adults, but a real purpose lay behind it all—a real purpose to promote the unity of the Empire, and though it was only expressed in a half-sad, half-humorous tone now and again, there was not one of the 'grown-ups' who did not realise that with him the old Valentine motto held true, and that 'absence only made the heart grow fonder.'

'Well, girls and boys,' the Doctor began after a formal bow to Evelyn, 'well, girls and boys, we should all be a great deal better in the fresh air and sunshine outside instead of being cooped up like a bunch of half-weaned calves in a corral, in this little school-house—however, it won't last long, ten minutes will see me through, and then it's "God Save the Queen," and out——' applause from two or three little boys for the suggestion of the ten-minute limit to his address, which applause proved to be premature. 'I'm to talk to you about Old Country folk and Canadians, and why they should have a mutual liking and respect for one another—for you know the Old Country boys stand rather aloof from the Canadian boys and are "rather English, you know," and the Canadian boys are not quite kind in their remarks about "green" Englishmen, who were not born with a wad of gum in their mouths and an axe in their hands.' Half a dozen sets of jaws that were previously grinding monotonously on the forbidden gum grew instantly rigid.

'Well, what's the difference between Old Country and Canadian boys, anyway? Boys and girls, it's just like this—all of you except the little tots know the old shed at the back of Pat Cassidy's store in town,' general nods of eager acquiescence—'well, when I first went to Minnedosa it stood on the north side of the river, and Pat kept his first store in it, and it was painted white—ten years ago he moved it on to the main street and fixed it up and he painted it grey—the year before last he built his new brick block and put the old shop at the back for a warehouse and painted it brown. If Johnnie Jones here were to go to the old shed and to take his jack-knife—the one he is cutting his desk with now——' (unhappy self-consciousness on the part of Johnnie, who finds himself the centre of attention for some fifty or sixty eyes)—'and were to scrape away a piece of brown paint very carefully, what would he come to?' Chorus of small voices, 'The grey paint, sir.'

'And then if he scraped away the grey?'

Renewed chorus, 'The white paint, sir.'

'That's right, children, and if he scraped away the white he would come to the lumber, and it's good, sound lumber, too, that lies hidden under the white and the grey and the brown.

'That's just the way it is with "Old Countrymen" and Canadians—there's the same good old timber at the bottom of them all. Here's Micky Dunoon, born and bred half a mile away from here—wasn't it myself that gave him his call name—he's a Manitoban, that is his brown coat of paint, let us scratch a bit of it off here on the cheek of him' (pantomime under which Micky looks rather nervous), 'why here's old Ontario maple syrup running out, and that is his grey coat of paint, and what have we got under that again? We will chip off a wee bit more Micky—why, here's a potato sprouting, and it's old Ireland we've come to, and sure Micky Dunoon, when you get the Manitoba paint and the Ontario paint off of him, is a "green" Irishman after all.

'Now look at little Pete M'Tavish—what are you, Pete?'

'Please, Doctor Casey, I'm a Canadian.'

'Of course you are, Pete, weren't you born at the old farm house down the valley yonder—but what's under the freckles on your nose, Pete?' (More pantomime.) 'Why, boys and girls, would you believe it? it's blue underneath; he's a "blue-nose" from Nova Scotia, and what have we underneath that? Why, there's a few porridge and some oatcakes—and listen—far away I hear a little boy singing, and I believe it's Pete's grandfather's voice, and he's singing about "Far Lochaber," and his pants hardly come to his knees, and it's a compliment to call them pants at all, and I do believe himself is a Highlander. Don't you laugh at raw Scotchmen, Pete, or you will be making fun of your own grandfather and—there's a strap at the farm house down the valley, Pete, and it's cut into tails in the old-fashioned way and applied in the old-fashioned spirit, and it goes by the old-fashioned name and the mark of the taws will remind you, Pete, of what is under your coats of paint.

40

'But who is that bullet-headed little chap next to you, Micky Dunoon? Billy Styles—and what do you call yourself, Billy? A Manitoban? That's you every time, Sonnie, but there is something else under that brown cheek of yours—why here are rocks and trout-streams and the spruce and the tamarac and a little log house in a clearing and we've come to Muskoka— we must go a little deeper, Billy, ah, here we come to the making of you— there's the red and the white and the blue, Billy, and we call it the "Old Flag," Billy, and there's a dog sitting down by the side of it, and he's a good bit like yourself in the build of him, Billy, he's short in the leg and stiff in the back and he's not much of a tyke to bark, but he has a little growl of his own—what does he say when he growls? He says what we have, we hold, Billy, and you'd better take his word for it.

'You're a Manitoban, Billy, true enough, but you are a chip of some fine old English blocks just the same, and as I listen to this side of you, Billy, your father's side, I hear an old song of the sea, and I see a frank-eyed sailor lad hanging to the tiller of a North Sea fishing-boat, and your father called him father in the long-off days before you were born, Billy. Again I listen to the other side of you, Billy, your mother's side, and I hear the snatch of a West Country ballad, and the cattle are coming home down a Somersetshire lane, and the tune of the song is the same that sings your baby sister to sleep in the stone house down by the Rolling River, and the cradle song of old Somerset, fifty years ago, is the cradle song of new Manitoba to-day, and you are a little English bull-dog, Billy, after all.

'Why, boys and girls, what have I done with my ten minutes—gone? I should say so—only remember, you Canadian boys and girls, you were English and Irish and Scotch fifty years ago, and you, you Old Country youngsters, in thirty years time or less your boys and girls will be singing "The Maple Leaf," and be proud to call themselves the children of the land where the maple grows.

' "Time," did you say, Micky Dunoon, you young villain—to hold me up—time it is—up on your feet, all of you, and get hold of the tune, Peter M'Tavish, and let her go for "God Save the Queen." '

Never was the national anthem honoured by a more vigorous and enthusiastic rendering, and on its close, at a word from Evelyn, the children trooped out of school, while the grown-ups thronged round the doctor with thanks for his address, for to more than one it had brought back memories of their own childhood and of the stories of the old land which they had listened to at their mothers' knee. The doctor himself became rather gruff and abrupt in his manner, for he was half ashamed of the under-current of feeling that had betrayed his more emotional side, and hastened out to his buggy under the plea that he had a patient waiting for him in town and he must start at once.

41

'I tell you what it is, Jim,' he confided to Mr. Hardie, as the latter untied the doctor's horse and handed him the reins, 'I'm getting an old man now, Jim, but the Old Land lies nearer my heart to-day though I may never see it again—than it did when I left it so many long years ago—so long, Jim,—I'm a confounded old fool,' and with a sharp jerk of the reins and a nervous flick of the whip the Doctor drove away.

CHAPTER IX

HOW TOM DENNIS KEPT THE SCORE

The Queen's Birthday ended as happily at the Dingle as it began, and the tennis party was quite the 'howling success' which Daisy—very moderately for her—described it as being to her mother in her final summing up of the happiness of the day before going to bed. In addition to Chris Raye and the Dennises who had been invited, two young Englishmen—old Dingle pupils—came over incidentally early in the afternoon, and although there were only the three girls, the boys behaved—Daisy's verdict again—in a way that was perfectly lovely,' and insisted on playing 'mixed doubles' till the girls went off to set the table in the shade of the black poplar bluff at the back of the house. Then indeed, they made up for the self-denial by some very vigorous 'singles' till Daisy came to call them to tea, very hot, very hungry, and still more thirsty—for the big crock of iced lemonade had been exhausted by the middle of the afternoon. Here they were joined by Mr. and Mrs. Enderby, the latter in a tussore silk gown trimmed with real lace, a carefully preserved relic of long past days, and reserved for such rare summer festivities as the present.

Mr. Enderby, who had been too long in the West to make many concessions to society in the matter of dress, had submitted so far to his wife's prejudices as to discard his working wear in favour of his town suit and a white collar, but pleaded that on such a warm day he might be allowed to dispense with his coat—as a set-off to the white flannels of the young men. It was a happy party, full of laughter and innocent chaff and repartee—no party could be very sedate that numbered Daisy among its members, and Daisy was on as easy terms with all the young men, except Chris Raye, as if they were her brothers—and Daisy's easy terms were very easy and very harmless. None of the 'Dingle' boys, as the former pupils were usually called, ever thought of flirting with Daisy, because flirting implies the presence of some modicum at least of sentiment in the person flirted with, and there was not a scrap of sentimentality in Daisy's nature. She described herself, and behaved and expected to be accepted as, 'one of the boys,' and the boys accepted her on that footing.

They lingered a long time round the table after tea was actually over, for as it was in the open air the boys had a dispensation to light their pipes

43

or cigarettes, but on a Western farm work can never be postponed beyond a certain limit. Mr. Enderby had slipped away quietly some time before to bring the cows in from the pasture, and on his return there was a general break-up and leave-taking. The two young Englishmen had already gone, and the Dennises and Chris Raye were sitting on the verandah step taking off their tennis shoes when Daisy had a swift intuition of the possibilities.

'There's a good half hour of light left yet—it's a shame to waste it—Mr. Chris, I'll play you a set of singles, and Evelyn shall come and see you play fair—do now.'

'I'm sure I should be very glad,' said Chris hesitating, 'only perhaps Mr. Hardie will be expecting me back to help.'

'Oh, no, I'm sure he won't,' said Daisy decidedly, 'besides, you left your rig down there, didn't you, Jack, well, suppose you go down and tell Mr. Hardie that Mr. Raye is just finishing a set—and then you can come up for Tom, and you can take Mr. Chris down to the lane in your buckboard—do you see?'

'You would make a great general, Daisy,' said Tom Dennis, laughing, 'you deserve to win your set, and I'll come over to the court and keep the score for you.'

'You don't know how glad I am, Mr. Dennis, to see my brother taking so kindly to the West,' said Evelyn a few minutes later, as she and Tom were seated on the rustic seat by the side of the court, 'although he was very anxious to come out, I was afraid he would not like the life when he found out how different it was to our life at home, but he seems to be perfectly contented.'

'Well, you see, he is more fortunate than a lot of young fellows; it's not often you find a fine little man like Jim Hardie to work for, and then the people at the "Dingle" are always awfully good to the English boys round, and we haven't all got a sister here who knows just what we really are and to take an interest in keeping us civilised.'

'Oh, I don't think Chris needs that, but he is rather shy and reserved—he never had many boys of his own age to mix with at home, and he got into the way of following little hobbies by himself. He was always collecting something—butterflies or beetles or fossils, and his room at home was a perfect museum of specimens, from a stuffed owl to the tooth of an antediluvian lizard.'

'Well, I don't fancy Mrs. Hardie would approve of his mussing up the house with anything of that kind—still, Jim has a great admiration for "learning" of all kinds, and though he probably would be secretly astonished at any one "fussing with the likes" of beetles or weeds—except to destroy them for the good of the farm—still, he would never be contemptu-

44

ous about it. Jim Hardie, though he is a slave to work himself, is not a mere money grubber like so many of the men here are.'

'Oh, he and Chris get along splendidly; Chris is very anxious to learn, and very particular about doing things properly, and he really takes an interest in the calves and pigs and hens and things like that, and he helps Mrs. Hardie in the garden.'

'Well, if he makes a friend of Mrs. Hardie he will have a good enough time—she is rather suspicious of English people and on the lookout for "airs," and she objects to muddy boots on her clean floor, or novels or papers lying round on Sunday—Jim's *Free Press* being exempted—if he is careful about a few little things of that kind and gets up when he's called, and keeps out of her way on washing-day, why, he'll be all right—and he mustn't talk too appreciatively of the Dingle and Daisy Enderby.'

'Why Daisy, Mr. Dennis, I'm sure she is unconventional enough——'

'Rather too much so, and she has a quick tongue and a freedom of repartee that shocks Mrs. Hardie's sense of the proprieties—even more, I expect, than it does you, because you are used to English boys' slang.'

'Well, she did startle me rather at first, and I used to feel sorry for her mother because Mrs. Enderby was so afraid I should take it as a serious lack of good breeding—but, do you know, I like Daisy better every day. She is spoilt, of course, but she is thoroughly good-hearted, and though she teases them all and is wilful about little things, it's only on the surface, and she is as penitently anxious as a little child to be "good" if she finds she has really hurt any one by letting her tongue run away with her.'

'Well, I'm very glad you like her, Miss Raye, it will make it much nicer for you all. I know Daisy and I used to have some great scraps when Jack and I were at the "Dingle"—she was only about seventeen then and more absolutely "tom-boy" than she is now. Of course I was a careless young beggar, and there was not a thing that a boy could do in the way of racing or climbing that she wouldn't try if I dared her to do it.'

'Oh, she has told me what great times you used to have; she often regrets the Dennis boys, and says there are no English boys so good as the Irish boys for fun.'

'I'm afraid Mr. Enderby used to find us rather a handful sometimes, and we boys would lead Daisy on just to see what she would do—well, we are punished now for our sins, for we find it slow enough "baching" on our own place and are glad to get away from it.'

'I'm sure it must be dreadfully lonely when one of you is away and your work is all done, and then it does not seem natural for a man to be doing all the cooking and sweeping and washing and all the domestic work of the home.'

'Oh, don't harbour any illusions about our housekeeping,' replied Tom, laughing rather ruefully, 'we don't live, we exist; honestly, Miss Raye, we live like savages—with apologies to the savages. Thanks to a neighbour Canadian farmer's wife, we get our washing done for us—that and the remnants of our bringing up in the Old Country enable us to appear semi-respectable when we go off our own place to town or come to the "Dingle"—but, our housekeeping at home—an Indian would not call it "housekeeping," and a dog wouldn't own it as "home," ' and there was a touch of scornful disgust in Tom's voice.

'I'm so sorry,' said Evelyn gently, and there was silence for a minute or two—broken by Tom.

'But I'm not kicking about it, you know, Miss Raye, I suppose it is our own fault. I am really getting to like the farm work part of the life very well, but I abhor anything to do with messing about the house, and Jack, who took to the cooking and so forth as a kind of picnicing novelty at first, has got sick of the whole thing.'

'I'm sure I hope Chris will not get tired of it,' said Evelyn rather anxiously, 'for I'm afraid I may have given him too bright a picture of Manitoba farm life. You see, when I was out before I was with the Swansons, and they were splendid housekeepers, and everything was beautifully clean and homelike.'

'Oh, he tells me you are to live with him when he gets a place of his own; that's quite a different story—lucky beggar!'

'Perhaps he may not be so lucky,' replied Evelyn with a blush at the honest impulsiveness of Tom's last words; 'you know I've been more of the "schoolmarm" than a cook since I grew up, and may prove a very indifferent substitute for Mrs. Hardie when it comes to cakes and pies.'

'It's not the absence of cakes and pies that makes our "baching" such a dismal failure. I'm always hungry and care very little what I eat as far as that goes—it's the squalidness of the life—we live like Connemara peasants—but I need not bore you with our grievances—you know an Irishman is never happy except when he's miserable.'

'Well, if you get too Irish happy, Mr. Dennis, you must come over here the oftener—there is your brother coming up the lane and Mr. Hardie with him. Daisy, is that set nearly over?—you will have to make peace for Chris —here is Mr. Hardie coming to look for his lost "hired man." '

'Oh, we finished five minutes ago, but you were so busy umpiring for us that you did not notice it—now, Tom, which of us won? I don't believe you even know that.'

'Oh, you won,' replied Tom laughing, 'no need to watch the game to know that; you would be chasing Raye with your racquet if you had been beaten—you know half the time your "serves" were in the wrong court, only Raye was so good-natured he never said anything.'

'You horrid fibber, Tom Dennis, I don't believe you ever saw a single stroke—you are too late for the tennis, Mr. Hardie,' she called out to the latter, who was by this time walking up from the lane, where Jack Dennis had stayed with the buckboard.

'Oh, you just rest easy with spoiling the young folks, Miss Daisy, without trying your hand on an old fellow like me,' said Jim laughing, 'it's not you I'm wanting the night, but Miss Raye there—I've a letter for you, Miss Raye, and a message for Bert and Tom Dennis here.'

'Oh, what is it all about, Evelyn? and what is the message for Bert, Mr. Hardie, and haven't you a letter for me?—Bert, Bert, come here, Mr. Hardie has a message for you, and I want to know what all this mystery is about.'

'Well, my part is not very mysterious, Daisy,' said Evelyn, who had finished reading her letter. 'This is just a note from Amanda Swanson asking me to go—as her old teacher—to her wedding next month up in Sweden.'

'Ah, I thought that was what it would be,' said Jim Hardie, 'young Carl Swanson brought it this morning on his way to town, and he brought a note to me written by Amanda for her father, and he wants me to drive Mr. Jordan up from our place to the Swedish Church—they've no minister of their own, you know, and Mr. Jordan is to marry them.'

'And he didn't ask you to bring me, Mr. Hardie?—that's too bad—a wedding in Sweden would be all kinds of a show.'

'Well, I cannot say he did,' replied Jim, 'but he did say as he would be proud to see Tom Dennis and Bert here if they would come—you see he thinks a lot of their kindness when they had the trouble last winter.'

'Oh, of course, Mr. Hardie,' said Daisy with mock indignation, 'we know how exclusive you men people are if there is any fun going—but shall you go, Evelyn?'

'I should like to very much if it can be managed,' said Evelyn, 'the Swansons were so good to me when I boarded there, and I promised Amanda in fun that I would come back to see her married.'

'Oh, the school here could have a holiday for a day for that matter,' said Jim, 'and I daresay Bert and Tom could see about taking you up.'

'Oh yes,' said Tom, 'I'd be delighted to take you up, if Bert cannot go, or we might all three go up together. I'll come over on Sunday and we can settle it then. There is the mare getting fidgety at the gate and we must be off—come, Raye, you can take the seat by Jack and Mr. Hardie and I will sit on behind—good-bye, Miss Raye, say good-bye to your mother for me, Daisy, and say, Daisy, try and play square the next time you challenge Raye to a set.'

Evelyn and Daisy watched the buckboard drive away and then strolled back to the house.

'My, but it has been a great day,' said Daisy with a sigh of regret that it was over, 'a regular top-notcher. Did you hear that last remark of Tom's about playing "square"—but an Irishman has no gratitude—absolutely none.'

CHAPTER X

BACHING AT CONNEMARA FARM

Connemara, as the Dennis boys had named their place, was a naturally good farm spoilt in the farming. It had been homesteaded some ten years earlier than the time of this story by a farmer's son from Ontario, who had come west with little more capital than a team of horses and money enough to pay his homestead fees and buy a wagon, a plough, and a set of harrows. He had no intention of making it his home and remaining in Manitoba—it was simply the means to an end—the creation of sufficient capital with which to farm on a more ambitious scale than a quarter section in one of the newer territories lying still further west. The homestead law required that he should break and crop a certain number of acres and spend a certain number of months on the homestead each year for three years. They also required that he should erect buildings which, by the favour of the homestead inspector, would pass muster for a house and a stable. He set to work with all the energy of a young Canadian who sees visions of many dollars in the future, and who has left old Ontario with his father's blessing, and an intimation that he need not return till he has made good. The first spring he camped on his homestead in a six-foot-by-eight tent and broke up twenty acres in not many more days. He worked as long hours as his team would stand it, and lived on porridge, fried bacon, and bannock, washed down with green tea. He worked from Monday morning to Saturday night, and on Sundays he rested, and stepped out his breaking to see how many acres he still had to do to complete his first year's quota—he might file a plough-point or two and perhaps bake a batch of bannock—this was not sufficiently work to trouble his conscience, and yet it saved time through the week. By the middle of May his task was done, and he was forced to turn his energies elsewhere. He went among the neighbouring settlers and hired out himself and, if possible, his team—no kind of work in which there was good pay came amiss—breaking, haying, harvesting, threshing, and so on, till the frost came.

During an idle interval in the summer he had gone up to the bush and cut and hewed enough poplar logs for a small house and a stable—these he now drew home, and before the snow came to stay both he and his team were adequately if roughly housed for the winter.

49

Such energy will not be denied—at the end of his third summer he had paid for his pre-emption of the adjoining quarter section of one hundred and sixty acres, his application for a patent or title to his homestead was accepted by the Dominion Land Department, and he had a nice nest-egg in the local bank at Minnedosa. His next step was to mortgage his whole farm for as much as a Loan Company was willing to lend on the security of the land—some three dollars an acre—and with the proceeds of his mortgage and his savings he went west to repeat the profitable venture in Saskatchewan. By his intentional failure to meet his repayments on the mortgage, the farm lapsed to the Loan Company and went out of cultivation. In four or five years the ploughed land was hardly distinguishable from the unbroken prairie except by the presence of wild oats and other weeds, the snake fences round the whilom fields were rotting and falling down, and the house and stable had ceased to be habitable even from a western point of view, which is not exacting.

When the father of the Dennis boys wrote to Mr. Enderby and asked him to purchase a farm on which Tom and Jack could launch out for themselves, it was this derelict homestead that he had chosen. The farm was a good farm, the price was reasonable, and the boys themselves were anxious to keep near the 'Dingle' and their English friends in the settlement. What Mr. Enderby had not taken into account was the demoralising effect upon the young men themselves of the comfortless makeshift surroundings in which the two boys found themselves when they entered on their possessions.

Bert Enderby went over with them for a few days, and with his aid the stable and house were replastered, the roof mended and the broken glass in the windows replaced by new, then he had to return to his own work and home and leave them to their own resources.

The novelty and sense of freedom carried them through the first summer—some thirty acres of the land which had been broken by their predecessor was ploughed up again ready for the next year, they put up enough hay for the winter, and they did a good deal of shooting of wild ducks and prairie chickens. More for the sake of company and a little variety than for the wages, they joined a threshing gang in the Fall—then followed the long winter with its deadly monotony, the occasional trip to the bush for firewood, the care of the team, the cooking of pork, porridge and bannock to-day, bannock, porridge, and pork to-morrow, the short days followed by endless nights when they sat by the stove and read and re-read untidy bundles of Old Country magazines and paper-covered novels, till in their weariness of life they turned into the towselled mass of blankets on a wooden bunk which was called bed!

Hundreds of well-born and nurtured Old Country lads, coming from re-fined and bright homes, have passed through the same experience and come out with the same result—a loathing of the whole prairie farm life—a contempt for those who have made a success of it with less opportunities than themselves, coupled often with a loss of their own self-respect and of what is due to their own manhood and their father's name and country.

The life at Connemara had told less severely on Tom Dennis than on his brother. His was naturally the stiffer character, and his failure was more due to the lack of any sufficiently compelling motive to work than a dislike to the character of the work itself, and Jim Hardie had said nothing more than the truth when he told him that if he would work as well at home as he did at Rosebank with Jim, that he would soon have a good farm of his own —but from his temperament a return in money value would never be a suf-ficient motive for Tom Dennis—his success, if it ever came, would come from an appeal to his sympathies or his affections rather than to an ambi-tion that could be expressed in material comforts. Then again, Tom had come to the life willingly and with a vague craving for adventure, for free-dom, for the open air. With Jack it was different—he came unwillingly—for him the Canadian West was a distasteful solution of the problem of what to do, since he had failed to qualify for the only calling for which he had a real craving—a soldier's life—a Western farm or a seat at an office desk in Belfast were the alternatives offered him by his father, he knew he would hate the latter, his brother Tom was a 'good sort,' so West he came, expecting little and finding it.

With the dead weight of his brother's discontent and indifference against him, Tom Dennis had well-nigh decided to cut the whole show and return with Jack to Ireland, when two events, entirely unconnected with each other, combined to wake him up to a fresh and honest effort to make their farming a success. One was the influence and friendship of Jim Hardie, resulting from a quite chance arrangement for him to help Jim draw up his hay from Jim's meadows in 'Sweden,' and the other was a let-ter from their father saying that owing to losses at home he would have to discontinue sending them an allowance, and adding: 'we feel that the sacri-fices we have made at home in order to give Jack and yourself a fair start in life entitle us to expect that you will settle down steadily to work—what you know would be a great disappointment to myself would be worse than a disappointment to your mother.'

While Tom Dennis was still under the influence of Jim Hardie's en-couragement and his father's letter came his first meeting with Evelyn Raye and their drive up from Minnedosa, and over the vision of the future which before was all hardness and duty came the glamour of love.

It was the morning after the tennis party at the 'Dingle,' and Tom and Jack had just finished their breakfast—porridge and bacon, with the unusual addition of poached eggs and bread—the last two a present from Mrs. Hardie the evening before. The few dishes were receiving a perfunctory washing from Jack while Tom was busy mending some harness—a task over which he was whistling with great cheerfulness and energy.

'You seem very gay this morning, Tom,' said Jack at last with a touch of irritation in his voice, 'I don't see anything very giddy ahead to-day to be so jolly cheerful about.'

'Well, we had a great day yesterday, and I feel as fit as a fiddle for work this morning—now, honestly, Jack, didn't you have a good time yesterday?'

'Oh, yes, I had a good enough time yesterday,' admitted Jack grudgingly, 'but that doesn't make to-day's drudgery any better. What's the good of a game of tennis every other week or so when there's this rotten show all the time between? You've taken to pretending you like it—I don't—that's all the difference.'

'That's not all the difference; I've made up my mind to work, whether I like it or not.'

'Have you?—well, I haven't; I've made up my mind to get out of this before long. If you like to grub along here you can—it's not good enough for Willie.'

'Why, what do you mean, Jack? Get out of it! What in the world else can you do? You never dream of bumming round some store in Minnedosa, like young Digby, for fifty cents a day and your board?'

'No, I don't mean to "bum" round Minnedosa, and I've no more idea of going behind a counter than you have,' retorted Jack warmly, 'I'm going to join the North-West Mounted Police.'

'Join the Mounted Police—whatever put that in your head?'

'I met two of them when I was in town last time, taking a horse-thief back to Yorkton, and I tell you they have a different sort of time with some life in it—different to rotting round a God-forsaken farm where you never see anything fresh in a dog's age. I made up my mind then that I would go this Fall anyway.'

'But why in the world didn't you tell me before? You've got to figure a little on what I say before you break away like that.'

'Well, I hated to say anything after——' and Jack hesitated and coloured up—' after the shape I came home from town, and when you seemed so keen on the farm—but I'm going,' and Jack's tone grew stubborn with the stubbornness of a weak will, 'and you're not my boss anyway, Tom, if you are three years older than I am—I'm twenty-two and my own master if it comes to that.'

'Who's talking about bossing you; don't be an ass; still, you cannot forget what the governor has done for us, and he has a right to be consulted before you go off on any wild scheme like that—besides, it's not fair to me —to leave me in the lurch.'

'Well, I don't think the governor can kick—he says he can't send us any more money, and I don't propose to stay here and starve to please either him or you—and that's jolly well what we should do if we depended on the farm to keep us. Besides, there are lots of gentlemen's sons in the Mounted Police—it's not like joining the ranks at home—though I would have done that before ever I came to this howling wilderness if it had not been for the fuss the mater and the girls would have made about it.'

'I know what you're thinking,' Jack continued as Tom remained silent, thoughtfully filling his pipe and lighting it and sitting down by the stove, 'you think I shall not keep straight. I can tell you I am a lot more likely to keep straight in a stirring life where there is some novelty, than grubbing along here—the same old thing every day in the year—only worse and more of it—why shouldn't you come too?'

'No, Jack, if you go you must go alone, and perhaps after all it would be the best thing in the long run—only don't go yet. Write home and ask the governor, and then help me out this summer. Then if you want to go I won't hinder you—you wouldn't mind staying here would you, if we had a chance of making it a comfortable home like they have at the Dingle?'

'What's the good of "ifs" when there is no earthly chance of them happening?'

'Well, will you leave me the "if" till the Fall, Jack, and then if this "if" fails, perhaps I'll go with you—I mean it—I'm not fooling.'

'You can't expect me to bind myself to some mysterious "if" in the dark, Tom; I've told you my plan openly and you must be square with me.'

'Did you ever know me not square, Jack Dennis? confound you, don't talk squareness to me,' retorted Tom with a momentary burst of temper, which was subdued as quickly as it came. 'You want me to be plain and I'll be plain—though, mind you, I'm talking to my brother, Jack Dennis, and not to every long-eared gossip in the country—I'm going to work this summer and work hard, and if I can make this place into a home—a home, Jack —and if we get off the crop in good shape and if—mind this "if," Jack—if you don't disgrace the old name by any low-down sprees in town—why, then,' and Tom blushed red to the roots of his hair—'why, then, I'm going to ask Evelyn Raye to be my wife——' and Tom rose from his chair, and picking up the harness, strode out of the house and down to the stable.

Half an hour later Jack joined him in the stableyard where he was hitching up the team to the wagon loaded with fence posts. Jack passed round the front of the horses to where Tom was stooping down doing up the last buckle, and as Tom raised himself erect Jack simply held out his hand—'I'll stay, Tom, and, please God, my "if" shall not come between you and happiness.'

CHAPTER XI

DAISY DEMANDS A SQUARE DEAL

Winter, rather than summer, is the season of social intercourse in the West, for it is the season of greater leisure, and there is little to record of the six or seven weeks which intervened between the tennis party of the Queen's birthday and the projected trip to 'Sweden' for Amanda Swanson's wedding. Tom and Jack Dennis worked hard at the fencing of their crop—a tight four-strand wire fence, which insured immunity from the wandering bands of their neighbours' cattle, and when that was done, settled down steadily to the breaking of new land for the next year. Twice on Saturday afternoons they had driven over to the 'Dingle' for tennis, and twice on church Sundays Tom had walked home from service with Bert Enderby and stayed for the rest of the day. The alternate Sundays Tom and Jack had spent at Rosebank with the Hardies—partly lest Jim should feel a slight on his ever-ready hospitality, and partly lest Daisy should put an embarrassing construction on the too hasty renewal of the old ties between Connemara Farm and the Dingle. It was left an open question till the church Sunday before the wedding whether Bert or Tom Dennis or both should accompany Evelyn on her trip to 'Sweden,' and Daisy had a talent for settling most open questions at the Dingle to meet her own views.

It was a scorching hot afternoon, and some rugs and the old deck chairs had been taken out to the shade of the poplar bluff—Tom had come back to dinner with the Dingle party, Jack Dennis and Chris Raye walking up from Rosebank in the middle of the afternoon.

The conversation, which had at first been general, had gradually drifted into little separate currents—Bert and Jack Dennis were talking 'horse,' the side of western life in which Jack took most interest, Bert having a young three-year-old which Jack, who was a fearless rider, was anxious to be allowed to break in. Evelyn in an old deck chair with Tom Dennis lying on a rug by its side were discussing *Lorna Doone*, which lay open on Evelyn's lap—she had lent the book to Tom two weeks before and Tom, rather to his own surprise, had found it interesting.

'I tried it once before,' he confessed to Evelyn, 'when I was just a big kid—but there was such a lot of description, and—and—really, I didn't see why John Ridd made such a fuss about Lorna—I liked his strength and fondness for fighting, but honestly I thought he was rather an ass——'

'You mustn't say a word against John Ridd to me,' interrupted Evelyn laughing, 'he is one of my heroes.'

'Oh, I liked the book all right this time,' admitted Tom, 'but you see, I am older now—boys at that age are natural heretics about—about Lornas —especially if they have sisters of their own to chaff them.'

'Well, I must forgive you as you recant now you have read it a second time—if you had still found it uninteresting I'm afraid I should have had no hopes of you. I wonder what Daisy and Chris are discussing so eagerly —at least——'

'At least Daisy is discussing and your brother doing the listening— Daisy's duets are apt to be one-sided—Daisy, what mischief are you plotting? I can see by the scared look on Raye's face that it is something desperate.'

'It's too bad of you, Tom, always to pretend that I am a wild, irresponsible person. We were thinking that it was not a square deal for Evelyn and you or Bert to go off and have a giddy time at a Swede wedding and for the rest of us to be left to our lonesome—the daily round and so forth, and so on——'

'Well, Daisy, why don't you come too?' replied Tom, 'I am sure "Sweden" would be highly honoured.'

'So Mr. Raye and I were thinking,' went on Daisy, ignoring Tom's suggestion with contempt, 'that the rest of us might have a holiday and little celebration of our own here; of course, we would have to imagine the wedding part of it, but we could have an afternoon's tennis, and you could pick Jack up when you brought Evelyn back in the evening, and if there were time we might even have a little dance—what do you say, Bert?'

'Oh, I will fall in with anything that suits the rest,' said Bert, 'I should have liked to go up to Sweden, but really I ought not to take the whole day off from the summer fallowing—do you think you could get away, Raye, for the afternoon?'

'I don't fancy there would be any difficulty for me,' said Chris Raye, 'Jim Hardie will be away with the team—he is taking Mr. Jordan up, you know, and Miss Daisy suggested——' and Chris hesitated and looked to Daisy to help him out.

'Well, you see, Jack,' broke in Daisy, 'you would drive over early in the morning with Tom, and as we couldn't play tennis till the afternoon you could get out at Rosebank and help Mr. Raye for the half day—he's doing something delightful—cutting scrub, didn't you say, Mr. Raye—and you are a dab at that, now aren't you, Jack? Now, say you'll come, like a good boy?'

'Oh yes, I'll come; I'm not struck on working at Connemara by myself, and say, Bert, I might have a shy with the colt in the evening?'

'All right, that will suit me if it suits you,' said Bert; 'I'll risk the colt if you'll risk your neck, and with the haying coming on there will not be much more tennis for a while.'

'Irish boys are the most delightful creatures in the world,' confided Daisy in an undertone to Evelyn; 'give them the chance of slipping out of their work or of breaking their necks with a horse and you can do what you like with them—but really, Evelyn,' giving the latter a sly pinch, 'don't you think Jack will be safer here with the colt than Tom will be driving to Sweden with the mare—and the schoolmarm?'

CHAPTER XII

THE ROSE OF SWEDEN

The June rains that year came in June, which is not such an unnecessary statement as might be supposed. No one knows when the term 'June rains' first came into common use in the West—probably it is the survival of some old Indian myth, which has been adopted as a conveniently short term to express the broken weather, with rain and thunder-storms, which may be expected to occur with some measure of confidence between, say, the first of May and the end of July. Whether they anticipate their title by keeping the settlers grumbling indoors when they are aching to be at their seeding—or defer their coming till all but the crop reporters of the papers are resigned to no oat straw for feed and ten bushels of wheat to the acre—the old-timer, faithful to the tradition of the past, still maintains his faith in 'June rains,' while admitting that the particular season is exceptional—quite exceptional. If there is any truth in the saying that 'the exception proves the rule,' the rule should be well established.

Following, then, the June rains there came a spell of intensely hot weather, a burning sun and a cloudless sky, and Tom Dennis, according to arrangement, was early at the Dingle so that the drive up to Sweden might be over before the heat of the day. Tom was tying up the mare to the fence as Daisy came down the garden path to greet him, with her blouse sleeves rolled up and her hair in unabashed curl-papers, for Tom Dennis did not count in such little domesticities.

'Good morning, Tom, did you bring Jack?'

'Yes, Jack is safe at Rosebank, and he and Raye are coming up right after dinner. Is Miss Raye ready?'

'Don't get in a fluster, my dear boy, Evelyn is just putting the finishing touches to her toilet, it is only half-past eight and the wedding is not till eleven. The mare must be getting slow in her old age if she wants two hours and a half for ten miles.'

'Oh, the mare's all right, but the new corded road is pretty rough for a buckboard, and there will still be some mud holes in the low spots.'

'How careful we are! Here comes Evelyn—now don't blush, Tom, it doesn't suit your complexion.'

But Tom did blush in spite of himself, and was glad to be busy arranging the cushions and rug for their knees till Evelyn reached the gate, when he turned round to greet her.

'Good morning, Miss Raye, we are going to have a lovely morning for our drive; I'll give the rig a half turn while you get in.'

'And I've made him promise to drive slowly, Evelyn, and Tom, you had better attend to the wedding service just to see——'

'Mind the wheel, Daisy,' and Tom tightened the lines, which was a sufficient hint to the old mare, 'mind the wheel—good-bye,' and they were out of hearing before Daisy, who jumped backward as the mare started, had time to complete her sentence.

At the end of the lane they came to the town line, the main road running from Minnedosa, twelve miles away to the south, far up into the Swedish colony to the north. For the first mile or two the road allowance, some thirty yards wide, was fenced, and on either side were fields of growing grain. Then the character of the scenery changed—they were at the end of the open prairie, and entering what a few years before had been solid bush, here the road had been cut through the woods, and the trail was still very rough and full of half-rotted roots and stumps. Not only did the scenery change, but they were soon conscious of a change in the whole character of the settlement. The first farmstead to which they came, in an opening in the woods, showed that they were among people differing widely in their ideals of life and beauty from the English and Canadian settlers to the south. They were in the land of the Norsemen—the fisherman, the wood-cutter and the peasant of Norway and Sweden had brought here the life and the spirit of the land of the Fells and the Fiords and were shaping out a new Scandinavia in the land of their adoption. Few of them had more than an acre or two cleared round their houses, but it was always neatly and tastefully fenced. Their log houses had an air of their own, entirely different from the log house of the Englishman or the Canadian. Here were wide projecting eaves, quaint little windows in the roof, rustic porches with trailing vines, with rustic seats, made from the spruce and the tamarac, on the shady side of the house.

The lake and woodland that had seemed too rough and broken for the Canadian who wished to grow prosaic wheat, or for the Englishman, unskilled in the use of the axe, appealed to the memory and the imagination of the Scandinavian, who loved to see in the new land and the new home, a scenery that spoke to him of the homeland of his people.

Tom Dennis had never driven through the woods in the summer time, and when he had been up to Jim Hardie's bush shanty in the previous winter it had all seemed to him as he said, 'a howling wilderness,' but it seemed quite a different world to-day with Evelyn by his side and the wide road allowance on either side of the trail, a wilderness of trailing vines, of wild hops and honeysuckles, with here and there glorious clusters of wild roses glistening in a sweet-scented loveliness of ruddy pink and dewdrops. The winter stillness of the bush that had seemed so sombre and lifeless was broken to-day by the rough melody of cow-bells, or the harsh scream of a bluejay as it darted through the woods, and as they passed by homesteads lying but a little distance back from the road the voices of a settler calling to his oxen, or of children playing round the house could be heard.

'I wondered last winter, when I heard an English girl had taught school in Sweden for two years, what kind of a girl she must be to have existed in such a place and among such a people, but it seems more possible to me now.'

'Now you know the English girl, do you mean, Mr. Dennis,' asked Evelyn, 'or now you see Sweden in the summertime?'

'I think it is a little of both; I know plenty of girls at home, who are nice enough girls too, who would seem absolutely incongruous if you were to set them down in Sweden—or even at the Dingle, while you seem to drop into all the ways of the West as if—as if—I don't quite know how to put it.'

' "As if to the manner born," to use the hackneyed expression—well, so I am in a way—to be a country parson's daughter in a scattered parish of farmers and farm labourers is not a bad preparation for the West. I'm used to going long walks by myself and to taking an interest in a lot of little things—things we call little, but which make up the lives of simple country people—then I am fond of children, and children I think are nicer in a comparatively wild state than when they are over-civilised into tidiness and the proprieties.'

'But you must have found the winter horribly long? I'll admit it is lovely up here now with the woods and the lakes and the wild flowers—but for how long? About four or five months. Then the cold and the solitude and the everlasting snow—the short days and the long evenings—whatever did you do?'

'Well, there was school in the daytime and in the evening I did a good deal of reading, or helped Amanda with her lessons, and occasionally we would have toboggan parties or snowshoe tramps, and some of the older people were delightful to talk to—old Mr. Nielson, Ludwig's father, and old Carl Swanson, Amanda's uncle, in their different ways. I could listen to them for hours, with their wild yarns of the sea and their old home life.'

'And the young people, were they equally charming?' asked Tom with a touch of sarcasm in his voice. 'I can't say I cared much for some of the fellows I met out threshing—they seemed pretty uncouth.'

'Well, perhaps they are not so interesting as the old people; they have lost the simple courtesy of the old world peasant and have picked up a good deal of the roughness of the railway gangs and lumber camps where they go out to work, and the girls who have gone out to service in hotels and so forth in the towns, and who have discarded their national dress, have lost the charm there is in girls like Amanda, who have stayed more among their own people and kept their old manner of life.'

'I expect I shall feel rather like a fish out of water,' said Tom, 'and you must give me a hint if I do not behave myself strictly according to Scandinavian etiquette.'

'Oh, I don't think you will get into any difficulties,' said Evelyn laughing. 'Mr. Hardie will take charge of you when we get there, and he knows most of them and is a great favourite in the colony. I hope you like coffee, for you cannot escape that—and when we go into the church all the men will sit on one side and the women on the other—we are nearly there now; just put your mind a hundred years back and you will find it all perfectly natural—and here is Mr. Hardie with Mr. Jordan close behind us.'

The road, which had been straight for a long stretch, swerved to the left, and here in a clearing of an acre or so stood the little log church, facing the blue waters of Otter lake. Here, too, apparently, was a goodly portion of the Swedish colony, for rows of wagons were already drawn up along the side of the trail, many of them bedecked with boughs of poplar and of spruce, the oxen which had drawn them tied to the church yard fence or in the shade of the trees by the roadside.

Evelyn was evidently expected, for as Tom drew up at the wicket gate a group of school girls came forward to greet her and she was carried off to where their mothers were gathered round the church porch, while Tom drove a little further along the road and was unhitching the mare when he was accosted by Jim Hardie.

'Good morning, Tom; a great day for a wedding, and I guess all Sweden will be here—you didn't hurry any on the road—it was half-past nine when we left Rosebank, and Mr. Jordan was getting fidgety we'd be late, but I told him they couldn't get very far on with the wedding without the minister.'

'Oh, we took it easy; the road's pretty rough, and you see——'

'And you didn't like to hurry the mare—I don't blame you, Tom; well, come along and I'll introduce you to some of the men folk, and then we'd better be getting into the church—there's Mr. Jordan just going in with his little black bag, and Ludwig is not the one to be late on his wedding-day.'

Even as Jim spoke a general movement of the scattered groups announced that the bridegroom and the bride had already come, and they had only time to follow the throng into the church itself, which was soon crowded to the door, while many of the younger men who could not find room stood without, hat in hand, at the open windows and around the porch.

The service which followed was a compromise between Mr. Jordan's loyalty to the Prayer Book and his dislike of the service not being understood by those who were taking part in it, and he was conscious that none of the older women and some of the older men had little, if any, knowledge of English. It began with the singing of a wedding hymn in Swedish, and during the singing of it a space was made for the bridal party to approach the altar and take their places in front of the 'Herr Pastor'—Mr. Jordan.

The dais on which the bride and bridegroom stood was covered with a crimson cloth, on which, in a regular device, had been arranged the pearl-white blossoms of the wood-anemone. The bridegroom, Ludwig Nielson, was a fine, handsome, young fellow, neither self-assertive nor yet abashed, simply and unaffectedly happy, with a sober reverence for the House of God, endowing his bride with an honest manhood worthy of the race of Vikings from which he was sprung. Amanda, the bride, looking indeed the 'Rose of Sweden,' as Jim Hardie had named her long ago, *simplex munditiis*, the pure white of her marriage gown untouched with colour, save where a cluster of wild roses nestled at her bosom. Who can tell how the simple beauty of her love and faith shone through the blue softness of her eyes as, in accents that hesitated now and again, she made her vows of wifely obedience and honour?

At the close of the simple service came a second hymn, a Swedish paraphrase of the twenty-third Psalm, 'The Lord is my shepherd,' and the mingled voices of young and old rose and fell with a full volume of sound to the evidently familiar words. Here and there, among the older women, there was a furtive wiping away of a tear, and it was not hard to guess what memories of other days and far-off scenes were awakened by this 'singing of the Lord's song' in a strange land. The true *heimweh* lies deepest and saddest in the heart of the woman; in the man it is his pride in his race and his fatherland, in the woman it is the deep fountain of her love of family and home.

The words of the benediction, 'The Peace of God,' uttered by the Herr Pastor with uplifted hands were followed by a solemn hush, and then the congregation filed slowly and quietly out of the church, forming as they did so, an avenue through which the bridal party passed to the church yard gate.

Here, too, Jim Hardie and Tom found their way, and were soon the centre of a little group of the older settlers who came to greet them and welcome them to Sweden, and Tom was secretly much amused to find himself being introduced, with much ceremony and taking off of hats, as Herr Dennis, to men in decent suits of broadcloth, full fashioned as to the coat-tails, and with much shirt front and cuffs. He could hardly realise that these grave, courteous men, every one of whom, as he told Daisy Enderby afterwards, might have been a churchwarden or a parish clerk at the least, were the same men whom he had often passed on the winter trail to town clad in rough and shabby skin coats, plodding along by the side of their oxen and loads of cordwood.

The greetings and introductions over, 'Old Carl' Swanson, Amanda's uncle, became their escort to the grove, a little nearer the lake shore, where the marriage feast was to take place.

It was a spot not only beautiful in itself, but possessed of that particular beauty which harmonised with the spirit of these good North folk. It was the beauty of long and stately avenues of spruce and pine, where green and golden moss sank beneath the footfall with the silent softness of an Eastern carpet. Above, through the long spreading plumes of the trees was the radiant blue of our Manitoba sky—a sky reflected in softened and rippling tones in the wavelets of the lake as it lay before them in the wide openings of the forest trees.

From the lavish preparations, it was evident that the marriage feast had grown from the modest quietness for which Amanda and Ludwig had hoped into the centre of a national festival in honour of the 'Rose of Sweden.'

Rows of tables, roughly formed of boards, yet covered with spotless linen, had been ranged beneath the trees and were soon covered with a bountiful repast—every family in the colony brought of its best, and great was the emulation of the housewives in the whiteness of their bread, the sweetness of their butter, and the richness of their cakes.

A certain formality and restraint, due to the presence among them of the Herr Pastor—as they invariably called Mr. Jordan—and of their other English guests, wore away by degrees, and soon the woods were ringing with mirth and laughter.

'I wonder what time we should be starting for home,' said Tom to Jim Hardie an hour or two later, as they sat under a big spruce enjoying a quiet smoke and watching the groups of children playing around. 'The mosquitoes will be bad in the bush towards evening, and I promised Daisy Enderby to be back early.'

'Here come the minister and Miss Raye; I guess we'd better ask them,' replied Jim as Mr. Jordan and Evelyn joined them. 'You two are the bosses to-day; Tom and I were wondering what the orders were.'

'We were just coming to see what you thought, Mr. Hardie,' said Mr. Jordan, 'I have promised to walk across to Pete Johnson's and christen a baby there, and Miss Raye is to go over with Amanda and her husband to see the presents at Mrs. Swanson's. I could be back at Ole's in an hour or so if that will suit you and Mr. Dennis?'

'That will suit me fine,' said Jim. 'I'd like as I'm up here to run up to my hay meadows—it's only a couple of miles north—just to see when my hay will be ready for cutting, and if Tom here will drive me up, why, we will be back and ready to start—say at four o'clock.'

Surely Tom must have forgotten his promise to Daisy Enderby, or the mosquitoes have neglected to use their opportunities, which is not like the mosquito, for the fact remains that the sun was setting as they turned into the lane at the Dingle. It is true they were delayed a little in the starting, for there were final libations of coffee at Mrs. Swanson's, to have forgone which would have cast a cloud over that good woman's hospitable soul; but still the slowness of the old mare would have been a scandal had there been any of Tom's sporting friends there to see. Perhaps the old mare herself was partly to blame: horses, like men, learn wisdom on a bachelor's homestead—the Sweden oats had been sound and plentiful—it was not for her to set the pace—if it were three miles an hour to-day it might be ten miles an hour to-morrow—*carpe diem*—though it is doubtful if her philosophy included the classics.

Yet they talked but little as the mare jogged quietly along—that was the danger of it—when a word is a sentence and a nod or glance of the eye an answer—when the one sees no peril and the other welcomes it, then it is that hearts are lost and won.

Old Doctor Casey, when comparing himself and his rival practitioner in Minnedosa, was often wont to say, 'I'm a darned fool and know it—Dr. Jones is a darnder fool and doesn't,' which, without any imputation of folly and in an entirely sympathetic spirit, may be a fair way of describing how matters stood with Evelyn and Tom as the result of their share in the bridal day of the 'Rose of Sweden.'

CHAPTER XIII

THE SHADOW OF A CLOUD

The romance of haymaking died with the introduction of modern machinery. It is no longer toil sweetened by a simple pride of skill in wielding the primitive tool of husbandry—the scythe—but toil that is accepted grudgingly as a necessary cog in the wheel of progress towards wealth. In the West 'the dewy call of incense breathing morn' is only an hour lost before the grass is dry enough for the mower to run. The emulation of farmer with farmer and rustic with rustic in the Old Land was the emulation that springs from a love of the soil, the joy of winning a coy consent from Nature to their wooing. The emulation of the West, with the farmer is the emulation of the biggest farm and the largest herd in the settlement, and with the 'hired man' the emulation to command the highest wage. The haymaking of the old days was toil, but it was companionable toil. The sturdy mowers followed one another at nicely adjusted intervals, scythe in time with scythe, a rhythmic harmony of sound and motion, the broad swaths falling with a sharp swish to the sweep of the keen-edged blades. Then as the sun reached towards its zenith came the 'nuncheon' hour, and scythes laid aside, they gathered beneath some wide-spreading elm growing in the hedgerow for their simple meal of bread and bacon and cheese. From under a cock of new-mown grass in the shade of the hedge was drawn out the little—perhaps not so little—keg of haying beer, and it was passed round in a recognised rotation from oldest to youngest, each as he took it giving a wipe to his lips with the back of his hand before he raised it to his mouth. How nice was the sense of delicacy to withdraw it before incurring a suspicion of greediness from his mates, and yet not too soon. Rough wit and humour enlivened the half hour left before the resumption of toil, and when night came they returned to their neighbouring cottages in the little villages, weary and grimed with the wiping of their faces with sweaty hands, yet redolent of the meadows, and with the sweet content of honest toil to be followed by well-earned repose.

There is no more sentiment in Western haymaking now than in a lawyer's bill of costs after a lost suit on a disputed lien note. The ties that bind the hired man and the farmer scarcely get beyond the atmosphere of work and wages, the one anxious to get the maximum of work, the other to do no more than he is paid for, and for a large part of the haying and harvest they work apart—the boss on the mower or the binder, the hired man on the rake or stooking the sheaves.

In the earlier days of settlement, when there was less money, there was more neighbourliness among the homesteaders; few dared run the risk of offering money wages to a stranger which the harvest might not enable them to pay. Neighbour worked with neighbour, exchanging work for work in return, and there was a larger spirit which was not careful to observe a nice balance of equivalents.

If Jim Hardie happened to observe to Bert Enderby that he was going to be a little 'crowded' to get his hay stacked before his early barley wanted cutting, Bert would take it up quite as a matter of course.

'I'll come along with a team and our chore boy and give you a hand for a day or two,' or perhaps Bert might say casually on a Sunday afternoon, 'Our wheat is all coming on together this year, I'm afraid it will be shelling before we can get it down,' and Jim would say nothing at the time, but just as Bert was leaving he might remark, as something which had slipped his notice at the time, 'Well, so long, Bert—oh, by the way, I can run up with the binder for a couple of days, I'm not figuring on using it at home before Wednesday,' and neither felt in the slightest degree that they were conferring or receiving an obligation—*tempora mutantur*—unfortunately.

Young fellows keeping 'bach' like the Dennis boys were a sort of freelances in the settlement, perfectly welcome to such hospitality on Sundays and other times as they might choose to put themselves in the way of accepting and very willing to lend a hand at the Dingle or Rosebank at busy seasons, and proving themselves much more strenuous in their labours anywhere than at home.

This year things were different at Connemara Farm. Tom worked with a feverish energy, not only at the farm work outside, but on rainy days to make the house less forlorn, and to build a granary for the crop, and Jack fell in with his brother's ambitions with a willingness he had never shown before—not truly because he was becoming more reconciled to the life, but because in Tom's promise not to force him to stay beyond the Fall there was a new horizon arising, full of promise, not only of escape from the hateful monotony of the farm, but of glorious possibilities of its own.

Early in the spring in the Old Country papers there had begun to be vague yet suggestive rumours of trouble in South Africa with the surly burghers of the Transvaal. These rumours, as the year advanced, began to take more definite shape—negotiations were always being reported as taking place—now in Cape Town, now in Kimberley, now in Pretoria, but as one difficulty seemed to be smoothed away, another took its place. Slowly the conviction was growing in Britain that the Boers were seeking, not a solution, but the gaining of time to complete their preparations for a struggle.

The spirit born of pride of race and community of blood began to stir and show itself in the other colonies—the farmers on far up-country sheep 'runs' in Australia realised that South Africa was a necessary link in the chain that bound them to the 'Old Land,' men these with whom action steps closely on the heels of realisation, and New South Wales came first with her offer of help. Canada almost smiled when she heard—at the foolish thought that the hour of need would come—smiled and followed suit, more to show the world the fulness of her ready loyalty than from any anticipation that serious danger to the Empire was ahead. By the beginning of July the scant cablegrams of British news in the Western papers began to be replaced by long despatches from London and Cape Town, by the beginning of August even the storekeepers in Minnedosa were watching for the Winnipeg train with its newspapers almost as eagerly as they watched the thermometer on still, cloudless nights for the first sign of early frost.

In the country settlements the excitement grew more slowly, especially among the Canadian farmers, who were not accustomed to take very much interest in matters of state or politics lying outside the Dominion, but there was an increasing spirit of unrest and eagerness for tidings among the Old Country people who, by letters and English papers, were kept more closely in touch with the progress of the controversy between Briton and Boer. Old Mrs. Dawson looked with cold disapproval at the rapidly increasing bulkiness of the mail-bag left week by week at the post-office—to her the big packages of *Graphics* and London dailies for the Enderbys, Dennises, and others were only a fresh evidence—to her mind not required—of the general extravagance and uselessness of 'them English folk.' In ordinary summers the distribution of the mail was apt to be rather casual, and the keeping of the post office almost a sinecure. Johnnie or Maggie might call for 'Father's' mail as they returned from school, and Johnnie or Maggie might be attended to or left to cool their heels on the doorstep till it suited old Mrs. Dawson or her daughter, Mary Ann, to attend to them; now the arrival of the mailman was anticipated for an hour or so by half a dozen horses or rigs tied to the garden fence, and half a dozen young fellows stamping round the office, talking loudly and maybe boastfully of the speedy wiping out of the Boers, if only old Kruger would come to the scratch. And when the mail did come they bustled the old lady almost beyond the endurance of her not very placid temper—'snatching the letters out of a body's hand,' as she said with great bitterness, 'before you seen where they were from or even look at the back of a post card, and "himself" leaving what bit of work he ever does about the place to come and join in their foolishness about fighting and the like—fighting indeed—and him with a lame back that won't let him—so he says—even lift the bit patch of potatoes.'

Old Dawson's lame back was rather a sore point with his wife and Mary Ann—possibly more so than in reality with the old man himself. The strangely intermittent character of the attacks of 'lameness' had long since worn out the family sympathy; little was heard of them during the slack seasons of the year, but they recurred with the advent of spring work and were far too acute during the haying or harvest to endure the jolting of the horse rake or the stooping to pick up sheaves in the stooking of the grain. The 'lameness' was always at its best round the 12th of July and could stand a long tramp in an Orange march, or the sitting on a hard, backless bench in a hot, stuffy hall to listen to rousing orations of King 'Billy' and the Boyne; it was not injuriously affected by an occasional lapse from so-briety—lapses for which there was even less domestic sympathy for the lameness of his excuses than for the lameness of his back.

To 'Old' Dawson the war excitement came rather by way of a godsend. Early in the spring, moved by a curious freak of mingled pig-headedness and bigotry, he had resigned the office of postmaster, and though he had subsequently withdrawn his resignation on the request of the Enderbys and some of the other settlers, he knew full well that the request was based less on appreciation of his own merits than on the difficulty of getting any one else to take it who would be equally conveniently situated to the town line. During the week or two which elapsed between his resignation and its withdrawal, the old man had talked rather freely of his loyalty and Protestantism which would not allow him to keep a government office—it was worth twelve dollars a year—under a Grit government with a 'Roman' for prime minister, and though Jim Hardie and Bert Enderby had treated his troubles quite seriously—at any rate to his face—Tom Dennis and some of the other English boys had not been quite so considerate, and had fallen into the way of chaffing the old man and affecting to believe that his resignation would create quite a stir in official circles at Ottawa. The chaff was really very harmless, but it touched him on his tenderest spot, and Old Dawson, though he affected to treat it with good-humoured contempt, in reality resented it deeply, and was much relieved when the war excitement caused the whole incident to be forgotten by all but himself; he might have easily forgiven a jest at the expense of his wife or Mary Ann, but never at the expense of his conceit of himself.

68

CHAPTER XIV

A TELL-TALE 'LOCAL'

It was the first Sunday in September and Daisy Enderby was finding it very quiet at the Dingle—far too quiet for her mercurial temperament. Not only was it Sunday, but it was Church Sunday with not a sign of a young man round the place, and Daisy felt that she had a genuine grievance against the world in general and young men in particular.

It was dull and chilly outside and yet not cold enough to have a fire in the box stove. Mrs. Enderby was resting upstairs; Mr. Enderby, Bert, and Marion had walked over to the anniversary service in the Presbyterian Church, a mile away, 'condoning,' so Daisy declared at dinner-time when the walk was planned, 'heresy and schism for the sake of being neighbourly—and to humour Dugald M'Leod,' she added maliciously and pointedly to Marion.

Only Daisy and Evelyn Raye were left at home, and for the past hour Evelyn had been writing at a little table by the window. Daisy stood it as long as she could, then she took a walk up to the stables and scolded the chore boy whom she found smoking a surreptitious cigarette in the granary; from there she wandered to the end of the lane on the town line—not a soul in sight—and back to the house, where Evelyn was still writing. Evelyn looked up with a smile and a little nod as she re-entered the room and then went on with her letter—it was the last straw.

'Evelyn, if you don't put that writing away I shall do something desperate. For three mortal Sundays there has not been a soul near the place more interesting than Jim Hardie's chore boy, and he only came up for some horse medicine, and now everybody else has gone off to the Conventicle up the road and you have not said a dozen words to me since you came back this morning from your visit to Minnedosa, and you ought to have all kinds of news to tell me.'

'I'm very sorry, dear, if I've been unsociable, but I wanted to get my "home" letters finished to-day—your father is going to town in the morning—but I've almost finished, and then I'll tell you my news. I'm afraid there is nothing very exciting after all; but see, Daisy, here is the last Minnedosa paper; Mr. Jordan gave it me this morning for your father and I forgot to give it to him. I'll have finished my letter by the time you have read it, and then I'll talk, or walk, or do anything you wish.'

'Well, your letter must be nearly finished then, for the paper usually lasts me five minutes for the news and ten if I read the advertisements—thank you, dear, I'll read the "locals" first,' and Daisy settled herself down on the old lounge and proceeded to read the 'locals' with more or less audible comments to herself:

'Mrs. William Brown returned from a visit to relatives at Russell on Tuesday.' (How thrilling!)

'Our worthy young fellow-townsman, Mr. Fred Twopenny, returned from his wedding trip to the East last Saturday—congratulations, Fred.' (How horribly familiar!)

'A deputation of our leading citizens, headed by Mr. Pat Cassidy, waited on the local government this week with regard to a rearrangement of the town debenture indebtedness. They report a very sympathetic reception and returned with the assurance of material assistance if the Government is sustained at the ensuing election.' (I call that rather barefaced, even for Manitoba.)

'Mr. Tom Dennis——'

'There, Daisy, I'm ready now,' broke in Evelyn, locking her desk with a sharp click and rising from her chair as she spoke.

'Just a moment, Evelyn, I must see what the *Star* has to say about Tom ——'

'Mr. Tom Dennis of Connemara Farm brought in some very fine wheat in the straw on Saturday morning; he says he has forty acres of it ready for the binder. He came in for an additional supply of twine.' (Did he really now!) 'He expects it to run close to thirty bushels to the acre. Keep an eye on Connemara Farm, girls, if that's the kind of farmers they are.' (Well, I call that the limit; Tom and Jack will be furious when they see it.) 'By the way, Evelyn, did you see this wonderful wheat—and Tom—on Saturday?'

'Not on Saturday, but he was in at the Rectory after church on Sunday.'

'After church on Sunday—oh, Evelyn Raye!'

'You see, he came in on Saturday evening so as not to waste any time, and it was very dark on Saturday night.'

'How very like Tom not to want to drive home in the dark. I hope he left in good time on Sunday, the dew falls so early and the damp is so bad for children.'

'Daisy, dear, don't be ridiculous,' said Evelyn, blushing in spite of herself, 'he left just after tea; we went for a walk with the Rectory children after dinner—and, oh, by the way, Tad Jordan is to come up to the Dingle the first time any one is down; perhaps your father will bring him to-morrow.'

'Of course he will. We all like Tad up here; he has a great time among the men and the horses, and he's a great boy to talk—not in a noisy, boyish way at all—but he says the oddest things in a quiet, simple voice, and he has a way of observing and drawing conclusions of his own about people and things that is quite capable of proving embarrassing.'

'I saw a great deal of him during my visit to the Rectory; we used to go long walks down by the river and through Cowan's Bush, and I got into the way of talking to him as if he were grown up.'

'Everybody does, I think, and he's as safe as his father to tell anything to in confidence; it's the little things he notices and says nothing about at the time that he is apt to reproduce to one's undoing, but it's entirely without guile and in simple, good faith.'

'He always spoke enthusiastically of the good time he had when he came up to the Dingle, and this time he is to be allowed to go over for a day's shooting at the Dennises—Mr. Tom Dennis promised to take him out for a day—the day I came up to the Dingle.'

'Well, Tad won't forget—if Tom is not too busy to come over for him —he might be, you know; perhaps he will come over on a Sunday—not in the dark, you know——'

'There are the others back from church,' said Evelyn, who had gone to the window, ignoring Daisy's last remark. 'I'll ask Mr. Enderby now if he can call for Tad. Why, I wonder where Marion is—it's just Mr. Bert and his father.'

'Oh, she must be there,' said Daisy, joining Evelyn at the window. 'Why, there she is coming up the lane with Dugald M'Leod—and see, Evelyn, he's carrying her Bible—watch him holding the garden gate open for her; if those flowers in his coat are not the very identical sweet peas I pinned on Merry's blouse, I'm a Dutchman, or at least a Dutchwoman; he's done it—as sure as eggs is eggs—and on the Sabbath too. See how innocent Merry will be when she comes in; but mum's the word—here come Dad and Bert both looking as unconscious of the sky falling as the Babes in the Wood.'

'Well, girls, here we are,' said Mr. Enderby as he and Bert entered the room; 'did you think we were never coming? It was all very nice and friendly down there; the minister they had up from Winnipeg was a very good speaker—he gave us more of a lecture than a sermon. I suppose Mr. Jordan with his twenty minutes has spoilt us for——'

'For an hour and twenty minutes—eh, Dad?' interrupted Daisy. 'Well, if Ephraim will go after strange idols, it's his own fault if he's bored. I suppose there was a great crowd?'

'Yes, the place was packed; there are a lot of themselves, and then the Methodists closed their church for the day, and there was a sprinkling of our church people as well as ourselves.'

'I guess it was a pretty thin sprinkling,' said Daisy. 'I'll say this for our boys generally, that if they don't go to their own church, they never go anywhere else.'

'Was Chris there, Mr. Enderby?' asked Evelyn. 'I hoped he would come up to-day, I have some letters for him to read.'

'Oh yes, your brother was there with Jim Hardie; he is coming up after supper. Jack Dennis went back with him to Rosebank——'

'You never mean to tell us that Jack was at the "Oatmeal" service?' said Daisy with affected horror.

'No, Jack was not at the service—I wish to goodness he had been,' replied Mr. Enderby, looking vexed. 'We met him on the town line as we were coming back—near Old Dawson's; he had been up to try and get his mail, and Old Dawson wouldn't give it to him—said the office was closed.'

'The old curmudgeon,' said Daisy indignantly; 'why, I know we've got mail on a Sunday before now when we've not been able to send up on a week day.'

'I know we have, but he doesn't have to give it out on a Sunday; it would have been all right if Mary Ann had been there, but she and the old lady were away to church, and I expect the old man wanted to pay the Dennis boys back for chaffing him. To make it worse, he told Jack there was a big packet of English papers for them—and you know how keen Jack is for war news—and finished up by telling him that there was no mail "for the likes of him" except in office hours.'

'What did Jack do then?' asked Daisy eagerly.

'Why, he could *do* nothing, but judging by the rage he was in when we met him I imagine he said a good deal.'

'And Jack can talk plainly,' remarked Daisy appreciatively, 'when his "Irish" is up—serve the horrid old man right too.'

'Well, I'm sorry it happened,' said Mr. Enderby. 'I hate any fuss and ill will in the settlement; however, it cannot be helped. By the way, Jack said something about Tom coming over for Tad Jordan—when is the boy coming up?'

'He was to come up the first time any one was down and had room for him; Evelyn thought perhaps you could bring him up to-morrow.'

'I suppose I can; he will have to ride on a load of twine, but I don't suppose he will mind.'

'He will be perfectly happy so long as he gets here, I think,' said Evelyn, 'he's longing to come up.'

'And,' added Daisy, 'he's to go over to the Dennises for a day's shooting. Now, Dad, if you and Bert will "vamoose" we girls will get supper ready. Oh, Merry, here you are at last—and Mr. M'Leod too! Now if you two can entertain each other for just a "leetle" bit longer, Evelyn and I will have the table set in no time. I do hope, Merry, the walk was not too much for you?'

Later on in the evening Daisy discovered to her great disgust that she had not yet made sufficient allowance for the diffidence of Dugald M'Leod in his wooing, and she had no reserve in expressing her disappointment to her sister:

'Well, Merry, if you can put up with the slowness of the pace I suppose the rest of us will have to—but it is an Englishman or Irishman for mine, when the time comes. After all I expect it is half your own fault; you know Dr. Casey says—There's many a good fish lost through not knowing when to strike—but you never were a sport, so what's the use of talking?'

CHAPTER XV

'A WHALE OF A TIME'

Tad Jordan did not in the least mind riding up on a load of twine; in fact, he probably preferred it to the more conventional buckboard, and the two following weeks more than realised his confident expectations of having a good time.

The broken weather of the previous week wound up with a sharp frost followed by perfect Fall weather, and Manitoba Fall weather at its best is without a rival—the gentle breeze rising with the dawn to dispel the fog through which the sun passes to a cloudless sky; the hoar-frost on every twig and branch and blade of grass dissolving into jewelled dewdrops, and they, in their turn, evaporating into the clear, pure atmosphere; the long, still day keeping its genial warmth till the sun sinks again, a crimson disc, in the gathering haze that precedes the evening dew fall, and leaves the landscape to the paler beauties of the rising harvest moon.

Tad loved the Fall, but he did not analyse the part which the phenomena of nature had in his enjoyment of his visit, and the account of it which he gave to his mother afterwards was at first singularly lacking in details; he was content to sum it up in the general term that he had had a 'whale of a time'—a term lacking, perhaps, in delicacy of expression, but which to him seemed the only one adequate to the occasion. It was not at all that Tad forgot the component parts of the 'whale of a time'—it was far otherwise —for they recurred intermittently and in a reminiscent fashion in his conversation at home and at school for the next six months, and 'when I was at the Dingle, you bet, I' grew to be familiar to the maternal ears—even to monotony.

The crown of glory of his visit was the day's shooting with Tom Dennis at Connemara Farm—not that the other days fell at all below Tad's expectations, for they were all good of their kind, but a string of pearls is not the Koh-i-noor. Nothing that bore the taint of 'work' could have been better than the long mornings out in the harvest field with Mr. Enderby and Bert, when Tad drove the team while Bert pitched the sheaves to his father on the load, or the afternoons when he stayed behind at the Dingle when Bert and his father returned to work, and had singles at tennis with Daisy, who served to him 'good and hard overhand, as if she expected a fellow to be able to play,' as Tad expressed it—'none of your bally lobs just toted over the net as if a fellow was an old married woman with the skirt of her dress tucked over her arm and tumbling into her petticoats every time she receives.'

Then on the first Saturday afternoon there was a picnic down to the cranberry bush with Miss Enderby, Daisy, and Evelyn, and it was fine fun climbing and scrambling among the fallen timber where the cranberry bushes bore their reddest and thickest clusters of ripening berries—and Tad enjoyed it thoroughly—racing with Daisy to see which could fill their pail first, or even helping Evelyn with shamefaced boyish courtesy over some big fallen trunk. Tad felt at first that there was a little danger of its being 'too much of a girls' ' affair to form a matter of boasting when he should come to talk over his visit with his 'fidus Achates,' Ralph M'Neale, on his return to town, but it was relieved even of this suspicion by Bert joining them in the bush just as they were lighting the fire to boil some water for the tea at their camp supper; for Bert brought his gun with him, and the addition of a man and a gun, Tad thought, would give a correct tone even to a berry-picking which started out with a boy and mere girls.

They were walking home through the silent woods in the gathering dusk, Bert carrying the cranberries in a big bag and Tad the gun—as yet unloaded—a quite unnecessary and rather derogatory precaution, as Tad thought, when a swift scurry through the dead leaves on the bush trail was followed by a whirr of wings, and a partridge flew up almost at Tad's feet.

'Oh, if the gun had only been loaded,' cried Tad with keen disappointment, 'I'd have had a whack at it.'

'We may get it yet if we're careful,' replied Bert, amused at Tad's confidence in his ability to shoot a partridge on the wing in the bush. 'You girls stay just where you are, while Tad and I go on—he won't have flown far.'

The two proceeded quickly some twenty yards along the narrow trail, scanning the bush closely on either side. Suddenly Bert stopped and beckoned Tad to his side.

'There he is, Tad, on a limb of that white poplar—follow my hand—you can see him against the sky; he's made up his mind to take chances by sitting still in the hope we will not see him.'

There he was, sure enough, absolutely motionless—not the stir of a feather or even the wink of his eye. Bert took the gun from Tad, fitted in a single cartridge, cocked it, and handed it back. Tad took a careful and long aim—too long and too careful, for he gave the gun a nervous jerk upward at the critical moment. Bang! The smoke hung for a moment, and as it cleared revealed the partridge still motionless on the bough. Bert put in a fresh cartridge and handed the gun back again to Tad—a long pause, during which the partridge wiped his beak a couple of times on a twig in front of his breast—'if he misses this time I'll try a fly,' he was thinking to himself, 'or the little beggar will pot me by accident.' Bang!—he had stayed too long—a wild flurry of wings among the dead leaves at the foot of the poplar, a sobbing gurgle in the outstretched throat, a shudder through the ball of black and golden feathers, a mate that will sound her tender call in vain through the gloaming woods. Tad was a boy—the twinge of conscience when it comes will be too late—twenty years perhaps—afterwards.

The great day was the following Saturday. Tom Dennis drove over for him on the Friday evening, so that they could make an early start on the following morning. Only Tad himself could be a fitting Homer for such an Iliad of slaughter. It was a foot-weary and stiffened hero that Tom brought back to the Dingle long after dark on the Saturday night; but Tad never grudged the price of glory, and Tom Dennis little realised the whole-souled, boyish appreciation that lay behind Tad's words of thanks as he crawled painfully out of the buckboard, 'Thank you awfully, Mr. Dennis, I've had a "whale of a time."'

Bert Enderby was just coming in from the stables carrying a lantern as Tom and Tad drove up the lane—he had been having a last look round for the night—and he came down to the gate to greet them.

'Back again safe and sound, Tad? Come along in, Tom, for a while.'

'Well, it's pretty late, I don't want to disturb your people———'

'Oh, you won't disturb them, they are just having a cup of cocoa and a bite before we go to bed———'

'Well, I'll tie up for a minute or two—Tad here is getting pretty sleepy —we were up at five this morning and we've had a long day's tramping.'

Mrs. Enderby and Marion had already retired, but they found Mr. Enderby cutting the kindling for the morning fire, and Daisy and Evelyn sitting by the table, chatting over their cocoa.

'Oh, here you are, Tom, after all; Bert, you had better take that poor boy up to bed,' for Tad, who had come in with Bert, was blinking in the sudden light of the room in a very dazed and bewildered way. 'I was just saying to Evelyn that I thought perhaps you would wait till the morning, as it was so dark—wasn't I, Evelyn?'

'Oh, I guess the old mare and I are quite used to that,' replied Tom, laughing and wondering why Evelyn blushed. 'The kid is to go down with his father to-morrow after church, so I thought he had better get a good night's rest in a comfortable bed here—we are a little primitive in our ways at Connemara Farm—besides, I wanted to speak to your father and Bert about the threshing.'

'What's that about the threshing, Tom?' asked Mr. Enderby, who was hanging up the draw-knife on the wall.

'Why, you see, Mr. Enderby, Jack and I have the chance of going out threshing with Cameron's outfit for a couple of weeks before we thresh at home, but I did not want to leave without knowing when you would be threshing here, in case you would be wanting us.'

'Oh, that will be all right, Tom,' replied Mr. Enderby; 'we have a week's stacking to do yet, and then if the fine weather holds we are going to get on with our Fall ploughing, and I don't expect to thresh till "freeze up." We have too much ploughing to leave it till spring; besides, it does not make such a rush of work now.'

'When will you want us for your own threshing, Tom?' asked Bert; 'of course, I can come with a team any time you send word.'

'Thank you, Bert; I was depending on you and Jim Hardie to give us a hand—I suppose a day or a day and a half will finish us off. Cameron intends to begin threshing on Monday east of us and to work west. If we have no bad breakdowns he should be at Connemara in a couple of weeks or so, but I'll give you a day's warning ahead.'

'That will be all right,' said Bert, 'we will be ploughing by then, and one day will be the same as another. I hope you have your own stacks well fire-guarded; the prairie grass is very heavy in the low lands this year and this fine weather is making it as dry as tinder.'

'Oh, I think they are safe enough; we have all our crop, except a small stack of oats which is back of the stable, stacked on the narrow strip of unbroken land that runs in between the two big fields, and Jack was ploughing a broad guard to-day on the stubble on either side of the strip.'

'That leaves it open on the west side,' said Bert doubtfully.

'I know, but that is so rough you could not plough across it without rooting out all the old stumps—there used to be a bluff there—and anyway there is the road allowance and a good, bare trail west of that again; the fire would hardly jump the trail, and then the grass along the road allowance has been eaten pretty close by stray cattle.'

'I suppose not, but you never can tell what it will do. Well, when you are ready we'll come.'

'Thank you, Bert; I hope I have not been keeping you all up too long. Good-night, Mr. Enderby—good-night, Daisy—good-bye, Miss Raye—so long, Bert,' and Tom, who had been standing with his hand on the door knob during the latter part of the conversation, opened the door and was gone.

CHAPTER XVI

TOM KEEPS THE LETTER OF HIS BOND

The fine weather lasted, but there were one or two interruptions to the plans which Cameron had mapped out for his threshing run—there always are. The stub of an old oak root which had been caught up into a sheaf of wheat escaped the eyes of the feeder of the separator, and passing into the cylinders wrought havoc which took two days to repair. A third day was lost through the wind being so boisterous as to make the danger of flying sparks too hazardous to the machine and stacks alike, so it was nearer three weeks than two before Tom Dennis went to give Jim Hardie and Bert Enderby their 'bid' to the threshing at Connemara Farm. At the last minute Tom deferred his own threshing for a day, partly to oblige a neighbour, old Mr. Berg, just across the road allowance to the west of the Dennis farm, and partly because he was rather nervous about taking the machine on to the dry, scrubby land on which his own wheat was stacked till the gusty equinoctial wind should show some signs of moderating. Tom left the gang at Berg's as they were returning to work after dinner and walked the short half mile back to his own place, for he had two or three hours' work to do at home—clearing out his granary and hunting up all available grain sacks for the morrow. It was growing dark when he threw a saddle on the old mare and started for Rosebank; the thresher was humming busily at Berg's as he rode by, and Tom could just distinguish his brother's tall form among the pitchers on the top of the last stack.

'Jack has stuck to his promise like a man,' Tom thought to himself, 'it won't be his fault if all my hopes are crushed in the end; he's stuck to it like a man and it's been for my sake,' and Tom's heart was very soft towards his brother. 'It's not been any too easy for him either, for at the bottom I know he hates the whole life just as much as ever he did. I wonder if he has made up his mind about the future if Evelyn should say "Yes," ' and Tom blushed at the very thought of the unspoken word—'would he be content to stay then? No, he'll never stay—Connemara Farm and Evelyn might be heaven for me, but it would kill poor Jack even if he were willing to try and content himself for my sake, and I promised him that I would not stand out against his own plans after I knew—and I'll soon know now; and all this war excitement about Africa—that has wrecked the last chance of

78

his settling down—if there is a chance for him to go, he'll go and nothing will stop him. What will they say at home? If there is real danger to the old flag the governor won't say a word against it—he's the last to hold a Dennis back when the country calls; and if there should be a "No" for yourself, Tom Dennis, when the question is asked—if you have been living in a fool's paradise of your own all summer—why, then there shall be two Dennises instead of one to stop Boer bullets, and I'll thank the man that shoots the quickest and straightest. Twenty-four hours and I'll know—when the last bushel goes into the bag to-morrow night I'll go over to the Dingle. Evelyn will give me a straight answer, for she's a true and honest girl if the sun ever shone on one. Four and twenty hours—good God! it's an eternity to wait. I might ask her to-night—but no, I'll keep to the letter of my bond with Jack, but not five minutes beyond it. I'll not go up to the Dingle to-night for fear I might break it; I'll ask Jim Hardie to let Bert know about to-morrow, and then back to Connemara. Heavens! I wish the wind would go down—another day's delay would be more than I could bear. Come, old girl, let's travel and forget our cares if we can.'

The mare answered to his voice and the tightening of the rein by breaking into a 'lope' which she kept up almost without a break till they reached the end of the lane leading up to Rosebank from the town line, when she slacked down for a hint as to which of the equally familiar roads—to Rosebank or to the Dingle—her master wished to take. For a moment Tom hesitated. 'I could see Evelyn to-night'—it was a sore temptation—'no, I'll stick it out,' and he turned the mare up the lane. He was within some thirty yards of the house when he heard the click of the door opening and two figures stepped on to the verandah, and the door was again closed. Though the light from the open door was only for a moment it was long enough for Tom to recognise the two figures—Evelyn and her brother. What luck! to have the merit of self-denial without paying the price!

Tom slipped hastily off the mare, and throwing the rein loosely over his left arm advanced to meet them through the gloom.

'Hello, Raye—good evening, Miss Raye—I hope I did not scare you in the dark—it's only me, Tom Dennis.'

'Oh, I wasn't much alarmed,' said Evelyn as they shook hands; 'one doesn't expect to meet anything very formidable between here and the Dingle, though Chris insists on coming with me if it is at all dark. I came home from school with the Hardie children and stayed for supper, and then Mrs. Hardie was showing me some fancy work and the time slipped away.'

'Well, I'm very glad it did,' replied Tom, 'or I would have missed seeing you. Will you ask Bert, Raye, if he can come to our threshing to-morrow—I'm just going to ask Jim Hardie if he can come too.'

'Very well, I fancy they are expecting to hear from you,' said Chris. 'Mr. Hardie heard to-day that Cameron was at Berg's.'

'Oh, that's all right, then; I'll just go in and have a word with Jim, and then I must get back and see that we are all ready for an early start.'

'So you won't be coming up to the Dingle, Mr. Dennis?' asked Evelyn.

'Not to-night—if you'll tell Bert, Raye, and ask him to call for Jim in the morning. Good-night, Raye—good-night, Miss Raye,' and Tom held her hand a moment in parting, it was such a kindly, blessed dusk, and Chris had already turned away down the lane. 'Not to-night, not till my harvest is safe, and then—may I come—may I come and ask you how much it means to me?'

'Come along, Evelyn, or you'll get lost in the dark,' called back her brother, and a faltering good-night, a moment's lingering pressure from the hand within his own, was all the answer to Tom's question.

'I'm coming, Chris; good-night, Mr. Dennis, and success to your threshing.'

Tom stood and watched them till not even his lover's imagination could give a form to the shadows down the lane, and then he turned back to the house, tied up the mare to a nearby post, and stepped on to the verandah and knocked at the door and entered.

Mr. Hardie was sitting by the stove smoking. 'Ha! it's you, Tom,' he said as the latter entered, 'I was kind of looking for you to-night. Did you meet the folks in the lane?'

'Yes, I've just left them; we are threshing to-morrow and Raye is going to tell Bert—I suppose it suits you?'

'Oh yes, it fits in fine; I finished my wheat stubble to-day and I'm not threshing myself till the middle of next week—we'll be along bright and early; won't you sit down and have a smoke?'

'Not to-night, Jim, I'm anxious to get back and see what Cameron is doing; they were on the last stack as I came by, but I hope they won't shift the machine to-night—it's a rough road across the creek bed in my hay meadow even in daylight, and if they got stuck there they might have all kinds of a time to get out of it.'

'Well, I won't keep you; we'll be there by the blow of the whistle anyway. How's the wind—is it letting up any? It was pretty strong when I came in from the field, but here in the shelter of the bluff it can blow like forty outside and we never know.'

'Oh, I think, if anything, it is rougher than before sundown, but not so steady—more in sudden gusts. I've noticed that very often when it does not go down with the sun it will blow all night and then fall at sunrise.'

'Well, I hope it will,' replied Jim, 'if it doesn't, I'd call the gang off for a day rather than take chances.'

'Oh, it must go down—hang it! I've lost a day now,' said Tom impatiently.

'It's too bad, too bad, but if Cameron thinks it's risky he'll not fire up; however, we'll come over anyway.'

'All right, Jim, I'll look for you, and now good-night.'

'So long, Tom; never mind the door, I'm going down to the stables before I turn in—so long.'

CHAPTER XVII

FIGHTING FIRE

Tom's impatience kept the mare on the canter for the first mile down the town line, but she dropped down to a walk as he turned on to the eastern trail leading home to Connemara Farm. It was now quite dark, the last fiery glow of the setting sun had faded from the western sky behind him and the moon had not yet risen. The road was fenced on either hand, but between the well-worn trail and the fences clumps of small willows and poplars fringed the road and added to the gloom.

For the first time since he left home two hours before Tom became conscious of a great weariness of body and lassitude of mind; he had been up since daybreak, and the hurried noontide meal had been all the food he had had since breakfast. The varied emotions to which he had given free course as he rode over to Rosebank, the wild flutter of happiness as Evelyn's hand rested in his own, the hot waves of a flowing tide of passion on which his heart had seemed to be carried to the assurance of victory as he felt the gentle answering pressure at parting, followed by the cold ebb of a despairing presentiment that victory would fail of realisation at the very moment of fulfilment—no wonder that as he watched his way in the shadows of the lane, drowsiness, almost a sense of stupor, fell upon him, while the mare picked her way more slowly and more warily through the blackness of the night. Once and again he almost reeled in the saddle to recover himself with a start, and forced his eyes to attempt to penetrate the gloom before him—'Surely that is a faint glow of crimson purple thrown high on the eastern sky,' or is it the self-created figment of his weary, straining eyes? 'No, that is scarcely a delusion.' Higher and clearer it mounts the black vaults of heaven—where had he seen such a weird sight before? Ah! he remembers—as the steamer dropped down the river to the sea when he left the old land—as he and Jack stood on the deck at midnight and watched the far-off lights of Liverpool reflected on the smoke-laden atmosphere of the sleeping city. But there is no great city beyond the rising land that lies between him and Connemara Farm. Ah, there is a hotter and more lurid gleam mounting straight up into the upper darkness, there is more than a trick of the imagination lying beyond that crimsoning flame! Tom is awake and standing up in his stirrups. 'Even though his own grain is safe in his granary—surely—surely—Berg would never fire his straw stacks in such a gale of wind.'

With a swift realisation of what that flood of light in the skies might mean to himself—a realisation that went to his heart like a dagger stab— Tom gave a wild cry to the mare and put her to the gallop, and in a few minutes reached the crest of the rise, and dread passed into certainty. The half mile of prairie and stubble land and summer fallow that lay between the crest of the hill and Berg's homestead was lighted up till every bluff and bush and fence was as clearly outlined as by a noontide sun. To one side of the blinding light shed by the mass of burning straw piles Berg's house and outbuildings were silhouetted against the blackness of the night beyond, and even in that tense moment Tom recognised the figure of old Mrs. Berg, with despairing upraised arms, before the door of the little log house. The old mare, as wild and excited as himself, is pounding along the trail nearer and nearer—now Tom can hear loud cries above the gusts of the wind and see weird figures of men and horses—now only the fence and a narrow strip of prairie divide him from the holocaust, and Tom, jumping from the mare and clambering over the fence, is racing towards it. There, to the one side of the burning straw stacks, labouring and plunging horses are dragging the engine over a bare potato patch into safety; closer in to the circle of blinding light and flame stands the separator, and a desperate attempt is being made to save it. No horse could be driven to face the sweltering heat and glaring light of the burning straw piles, but big John Cameron himself, his clothes drenched with water from the tank and with a soaking grain bag round his neck and face, has rushed into the torrid vortex and passed a cable through the tongue of the separator, and with scorched hands and blackened face made his way back. Now a score of hands are straining on the cable, and with hoarse cries—'Together, boys, together, boys'—the big, unwieldy machine is moving. 'Keep her going, boys, keep her going,' and as the separator slowly moves in response to their desperate efforts, four or five, more reckless than the rest of heat and danger, rush in and grasp the blistering spokes of the wheels and strain and labour till the torrid heat drives them back and Tom Dennis is among them. Now the greatest heat is passed, and Cameron himself is on the separator beating out with a wet sack the last sparks of some loose sheaves that had been lying on the grain table. Farther and farther, now with two teams of horses, the machine is drawn on to a bare strip of summer fallow to absolute security, and the threshing gang cheer and cheer again as they gather round Cameron with rough congratulations. The 'outfit' is saved, and in the hot fight for its salvation there has been no time for thought of aught else—but what of the thin lengthening line of fire that unnoticed and forgotten till now is sweeping across Berg's stubble to the road allowance to the east?

Not one thought but to save the separator had been in Tom's mind till now —not a thought or a glance beyond the strenuous labour of the moment and the burning mass before him. Now with a flash it comes back to him—his wheat stacks—and he gives a wild cry.

'Good God, Cameron, the fire is half across the stubble—if it jumps the trail——' and grasping one of the sodden sacks that lie around Tom is racing across the burnt and blackened stubble towards that line of fire, followed by the gang, swift as himself now to realise the danger that had passed undreamt of in the wild excitement—'Save Dennis's stacks'—and big Cameron is by Tom's side.

The lane of fire is a quarter of a mile wide by now and still sweeping onwards; the men scatter along the line, some at the ends stamping with their feet, beating down with bags or even their coats the flames which, crushed for the moment, flare up again, and each fresh gust of wind carries sparks of burning stubble nearer and nearer to the trail. There at the bare-eaten road allowance for a moment the line of flame dies down, for that moment hope and courage comes back to Tom's heart; but only for a moment—a blazing tuft of dead, matted grass is lifted skyward by some devilish spirit of the gale and whirled high and wide across the road allowance to fall into the long, sun-dried tangle of rank-grass in Tom's meadow land —to fall and spread flames and destruction as it falls.

Greedily lapping, the flames seize on their new prey; it is in vain that Tom and Cameron and half a score of men dash into the strip of scrub land, matted with dead and dry veitches and pea vine and impeded with half-rotted stumps, on which the doomed stacks are standing, lit up now and outlined clear against the sky.

Beaten and hopeless the brave fellows keep up the unequal fight, torn and wounded by thorn-bush and sharp-pointed stumps—beaten and hopeless. A wilder gust of storm has carried a sheet of flame to the foot of the nearest stack and it sweeps up the side of the stack, and in less time than it takes to write the words, the whole eight stacks are in a blaze. Tom, in his frenzy, dashed through the smoke and welter and attempted to tear out with his bare hands the sheaf on which the first spark fell, and it took all big John Cameron's strength—big John, the Anak of the Minnedosa country in those days—all big John's strength to drag him back from the helpless fight and from death—back from the deadly heat that grew and grew in fierce intensity as every gust of storm drove the fire inward to the solid hearts of the stacks, till to Tom's scorched and straining eyesight it looked like the very pit of a lurid hell. For a moment Tom struggled desperately and madly against the tense chain of John Cameron's encircling arms—he even cursed him with a bitter oath for holding him back—then as quickly as the mad words came, came a realisation of the truth of the hopelessness of the struggle.

'Forgive me, Cameron, my life's hope was in those stacks, and my life's hope has gone with them—I'm all in,' and Tom slid limp and inert to the earth at big John's feet.

With a rough carefulness Cameron gathered the unresisting form in his arms, as a mother might take up her sleeping child, and carried Tom across the field to the house and laid him down in his bunk. Then after removing his boots, throwing open his shirt at the collar, and covering him with a quilt, Cameron returned to the burning stacks. There was nothing there to be saved, but the burnt-out piles of smouldering ashes must be watched lest the fire, now confined to the strip of scrub land, should burst its bounds and be carried by some wind-borne sparks and start again a general conflagration of the stubble and prairie land to the east of Connemara Farm.

CHAPTER XVIII

'WHY DIDN'T JACK COME?'

From the utter collapse of body and mind into which Tom Dennis had swooned as he fell back into Cameron's arms, he passed into a heavy stupor of slumber which lasted till daybreak, when some unconscious movement in his sleep brought with it a sharp twinge in the muscles of his overstrained and stiffened limbs. With an involuntary expression of pain he sank back on his bunk, and in a dull and unrealising way his mind slowly reconstructed the scenes of the previous night—the first glow of light in the sky—the rescue of the separator at Berg's—the wild fight with the flames in the scrub land—ah, and the stacks were gone! and what else? Memory came back only too cruelly now: this was the dawn of the day— struggling through the haze—the day he was to ask Evelyn for her love— what would the stacks matter but for that?—and Tom rolled over and buried his head in his folded arms and tried to drive back into oblivion the cruel blows that memory, that would not be denied, thrust with reiterating cruelty before his awakening mind. Dimly he became conscious of some one moving with careful but heavy footsteps beyond the rough curtain that separated the sleeping bunks from the living-room—the subdued rattle of stove lids and cooking utensils. Some one was getting breakfast ready. What did breakfast matter—what did anything matter now? Could he take up life again and work and work without a word to Evelyn of such a dim hope as might be behind such a time of waiting—had he the courage?— would it be fair to her?—or could he ask her to link her youth and beauty with one so marked by fate for misfortune—it would be Africa for Jack— why not?—Jack! Where was Jack? Good Heavens! Where was he—last night and now? That was no step of Jack's lumbering so carefully behind the curtain—and with a leap Tom was on his feet and the curtain pulled aside.

A stable lantern, burning in sickly competition with the dawning light, stood in the middle of the rough kitchen table on which were set two or three plates, some cups without saucers, some butter and the half of a loaf of bread, while big John Cameron was at the stove turning over with a fork some thick slices of pork in a frying pan, whistling softly to himself the while.

'Ah, Tom—so you're awake—I've been making myself to home to try and get a bit of breakfast for you—you'll be needing it.'

'Cameron, where's Jack?'

'Well now, to think of it, I couldn't rightly say—but I guess he'll be over at Berg's with the boys—that is if he's back from town yet.'

'Back from town—where was Jack last night—where was he during the fire—why wasn't he here?'

'Oh, I'm forgetting you don't know how the trouble began. You see, Jack went to town for some teeth for the separator.'

'Why it was all right when I rode by on my way to Hardie's just at dusk.'

'Yes, it was near an hour after that it happened—you see, it was this way—we'd got well down to the butt of the stack, and I'd left the boys to finish while I went in to tell Mrs. Berg we'd be in to supper in half an hour, and just as I came out of the house again, the whistle blew and I heard a shouting. I ran up to the machine as fast as I could, for I was skeered some one was hurt, and I found they had thrown off the big belt and had just brought the machine to a standstill. It seems when they got to the last dozen sheaves or so the boys got larking and throwing up the sheaves faster than the band-cutter could take them, and some crazy galoot let his fork handle slip through his hands, and the first thing they knew it had got in the cylinders and everything was flying. Nobody was hurt, but the chap that lost his fork would have been if I'd known who he was; but when I got up on the separator I found six or seven teeth broken. It was no use talking or telling the boys what I thought of them—though I did that too; some one had got to go to town to Shaw's for some fresh teeth or we'd be in trouble half the time if we tried to run the separator without them—so your brother, he up and said he'd drive down if Berg would lend him a horse and his buckboard. He ran into the house and got a bite of supper and started right off, while the boys and myself got everything ready to move— let off steam—damped the fire down and went in to our supper. We'd just finished eating and Tim Ryley got up saying he'd left his pipe in the caboose, when, as he opened the door, he gave a great shout—'the straw's afire'—and so it was, and we were all out mighty quick, and—you know the rest. How did it happen? Lord knows! it may have been a spark from the engine, though I don't think it—I expect one of them furriners had chucked a cigarette away when he came in to supper and it had smouldered —they'd light their cigarettes on a barrel of powder if you didn't watch 'em—but lit it was, and I'd sooner have lost the outfit than have you lose your year's work in the way you did—so I would—and if I can help you out you've only to say the word now and I'll do it,' and big John Cameron reached out an awkward but hearty hand of sympathy, for, though they were there, the expression of the softer emotions did not come easily to big John Cameron's disposition.

'Thank you, Cameron, I know you would—I shall be all right—but I wonder Jack is not back.'

'Well, it's been a rough dark night, and maybe Shaw wasn't at home when he got down to town.'

'That may be it—but the night would not keep him if he got the teeth, and he'd know we would be anxious to start early on account of the neighbours coming to help.'

'I'll step over to Berg's and see what's doing; you just bide here and get a bit of breakfast, and I'll meet him when he comes up and tell him to come over—poor fellow, it's pretty rough on him too.'

'Thank you, Cameron—and say—just let Jack come over by himself; and don't let Bert Enderby or Jim Hardie come over for a while; I can't stand seeing them—not just yet,' and poor Tom turned his back on Cameron, and made a pretence of putting some wood in the stove to hide the emotion which almost overmastered his control at the mere thought of the sympathy which he knew would fill the hearts of his two true-hearted friends.

As Cameron closed the house door Tom turned back to the table and sat down wearily. Cameron had told him to eat some breakfast—well, he would try—no, the half cold fried pork on his plate was impossible. He cut a slice of bread and butter and started to munch it slowly—how dry and parched his mouth was. Tom got up and took the teapot from the side of the stove, and poured out a cup of black and steaming tea—ah, that was better! Though with no sense of taste or relish he finished his round of bread, and poured out a second cup of tea and turned round to the stove and put his feet on the apron, and felt mechanically for his pipe and tobacco. Mechanically he cut the tobacco into the palm of his hand and rubbed it out and filled and lit his pipe. Where was Jack?—His thoughts seemed so dull and leaden and never to get beyond that point. At the end of half an hour he rose and went to the window and looked out; the sun was winning a dubious victory over the thick haze of the morning, and he could distinguish dimly the outline of Berg's house and buildings, but there was no sign of life outside.

'Why didn't Jack come?' and he went back to the stove, refilled his pipe and sat down again to try and wait with such patience as he could—another half hour passed, 'surely Jack must be back by now,' and he went again to the window. Ah, there was a group of men in Berg's yard—a wagon and team before Berg's door—and there was Berg's buckboard with some one standing by the horse's head—Jack's back! He watches anxiously, trying to distinguish his brother's form—perhaps he is in that group

88

evidently talking eagerly in the yard—perhaps they are telling him of the disaster to the crop—poor Jack!—some one has left the group and is walking slowly across the summer fallow towards the house—but that's not Jack—it's too short and too deliberate—it's Bert Enderby—yet Jack's back, for there is the Berg buckboard. What can keep him from being the first to come to him in his trouble? Tom stood watching till Bert had crossed the burnt hay meadow and was coming across the farmyard, then pulling himself together as one prepared to meet all of adversity that can come, he walks across the floor, throws open the door, and meets Bert on the threshold.

CHAPTER XIX

SOMETHING WORTH LIVING FOR

There is nothing harder for a proud and reserved nature to endure than the fully expressed sympathy of an undoubted friend, and Tom's nature at bottom, beneath his usual free and easy Irish manner, was essentially reserved and proud. It was this highstrung temperament, taking alarm at the evident emotion under which Bert was labouring as the two friends clasped hands, that led to a swift change in Tom's manner in the very moment of greeting; the swift resolution that if all else was lost he would not betray what he conceived to be his manhood by a weak giving way to womanish emotion and maybe to womanish tears.

'Tom, old man, Tom, I cannot tell you——' and Bert turned away to hide the feelings which his broken voice expressed too well.

'Oh, dash it all, Bert, don't let's slobber over it,' and Tom's voice was sharp and almost angry in its tone. 'The blooming crop's gone and that's the end of it all—careful chaps like you and Jim Hardie would never have left that opening in the fireguard—and if you had, the wind would have turned round and blown the other way—an Irishman's luck is like a boomerang; you think it is going to knock the other fellow down, and then it turns and wipes your own eye. The crop's gone up in smoke and my farming ambitions have gone up with it—so there's no more to be said about it.'

'Oh, Tom—for heaven's sake don't take it like that. There's not one of us that would let you go under because the crop's gone—if it were only the crop——'

'Only the crop—well, that's a pretty tidy slap in the face for poor beggars like Jack and me—of course, a crop more or less, I suppose, doesn't matter to old established people like your father and Jim Hardie——'

'Tom, you know I don't mean that, but, Tom, there are worse things than losing a crop—don't make my task harder—be yourself, Tom.'

'Man alive, Bert, don't talk in riddles.'

'There's Jack——'

'Of course there's Jack, why didn't he come over himself? He knows very well it has hit me harder than it has him,' added Tom bitterly.

'Jack is not back from town—Jim Turner brought the horse and rig back—Jack was kept in town.'

'Jack not back—I suppose you are going to tell me Jack spent the time our crop was burning by celebrating the family good fortunes in a drunken spree—if that's it he was a day short in keeping his promise—thank God, I wasn't—you've only got to tell me he's got locked up for some rowdy quarrel and the thing will be complete—I have provided the ruin and he caps it with the disgrace.'

'Tom, you don't know what you're saying; come inside and pull yourself together—be a real man for your mother's sake,' and Bert drew Tom into the house and closed the door. 'Now, Tom, listen to me, and don't say a hard word till you know the truth.'

Awed by the impressiveness of Bert's manner and by the almost sternness of his voice, Tom took his seat by the table, and resting his head on his open hands, he looked his friend steadily in the eyes.

'All right, Bert, go ahead—I can take all you've got to give me—where's Jack?'

'Jack is in the prison cells in Minnedosa Town Hall—no, Tom, don't break in,' as the latter started and uttered a meaning 'Ah,' under his voice; 'I must tell you the whole story as Jim Turner told it me, and then there's a note from Mr. Jordan to confirm it.'

'When Jack got to town last night he found that Shaw was in the country and would not be home till late, so he put his horse in the stable and went down to the Chinese restaurant for supper and to wait—he wouldn't go to the hotel because he didn't want to run across any of the fellows he used to go with. After supper he went up to Shaw's house and waited there till nearly ten o'clock, when Shaw got home and went down with him to his warehouse and got the separator teeth. Then Jack started to go across the river to get his horse and come home. Just as he got to the railway crossing he met a crowd of fellows cheering and shouting on the station platform—among them two of the Burke boys from the north of you, and one of them rushed across to Jack waving a telegram in his hand, and shouting that the war had begun and there was a call for volunteers from Canada, or something of that sort' ('For God's sake, cut it short,' poor Tom groaned). 'Well, they hustled Jack along with them, and he, poor fellow, was excited himself, into one of the hotel bars, and one of the Burkes called for glasses round to drink the health of the Queen, and good luck to the Canadian volunteers. Just what happened I cannot tell you, but there was a half-drunk fellow loafing in the bar, and when the crowd pushed up to the bar to get their glasses, he drew back and spat on the floor with an expression of contempt for the Queen. Jack was as excited as the rest and pulled the fellow forward by the arm and cried—'Come along'—and backing out, the man—they say he is an Irish American working on the section —jerked himself free and struck at Jack with a curse on the Queen and an expression to Jack that no man could endure. With swift passion Jack struck him between the eyes and he went down like a log—and he did not get up again—his head struck a sharp corner of the bar and soon there was blood trickling across the floor——'

'Don't tell me, Bert, don't tell me the man was dead?' and Tom's face was full of horror.

'No, he's not dead, but when Jim left he had not become conscious. The crowd, whose sympathies were all with Jack, hurried him out of the hotel and wanted him to strike for Brandon and the boundary line, but Jack wouldn't go—he was sober enough now—in fact, he hadn't touched a drop of liquor in town—and he went straight up to the town constable's house and gave himself up.'

'Is that all, Bert?' and though Tom's face was drawn and white from the intensity of the struggle with which he maintained his self-control, still his voice was quiet and firm, 'Is that all?'

'Jim Turner was in the crowd and went with him to the Town Hall and then went and fetched Mr. Jordan, who went right over with him to Jack, and Mr. Jordan sent up this note by Jim,' and Bert handed to Tom a half sheet of paper twisted into a note.

Tom took it mechanically and smoothed it out on the table, and read it slowly, first to himself and then a second time aloud.

'DEAR TOM,—Jim Turner will tell you the truth of Jack's trouble. I am with him now and will stay with him till you get down. Jack is filled with remorse for the disgrace he feels he has brought on you, and he says for failing in his promise to you. Dr. Casey is attending the wretched cause of all this trouble, but can give no opinion yet. Remember, Tom, Jack is your brother, and honestly as a man, if not as a parson, I cannot blame Jack for what he did. When you come down drive straight to the Rectory, and be sure what can be done shall be, by, Yours,
'E. J.'

Tom folded the letter and put it carefully in his breast pocket, and then turned to Bert who was watching him, anxious as to what lay beneath this quiet in Tom's voice and manner.

'Will you hitch up the mare for me, Bert, while I wash myself and put a few things together? and say, don't let any of the other fellows come over from Berg's.'

'And I'll come down with you, Tom.'

'Thank you, Bert, and the sooner we start the better, and Bert, forgive me my thankless reception of your first coming—I thought I had nothing worth living for when I saw my summer's hopes burn away in last night's fire—and when I was so ready to blame poor Jack—but I have one thing left to do if I can—to try and keep the promise I gave my mother when I left home, that looking after Jack should come first. If I can save him and the old name the rest may go, and be—no, I won't say that in the same breath with my mother's name.'

CHAPTER XX

JUST TILL TO-MORROW

It was to the credit of Tom's modesty, if not to his knowledge of the quick intuition of a maiden's heart, that in his troubles he should be able to find a painful consolation in believing that he had, on the very brink, drawn back from a premature avowal of his hopes and love. He could not know, and happily was not so conceited as to imagine, that behind Evelyn's ever quiet, self-respecting reserve there had been taking form an ideal of frankness, courage and manly beauty which only needed a spark to flash it into her consciousness as finding its material embodiment in himself.

Evelyn was one of those who have the strength of mind to put on one side till the time comes—if it ever come—the asking of intimate questions of their own heart, and the greater resolution not to let the mind dwell on answers which may never be required. But Evelyn, no less than Tom, had been taken unawares in that brief meeting in the gloaming in Jim Hardie's lane, and knew full well as she hastened to follow her brother that, in that parting pressure of Tom's hand, a question had in all but the words been asked, and that her heart had found a swift but undoubting answer.

Her brother stalked along by her side in silence, with all a brother's indifference and unconsciousness of aught but the most prosaic surroundings—if, as they turned into the Dingle pathway, Evelyn took his arm and pressed more closely to him—why, here in the open the wind was rough and gusty, and he sought no further reason why, when they reached the garden gate, she should turn her back to the wind and ask him to go on alone while she rested there for a moment and gained her breath.

Evelyn was relieved when she entered the living-room a few minutes later to find Daisy and Marion busily engaged in the difficult problem of making over for Daisy a winter dress of one of Mrs. Enderby's more prosperous nieces in the Old Country, and which the latter thought might still be sufficiently up-to-date and serviceable for the colonies. Thanks to this preoccupation Tom's message had evidently been delivered without exciting remark as to when and where Chris had met him, and after a few minutes casual talk with Bert about what was being done at Rosebank and when Jim Hardie expected to thresh, Chris took his departure, while Evelyn was called into consultation at the sewing-table as to how best might be concealed from critical feminine eyes the fact that Daisy's new frock had had a previous and more fashionable existence.

Gifts of this kind came to the Enderby girls nearly every autumn from their aunt at home, and were received in a very different spirit by the two girls—to practical Marion they were a happy solution of the problem of being comfortably and warmly clad without running into debt, but to Daisy they were a mingled source of gratification and resentment. She always spoke of them when they came with great scorn as Cousin Mary's 'cast-off duds,' and wore them afterwards with a certain pride in the undoubted superiority of their material to anything procurable in Minnedosa, tempered by a misgiving lest some sharp Canadian eyes should discover that they had been 'made over.' With Evelyn, of course, no secrecy was attempted, and it was a great relief to Daisy's soreness when she found that the making and receiving of such a gift was looked on by Evelyn as quite natural and matter of course.

The three girls were kept busy till bedtime, planning and scheming how front lengths that were a little rubbed and worn might be relegated to less conspicuous positions, and in the letting out of 'gores' and 'bands,' for Daisy's form was evidently more buxom than that of her far-away cousin, but at last Evelyn escaped to her room, and sitting at its little window, looking out on the moonlit night, was free to let her thoughts wander back and linger on the sweetness of that brief but revealing meeting with Tom, while her heart looked forward with a confident, yet trembling happiness to that meeting on the morrow. How well she knew Tom loved her—how well she knew now how fully her heart answered to that love, yet was there a shy happiness in the keeping of her secret till to-morrow—just till to-morrow—when Tom should come in his innocence of a woman's ways to ask for the answer that was already given.

The happy thoughts with which Evelyn fell asleep were there to greet her as she woke to consciousness to find the grey dawn bringing into dim outline the familiar surroundings of her little room. Once or twice during the night she had been half-awakened by the gusts of wind blowing round the gable of the house and rattling the ill-fitting casements, but now there was no lightest sound without, and her first thought was of Tom's threshing, and swiftly on to that question to which she hoped she had not betrayed too readily the answer. But there was all the day to wait, and she set her mind to find for itself other occupation till it should be time for her to arise for breakfast. Already she could hear the furtive sounds which ushered in another day's toil for the Dingle household. Mrs. Enderby always maintained an innocent fiction that she never slept after the earliest hour of dawn, but the household, while accepting the fiction with kindly consideration, acted on the reality, and went softly about the necessary duties of the farm. Evelyn lay and listened, and let her imagination fill in the gaps between the audible sounds—that is Bert stealing past her door in socked feet like a burglar—and unlike a burglar who knows the niceties of his calling, he drops one of his heavy boots with a clatter on the floor, and she catches a subdued growl of vexation—now he is tapping lightly on Daisy's door—a little louder and a whispered controversy—'It's six o'clock, Daisy,'—'Oh bother, Bert, it's the middle of the night'—'I've got to get off to the threshing at Dennises—hurry up,' and Bert has passed on to the end of the passage to rouse Sam, the chore boy—a task always of some difficulty, and Evelyn's mind runs on to what Bert had told her of Sam's first coming to the Dingle, and of how, if Sam was called suddenly, his first sign of awakening was to put up his arm to protect his head—poor boy! evidently a survival of early unhappy days in the slums of London, before he found the safety of the Barnardo Home. Now Bert is stealing downstairs, and a faint clatter betrays the fact that he is lighting the stove fire. The outer door opens and closes, and he is off to the stable to feed and harness his team. Evelyn gets up and proceeds leisurely with her own dressing—shall she wear her blue serge to-day instead of her usual school-dress? Will Daisy notice it? She is so quick to notice—and so sure in her deductions! Yes—she will wear it and not go down till she has her jacket on and there is just time to have a hasty breakfast before starting for school—what does it matter if Daisy does?—it is cold enough now in the mornings to justify the change—that was the dress she wore that day she came to Minnedosa, when she first met Tom, and had that drive up from town with him—but no—it is part of her bargain with herself not to think of Tom till the day and its duties are over—but poor Tom is like King Charles' head and Evelyn is as helpless as poor Mr. Dick—for all her thoughts, however well they start out from her mind, will run back again to the forbidden spot. She will be very firm with herself, and she lights her lamp and sits down deliberately to set an Arithmetic examination paper for her older scholars, and holds her own with herself very successfully till she tries to evolve sundry problem questions to test the intelligence of Pete M'Tavish and his shrewd and worldly wise classmates.

'If a farmer—(no, he's not named Tom)—if John Jones has twenty-seven and one half acres of wheat and it yields thirty-five bushels to the acre (wouldn't that be lovely for the poor, dear boy!)—no—and it yields thirteen bushels to the acre (Oh, Evelyn, how can you be so hard on him after all his hard work?), and he sells two-thirds of it for seventy cents a bushel—(now, that is being quite fair, and I'm sure it is Mr. Jones')—how many cows could he buy with the money at forty-seven dollars and fifty cents each? (and you know you can hardly milk—such a farmer's wife).

'Problem Number Two. If Tom—Mr. Jones sold the remainder of his crop for forty-five cents a bushel, what would be his profit on the whole crop, if his seed grain, labour, and his threshing—no,—and his other expenses came to nine dollars an acre? (poor fellow, I don't believe he will be a bit better off after all). Now, Evelyn, there shall not be another problem,' and she resolutely completed the paper with a complex compound vulgar fraction that was absolutely incapable of the slightest romantic construction, and so down to breakfast and to school.

And so through the day—and a busy day, for the attendance at school was increasing as the bigger boys, who had been kept at home for the harvest, were returning to school for the winter and needed a firm hand till they settled down to work—but four o'clock came at last.

As is so often the case in the West, the wild stormy night had been followed by a still, calm day, and Evelyn started homewards, walking briskly, with her little strapped bundle of schoolbooks in the one hand and her dinner pail in the other, and accompanied by two or three of the children whose way lay the same as far as the town line, and who looked on the home walk with 'teacher' as the bright spot in the school day.

With her 'good-bye' to Pete M'Tavish, the last of her companions to leave her, Evelyn's compact with herself ended, and she let her thoughts come back to Tom's question, 'May I come and tell you?' The sun was drawing near to his setting—she knew the routine of the threshing so well —the day's work would soon be over, and then there would be the gathering of the threshing gang for their supper; and Tom would have to be there and perhaps have to stay and help move the machine to his next neighbour's, and it would be dark before he would be able to slip away—'Would it be too late for him to come?—no, surely.' She knew full well that he would not be turned from his purpose lightly—not if he cared to come. But that was hours away, and she did not want to get back to the Dingle till it was dark and supper-time and the family were all gathered together. There is safety in numbers and a general conversation—and she had not been entirely successful in evading Daisy's sharp eyes in the morning—for Daisy came into her room as she was putting on her jacket.

'Why, how smart we are this morning—Sunday frock and go-to-meeting hat—I must come and see what big boys you have over at Lakeside,' and though Evelyn had put her off with a remark about the chilly evenings, she knew that she blushed and that Daisy was quite equal to drawing very embarrassing conclusions on very slight evidence.

A buckboard jogging slowly along before her and to which she had given no thought, turned off the town line into Dawson's lane—'The mailman from Minnedosa'—'why should I not go up to the post-office and wait for the Dingle mail? I can still be home by dark, and Daisy always makes such a fuss over the English letters that she will never think of me,' and Evelyn followed slowly in the mailman's wake to the post office door. The solution of her difficulties was so simple that Evelyn wondered she had not thought of it before, for during the busy harvest season she had fallen into the way of calling for the mail on her way from school so as to save Bert going for it specially, and she was on very friendly terms with old Mrs. Dawson and Mary Ann.

She had won old Mrs. Dawson's goodwill from the start by the carefulness with which she wiped her shoes before stepping on the well-scrubbed floor, and by the entire good humour with which she waited on the sorting of the mail—'different to some young women I could mention,' as Mrs. Dawson often observed, 'as don't know what's coming to a clean floor by reason of not having one to home.' A remark which Daisy took as being very personal to herself when Evelyn told her what the old lady had said.

Evelyn's good footing with Mary Ann rested, so Mary Ann believed, on a higher level than any mere question of the proper use of a doormat. Mary Ann recognised in Evelyn a fellow-disciple in the paths of literature and in the cultivation of the emotions. Mary Ann was forty-five by the candour of the Family Bible and at least thirty-five by her own, she was stout of figure and heavy of countenance, but the fairies who had been somewhat unkind in their gifts of form and feature, realising their mistake at the last moment, had thrown in a double portion of imagination, and of a capacity for emotion entirely out of proportion to her destined environment. Her love for her mother was true and deep, and happily it was mutual, but as is often the way with Canadian farm women, it found too little outward expression in the little amenities of daily family life. Mother and daughter were in staunch alliance when Old Dawson came home from town, as he did three or four times in the course of the year, in a state of too exuberant loyalty and whisky; they had identical views as to the lameness of Old Dawson's plea of a 'lame back' when there was work to be done around the house; they watched with equal rigour lest the mailman or any passing neighbour should bring him a surreptitious flask to be hidden in the barn and consumed in attempted secrecy; but the morning and evening kiss, the smile answering to smile, the passing caress of a touch of the hand, were long since but memories of childhood in the minds of both, and which, though both cherished them deep down in their hearts, neither could have attempted to revive without embarrassment and shame-facedness. Still, stunted and dwarfed as it was in its expression, it was the soundest and sweetest remnant of the divine in Mary Ann's nature—it was the flower in a wilderness of weeds which Evelyn's sympathetic eyes had been quick to discover and to seek to win to a fuller and happier blossoming.

Mary Ann's imaginative gift was also of Evelyn's finding out, but she was not quite sure whether it were among the weeds or the flowers. It was sufficiently exuberate but not quite lovely in all its manifestations. On its literary side it had battened on the short stories of the weekly papers and the *Family Herald*, and constructively in deducing the family or financial affairs of her neighbours from as close an examination of their mail as was possible without actually opening their letters, and from keeping her eyes open at church and other gatherings of the settlement folks. Of the rather scant materials thus furnished Mary Ann had fallen into the way of erecting castles in Spain—things of beauty or otherwise as her rather strong prejudices might dictate.

The chance coming of a new novel from a friend in the Old Country, and which Evelyn had opened and shown to Mary Ann on one of her visits to the post office, had been the incidental means of revealing to her the romantic side of Mary Ann's temperament, and she had fallen into the way of lending Mary Ann books from her own store at the Dingle and from the school library which she had started at the Lakeside School.

Mary Ann devoured with avidity the love stories of Rosa Nouchette Carey and L. T. Meade, but the book which completely captured her heart was *Jane Eyre*. Frankly conscious that she hardly possessed the qualities of youth and beauty in her own person commensurate to the part of heroine in a romance of real life, she had generously allotted the leading part to Evelyn; the friction with the Dennis boys over their mail provided her with a choice of villains, and the finally successful hero was to be Bert Enderby. She hesitated a little over Bert—he was somewhat lacking in the way of raven locks and flashing eyes and other physical qualifications for a hero— but then he was 'that' kind-mannered and pleasant when he came for the mail—never a bit of mud on his boots to vex her mother, nor chaffing her father to lead him to make himself ridiculous. And then such a consummation would be probably distasteful to Mrs. Enderby and Daisy, who would not think a girl who had no rich relatives and who had to make her own living, good enough for their high and mighty English notions. Altogether, Mary Ann thought it would work out to quite a desirable 'daynoomong,' in which she, as Evelyn's trusted confidante, would occupy, if a subordinate, still quite a striking position. If it should seem that Mary Ann's superstructure was rather top-heavy for its base, it must be remembered that in a Manitoba country settlement open ears and quick eyes can gather many suggestive trifles, and that as a regular church member and the postmaster's daughter Mary Ann was fortunately placed for knowing all there was to be known—possibly a little more—of her neighbours' doings. That Tom drove Evelyn up from town, that he took her to Amanda's wedding, that it was after dark when they got back, that the Dennis boys were going to church regularly, that the only trip Tom had made to town was when Evelyn was staying with Mr. Jordan—these were commonplaces in Mary Ann's store of inside information. Many other details had been gathered quite incidentally from Sam, the Dingle chore boy, when he was sent up to post letters. It gratified Sam's ready appetite to receive, maybe, a piece of cake or a cookie while he waited for the mail, and it increased his conceit of himself to find a ready listener, his native loquacity being rather at a discount among the ladies of the Dingle. He, too, was a great admirer of Bert and of Miss Raye, neither of whom laughed at his Cockney accent and figures of speech as did Daisy and the Dennis boys; that Mary Ann had any motive in her questions about life at the Dingle beyond an interest in his self-satisfied little self never entered Sam's mind—as why should it?

How little we dream of what fortune has in store for us of happiness or sorrow! Evelyn walked slowly up the Dawson lane indulging in a last tender thought of Tom and of his coming, as unconscious of the vagaries of Mary Ann's mind as she was of the swift fading of that vision of love and happiness born of the pressure of his farewell hand and of his whispered question, 'May I come?'

CHAPTER XXI

AN EMBARRASSING MEETING

As Evelyn opened the post-office door the mailman was just retying his bag preparatory to resuming his journey, and receiving directions from Mary Ann for the delivery of sundry parcels in 'Sweden,' for the mailman often acted as a means of communication between the two settlements. 'Here's a bundle from Mrs. M'Tavish for Mrs. Jensen who makes the rag carpet, and that plough-point agin the door is for Carl Swanson, and this little parcel is for "old man" Nielson—yes, that's all,' and Mary Ann held the door open for the mailman's departure. 'No, father does not want anything next trip from town,' she added decisively, for the mailman looked inquiringly at 'Old Dawson,' who was edging his way rather furtively towards the door with his cap in his hand, and Mary Ann closed the door sharply and turned towards Evelyn and shook hands.

'I am sure I am very glad to see you, Miss Raye, though you find us all of a muss—what with the work outside and the office and all; father's back is bad, so he says, and there's mother laid up with the bronchitis and not able to turn.'

'Oh, I'm so sorry, Miss Dawson,' said Evelyn sympathetically; 'I hope your mother is not seriously ill—she is always so brisk and busy.'

'Well, when mother lays up you may be sure it's not just fancy—she's one of the kind as'll work till they drop—she's not like some,' Mary Ann added, with a suggestive, if unintentional, emphasis on the 'some.'

'How long has your mother been ill?' asked Evelyn as she laid down her books and pail and took the chair Mary Ann had drawn forward to the stove. 'It's a wonder none of the children told me at school—they generally know everything.'

'Well, she has not been real well all Fall, and last week I was down at a neighbour's nursing for a couple of days, and mother, she took a chill; nobody round, it seems, so much as to put the cows in the stable and to milk them, or to feed the pigs. I packed her off to bed, you may be sure, as soon as I got home, and there she stays till she gets the cold off her chist.'

'I'm sure she will be well looked after now, but did you not send for the doctor, Mr. Dawson?' asked Evelyn of the latter, who having put on a pair of spectacles was commencing to sort out the letters and papers on the table.

'No, I didn't,' answered Old Dawson sulkily, for he was feeling rather sore for reasons of his own, 'common folks like us 'ens can't be sending for the doctor every day and paying him ten dollars to come and look wise. Mary Ann there has been a-nussing other folks for ten year and sure she can mind the "old woman" through a bit of a cold. I never sends for no doctor, though my back is that bad these days——'

'Oh, never mind your back,' interrupted Mary Ann sharply. 'It's not the money, Miss Raye, but you see I can do all as is to be done. I put on a couple of mustard plasters—front and back—as soon as I got home, and she's had a flannel with some goose grease on her chist night and day since, and I always keep a drop of whisky in the house, where it's safe, and she's doing nicely. I'll not be leaving her again to other folk's care—but she'll be real glad to see you, if you can stay a while till I sort out the Dingle mail.'

'Oh, I'm in no hurry at all,' replied Evelyn, 'and shall be glad to sit with your mother and will not talk to disturb her.'

'You'll not disturb her—she's lonesome while I'm about my work and it'll do her good to hear you, and she likes to talk a little herself—it's not nateral for her to be resting quiet all day.'

Mary Ann ushered Evelyn into her mother's room, which was partitioned off the general living-room of the post-office, and placed a chair for her by her mother's bedside. 'Are you awake, mother? Here's Miss Raye, the schoolma'am, come to sit with you and cheer you up while father and I sort the mail.'

The old woman drew out from under the patchwork quilt a thin and shaky hand, which Evelyn took gently and held in her own as she sat down beside the bed. 'I'm so sorry you have been so ill, Mrs. Dawson, I do hope you will soon be well again now you have your daughter home to care for you.'

'Oh, she does well enough,' admitted the old woman rather ungraciously, 'she's nussed lots of other folks as she had little call to—the Lord knows I'm not one to be hanging on to life when I can't do my own bit of work round the place. Has the mailman gone, Mary Ann, and where's your father?' she added suspiciously.

'Oh yes, I saw to that, mother, and father is sorting the mail.'

'Well, you'd best be helping him—if it's to be done to-night—when "himself" can hardly read book print let alone writing.'

'Don't worry, mother, we will manage all right—and I'll come and tell you when your mail is ready, Miss Raye,' and Mary Ann left the room, drawing to but not closing the door.

Evelyn had visited too many querulous and rheumatic old villagers in her father's parish at home to feel embarrassed by Mrs. Dawson's rather grudging reception. She told her in an easy and quiet way such little news of the doings of the settlement as she herself had heard from the school children, and under her sympathetic influence in a little while Mrs. Dawson was giving her—between rather short breaths and fits of coughing—a detailed account of how she was 'took' with the chill. As this involved some severe strictures on the deficiencies of 'himself' in looking after the cows and the stables, Evelyn endeavoured to switch the conversation on to more kindly lines by asking if her minister had been to see her since she was laid up.

She was only too successful. 'No, he's not, and it's not myself that would be sending for him. The last time they came round gathering for his salary, Samuel—that's my husband—only gave them two dollars, and grumbled at that. No, I'll never be sending, not if the Lord takes me without seeing the minister at all. Maybe the Lord knows I'm a sinner, but He knows I've never needed to be ashamed of the colour of my whites on the line of a Monday morning, and my house floor maybe is cleaner than some of them 'ens as goes trapsing to every 'vangelist meeting as comes along,' and the old lady relapsed from her energy into a fit of coughing which left her exhausted and choking for breath.

Evelyn leaned over her to try and catch the words the old woman was struggling to articulate between her gasps. 'A drink—the cup? Yes,' and Evelyn fetched the cup from the little stand by the window and gently raised her head and held the cup to her lips.

'Now, Mrs. Dawson, you must not try to talk any more or your daughter will think I am making you worse instead of better; and indeed I must be going if my mail is ready, or it will be dark before I get home. Good-bye, and I will be coming again soon and hope you will be better,' and gently pressing her hand in farewell Evelyn stepped quickly across the floor and into the post-office.

Mary Ann was tying together with a piece of binding twine a bundle of letters and papers. 'There you are, Miss Raye, I was just coming for you. I heard mother coughing; she will talk, if there's ever a body to talk to, but she'd be that vexed if I let you go without seeing her;—but there's some one just drove up to the door—maybe it's some of your folks and you'll get a drive home.'

'Oh, I don't think so,' replied Evelyn quickly. 'Mr. Bert is away threshing at—threshing, and the boy would not be sent with the horse. Good-bye, I hope your mother will soon be well again,' and Evelyn opened the door and stepped out to meet Bert Enderby on the threshhold and to see Tom Dennis's mare and buckboard a few yards away.

'There now, I told you, Miss Raye,' exclaimed Mary Ann, with obvious delight at the *rencontre*—could anything be more in keeping with the fitness of things? 'Now, that's real cute of you, Mr. Bert, to guess as how you would find the schoolmarm here and to bring the rig and all; I was just telling her as how it would be you when I heard the rig drive up.'

Evelyn and Bert were too mutually surprised and embarrassed for different reasons to catch the purport of Mary Ann's innuendoes, and were both glad too of a moment to regain their composure under cover of Mary Ann's chatter. Evelyn was the first to speak. 'I called round for the mail as I came from school and then stayed to have a chat with Mrs. Dawson; I thought I should be saving you a trip. Good-bye, Mrs. Dawson,' and then Bert, as he turned the buckboard so that she might get in, and taking his own seat by her side, 'Well, I happened to be driving up from town and thought I would call as I came by,' and both relapsed into silence as Bert gave the lines a shake and the mare started off.

A very awkward and embarrassed silence as they drove down the lane and turned into the town line, for in each mind there was a question clamouring for an answer—and a question that could not be asked without obvious implications. In Bert's mind, 'Has she heard of the burning of the stacks, and of Jack's trouble in town? If those confounded women at the office have heard, she knows it all and a lot more; and if she hasn't how am I, of all men, to tell her—to be kind to her and yet true to Tom?'

And in Evelyn's, 'Why is Bert here—why has he been to town—and why to-night, of all nights, is he driving home with Tom's mare and no word of Tom or the threshing? I must know what has happened and what lies behind his silence and brusqueness—I must know—but he must not dream why I must know.'

As always, the woman's courage to face the dreaded unknown was greater than the man's, and the woman's intuition quicker to divine that it is less self-revealing to question than to be questioned. Moreover, a woman guarding the secret of an unasked and unacknowledged love is more inscrutable than the Sphinx, and as unscrupulous as an Old Bailey lawyer.

'It's too bad that my benevolent intention of saving you a trip to the office should have been spoilt after all, Mr. Bert,' and Evelyn's voice was light and almost flippant, 'but you know it's your own fault, for you said last night you were going threshing or something, and would not be home till after dark—and I knew the girls would like to get the English mail.'

'Oh yes, I know I did, and it's very kind of you, but you see—they—we—did not thresh to-day,' and Bert hesitated. 'Ah—did you hear any news at the office?'

'Now, let me see—oh yes—"himself" has a lame back—but I'm afraid that isn't news—and poor old Mrs. Dawson is quite ill—that selfish old man won't send for the doctor—and oh—if you should see their minister I'm sure she would like to see him, though she won't send to ask him to come because "himself" is too mean to pay his share of the minister's salary. I suppose it was too windy to thresh to-day?'—the last very casually and in the face of a day-long calm! 'Or did the engine misbehave itself? I know Daisy says there never was a threshing yet when something did not go wrong.'

'Oh, there was an accident at Berg's last night—no one hurt, you know,' added Bert hastily, 'and Jack Dennis went to town for some new teeth for the separator and—and—after he left—Tom's spoilt this mare of his,' and Bert gave an irritated jerk to the reins; 'she wants either to go on a tearing canter or else just to crawl.'

'Poor old thing—I expect she likes to have her own way. You were saying after Mr. Jack went to town?'

'Some stupid ass dropped a light near Berg's straw stacks——'

'And they were burnt up?—oh, that's too bad!'

'Oh, that didn't matter—his grain was all safe—but——'

'Why, Mr. Bert, you are almost as slow in telling me as Mr. Dennis's mare's walk.'

Poor Bert was desperate, and in his despair made the inevitable *faux pas*—beautifully typical of his sex in a tight corner—a mistake that braced up Evelyn's self-protecting banter to the last notch. 'I'm slow in telling you because I hate to hurt you—because it hurts me to hurt you—the fire spread to the Dennises and their stacks were all burnt up.' Bert could have sworn he felt a start and quiver in the form pressed so near to him by the narrow seat of the buckboard, but the voice was as steady and as inexpressive as ever.

'Oh, that's too bad, I'm so sorry—do let her take her own time, Mr. Bert,' for Bert was again jerking on the reins. 'I suppose Mr. Jack will be more severe on the farm life than ever. So you and Mr. Hardie had all your hurry and early rising for nothing?'

Had the girl no feeling at all?—Bert was utterly at sea—or had he been blind all summer? If there was nothing where he had been sure there was so much what a fool he had made of himself—if she didn't care for Tom was it possible?—at least it made the telling of the rest of his story easier, and he hurried on with an account of Jack's mishap and his own visit with Tom to town.

Evelyn spoke but little; she was sympathetic now in such little questions as she asked, but it was purely a conventional sympathy—so it seemed at least to Bert, who alternated between hot flashes of a wild hope, of possibilities for his own love, and shudders of disgust at what surely was disloyalty to his friend. It was nearly dark as they neared the Dingle lane, and he brought his tale to a conclusion. 'So,' it was Evelyn who asked, 'I suppose Mr. Jack, if this wretched man recovers, and, as you say, can be bribed not to prosecute, I suppose Mr. Jack will volunteer for South Africa —he told me he was aching to go—and his brother will come back to the farm?'

By this time Bert's tender carefulness to spare Evelyn was quite lulled to sleep. 'Oh, if Jack goes, Tom will go too. After losing the crop he could not stay on the place without help from his people at home, and that he said he would not ask; besides, the disgrace of this affair of Jack's——'

'What disgrace is that to Mr. Tom Dennis, pray, that his brother would not allow a miserable wretch to insult the Queen? Who says it is a disgrace —his friends?'

'Oh no, I did not mean that—poor Jack has the sympathy of everybody in town—but Tom feels the shame of his brother being locked up in the cells and the trial, if there has to be one—and their name in the police news, and—you know Jack is the youngest boy in the family, Tom pledged himself to his mother to stand between Jack and harm—will you hold the lines while I open the gate?'

'Oh, let me open it,' and before Bert could protest Evelyn had jumped out and hastened to open the yard gate. 'No, don't wait for me, I will shut the gate and walk up to the house.'

'It was too bad of you not to let me get out—never mind the fastening —please tell them I've had my supper,' and Bert drove on to the stable. 'I wonder after all if she cares for Tom?—But she couldn't have taken it like that if she did—yet why did she snap me up so quickly about Jack?—and her voice as cold as an icicle—"his friends"—and I fighting my own heart all summer because I thought that she loved Tom—I wonder——' and still wondering, Bert put the mare in the stable and fed her and returned slowly to the house to find that Evelyn had gone straight to her room on the plea of a headache from the stuffiness of Mrs. Dawson's room, while Daisy was waiting for a full account of the happenings at Connemara Farm and of his trip to town,—a brief note which Bert had sent back by Jim Hardie in the morning saying the Dennis crop was burned and that he had gone to town, having left the Dingle family in a state of wonderment and anxiety.

CHAPTER XXII

A WEEK OF SUSPENSE

Never afterwards could Tom Dennis think of his first three days in Minnedosa without a shudder—it was a time of utter, unbroken shame and misery. It was in vain for Mr. Jordan to assure him that Jack had the sympathy of every one in town in his trouble—that did not undo the fact that his brother was a prisoner in a prison cell, and might soon be brought before a judge to answer for a serious crime. Anxious as he was to hasten to his brother's side, his first visit to the prison cell in the town hall was a cruel ordeal. Mr. Jordan procured the necessary permission for his visit from the police magistrate and accompanied him to the town hall. The town constable, who also acted as gaoler, admitted him into the building, and locking the door after them, led the way to the two or three little cells in the rear, unlocked the door of one of these and ushered Tom into his brother's presence, and going out, locked the door behind him:—

'I'll come round in a while and let you out—but there's no hurry,' and a minute afterward Tom heard him unlocking and relocking the outer door.

If Tom had had a hard thought in his heart it must have vanished at the sight of his brother's misery—his white, drawn face told not only of a night without sleep, but of an utter collapse of self-control and of a panic fear. It was not the dread of punishment that had kept poor Jack tossing on his pallet through the long, silent hours of the unending night, but the moral horror lest he should have killed the unhappy object of his hasty passion—was he a murderer? The coming of the morn had brought little relief to his suspense—it was well after eight o'clock before the town constable unlocked the cell door and handed in Jack's breakfast, and he was very non-committal in his answers to Jack's eager questions. His gaoler was a simple, kindly man, who had been a farm labourer in the Old Country, and who, having attained late in life to the dignity of town constable of Minnedosa, felt that it behoved him to maintain a certain reserve in his relations with his prisoner, and he was hampered by vague recollections of what he had read in the papers about not allowing prisoners to make statements without due warning. Consequently, his extreme caution in admitting that the man might die—or again, he might not—had only confirmed Jack in his worst fears, especially when he added, 'don't you go for to say nothing; it will be used agen you.' So Jack turned from the basket of food, and throwing himself again on his bed took up once more the asking of that question to which there was no answer forthcoming.

The last spark of resentment against Jack for the loss of his own happiness forsook Tom's breast as he knelt down by the pallet and put his arms about his brother's neck as gently as a woman and kissed him on the cheek —there was only brother and brother there—and it seemed to Tom that only the other day they were playing round the one mother's knee.

'No, Jack, don't turn from me,' as Jack put his hands to his face and tried to turn to the wall. 'I know all about it, I know there was no thought of crime in your heart, and there's not a Dennis of them all that would have done different.'

'Oh, Tom, I can bear any punishment if only the man doesn't die—and the shame to you and all your hopes——'

'My hopes went up in smoke last night, Jack—so you need not grieve for them—but of course, you've not heard—our stacks were burnt last night by a prairie fire——'

'Oh, Tom, after all your work, and now——?'

'We're as bare as we came into the world—and Jack, remember this, however your trouble ends, I'd made up my mind before I heard of it that I would—it was a hard pull, Jack—I would never say the words I meant to say to Evelyn Raye.'

'Thank you, Tom, for saying it—my punishment would be double if it had spoilt your life too—but Tom, you have seen Mr. Jordan; what does he think about the man—will he—will he recover?'

'Mr. Jordan was at the hospital this morning and Dr. Casey has been there all night—and Dr. Casey will not say "yes" or "no" to anything—but there's a chance, and we must rest on that—we won't talk about it, Jack; just remember I'm here, and here to stop till our uncertainty is over. Mr. Jordan insists on my staying at the Rectory, and I'll be here as often as they will let me, and here's the old chap unlocking the door—good-bye, Jack, keep a good heart—good-bye—I'll be back again this afternoon.'

In the afternoon Tom had a long talk with Bert Enderby in Mr. Jordan's study, in which Tom spoke of his own loss at the farm as a matter of quite trifling importance—how best to provide for Jack's defence if the wounded man, Tim Toole, should die, or if Jack should be brought to trial for assault if he recovered. Jack's present and Jack's future were the only things that mattered—for the rest he gratefully accepted Bert's proffered help to go over to Connemara the next day and arrange for the Dennis team to be sent to Berg's for the present, and to pack up and bring down in a day or two such clothes as were worth bringing, and Tom's desk and any letters there might be lying round.

'You'll be coming back north yourself, Tom, in a few days?' Bert asked hesitatingly just before he left, 'if all goes well, or even if——'

'No, Bert, no matter how it ends, I'll not show my face at the Dingle—their very kindness would kill me—if all goes well it will be Africa for Jack—if he can get on the muster roll—and where Jack goes, I go, and if that fails it will be to hide myself where I am not known till Jack is a free man and I can take him home—but what's the use of talking of the future —God only knows what it will be—good-bye.'

In the evening Tom was back with his brother till as late as the constable would consent to be kept out of bed, and was with him nearly the whole of the following two days, sometimes alone, sometimes with Mr. Jordan, and once with Mr. Darcy, the lawyer, who had thrown himself eagerly into the preparing for Jack's defence. Though Jack had by now recovered in some measure his nerve and self-control, and Tom had overcome his sense of shame in being seen stealing down the back lane with the constable on his trips to and from the town hall, still the strain of suspense told heavily on both brothers, and when, in Mr. Jordan's study on the third evening, Dr. Casey told Tom that Tim Toole would live, Tom fairly broke down and sobbed like a child. Because his own feelings were deeply moved old Dr. Casey took a very brusque attitude with Tom and was entirely unsympathetic—'You go down and tell that scamp of a brother of yours that thanks to a thick head and little brains Tim Toole will be out of hospital in a week and be fuddling himself with whisky again in a fortnight —the Fenian blackguard! I'd have let him bleed to death like a pig the night it happened if it had not been for the honour of the profession and to get you two Irish boys out of trouble—so I would. And it's trouble enough we will be having with the rascal yet before we have done with him—for since the devil decided to give him another chance to miss—what he deserves, I'll say, since Mr. Jordan is here—why, he's showing a very ugly temper, and is as full of revenge and black-hearted malice as an egg's full of meat. But get you down to your brother, poor lad, and make his mind easy, and between Mr. Darcy and myself we'll try and get Tim to a better frame of mind, with the help of a few dollars, maybe, and if that fails, why, Mr. Jordan here must get a papist priest over from Brandon to scare a little religion into his conscience or his pocket.'

It was late on in the following morning when Tom Dennis awoke with a start to find Mr. Jordan standing by his bedside, with a cheerful smile that was itself an answer to the half-uttered question that seemed on Tom's lips as he opened his eyes—'All's well, Tom, when you sleep you sleep soundly—do you know what time it is? It's half-past eleven!'

'Oh, I'm awfully sorry—but you see it's the first real sleep I've had—it seems for an age—and I should have been down with Jack long ago. He was to be brought before the magistrate this morning, and I should have been by his side—what has been done?' and Tom's face was very anxious.

'Well, that is all over, and you may feel easy. I came in to see you before I went down to the Town Hall, and you were sound asleep—poor fellow, the ordeal would have hurt you and it could do no good, so I let you sleep on and told Jack why you were not there, and he was as glad as I for you to be spared. As it was early, there were only one or two people in the court, besides the magistrate, Mr. Darcy and myself. Jim Turner and the constable were the only witnesses, and they were both as favourable to Jack as they could be, and when Dr. Casey gave his assurance that the man was out of danger and could appear in four or five days if he wished to press this charge, the magistrate committed Jack on a charge of common assault and adjourned the case till next Wednesday, and then I think you may rest easy that Jack will be a free man again, and it will only be a case of a few dollars fine.'

'And till then must Jack stay in pris—that place?' and Tom winced as he made the substitution.

'Well, you see, Tom, it was rather awkward——' and Mr. Jordan hesitated for a moment,—'I hope I acted for the best—the magistrate would have taken my bail—but I didn't see what we could do with your brother in the meantime—he would not go up north, either home or to the Dingle or to Jim Hardie's—I would have gladly had him here, but he could not stay in the house all the time, and if he went down town he would find himself a hero—not only on account of the very thing that has caused all the trouble, but it has got out that you are both volunteering for South Africa, and the whole country is in a blaze of patriotism. I'm certain your brother is as safe as a house as regards—you know the old trouble—but he would be in a hard place.'

'Thank you, Mr. Jordan, I hate to think of him being there—but you're right—and I—both of us can never thank you.'

'Oh, that's all right—it's all in the day's work,' replied Mr. Jordan lightly, 'Jack is a new man this morning, and I've taken him down a big budget of papers about the war, and his only anxiety now is about getting on the roll—and I suppose, Tom, your own mind is quite made up—you'll still volunteer yourself—I thought, perhaps, now,' and Mr. Jordan's voice was kindly and invited confidence, for he had had thoughts of his own in the past summer as he had seen Tom so often at the Dingle, 'I thought, perhaps, now Jack's trouble is so nearly over, you might stay with us. I hate to lose you both from my little flock up north.'

'Thank you, for saying so, sir, but——' and Tom's voice, which faltered at the first words, grew quite steady as he went on—'I go with Jack if it can be managed—I sent our two names into Brandon the day after I

110

came down on the off-chance, and Dr. Casey promised to write to the officer in charge there.'

'Well, he kept his promise, and this afternoon he is going to examine both of you physically, and if that is satisfactory he is going to write again and ask them to hold the two places till next Wednesday, and if all is well he will drive the two of you over on Wednesday night.'

'It's awfully good of the doctor—we'll never forget, Jack and I, both of you——'

'Oh, you're Irish—that accounts for the doctor—that, and your volunteering—why, the old doctor would go himself if he were young enough—I'm bad enough, if I see a red coat or hear the sound of a drum—but Dr. Casey is a regular fire-eater if any one slights the Queen or the Flag.'

'I'm afraid it's just your kind way of making it easy for us to accept your help, but now I can stay at the hotel till next Wednesday—I cannot be on your hands——'

'Nonsense, Tom, don't talk foolishness, we are delighted to have you till you go "off to the wars," ' said Mr. Jordan heartily, 'only you'll find it slow, as I expect you'll want to keep clear of the town, and you cannot be cooped up with Jack all day—you must get out and get braced up after all your worry—I tell you what—Bert Enderby is down this morning—brought your things—you can settle with him this afternoon about your farm affairs while you are away—and then after to-day, till you go, Tad can have a little holiday from school, and you can get off and have a little shooting down the valley, it's quiet and out of the way there, and you'll not meet people you know.'

'That would be just the thing for me—but Tad?'

'Oh, Tad won't grieve at missing school—you've been a great favourite with him since the summer, his mother and I had to lay an embargo on the words "Mr. Tom" and "Connemara" or he would have talked us to death.'

'Tad's a fine boy,' said Tom laughing a little and touched too, 'there's very little better company for a tramp, and if you and Mrs. Jordan don't mind, it will be the thing I would choose myself.'

'So that's settled,' said Mr. Jordan heartily, 'only don't let him get too much war spirit or he will want to go himself as a drummer or something. Now, when you're dressed you can have breakfast and dinner together, and Bert is coming up at two o'clock, and then you can get the business part of your plans off your hands.'

Though Bert Enderby and Tom Dennis had a real and honest affection for each other, they both found their meeting in the afternoon full of embarrassment, for each brought to it reservations of confidence which they, for perfectly honourable reasons, were determined at all costs to maintain. For Jack's sake Tom had given out from the first that the loss of the crop had decided him to abandon the farm, and that, and enthusiasm for the war, would be sufficient to satisfy the curiosity of their friends and neighbours in the settlement. To Bert Tom had extended the further confidence of his sense of obligation to his people at home to stand by Jack in his trouble and to go with him to Africa, if he should be free to go. But there his confidence ended, he trusted Bert's loyalty entirely, but from experience he distrusted Bert's capacity to withstand Daisy's cross-examination if that young lady had a suspicion that there was something to be known which Bert was hiding from her—and he judged rightly that ignorance would be Bert's best safeguard. Tom felt that if he were not free to himself tell Evelyn of his love, at least she should not be embarrassed by perhaps tactless and thoughtless innuendoes from Daisy.

A week before Bert would have been honestly relieved to be told that Tom had proposed to Evelyn and had been accepted, so sure was he in his own mind of how things were with them—not that the love with which Evelyn had inspired him from the first had grown less, but because he realised more completely its hopelessness. Having in his own mind accepted in his slow, quiet way, the inevitable, it was very disturbing to discover, as he believed that he had discovered, that as far as Evelyn at least was concerned, he had been under a delusion.

His imagined discovery, after the first flush of a new hope for himself —a hope so uncertain that it gave him no confidence—left him only anxious to spare Tom the knowledge of Evelyn's feelings, which he thought she had revealed to himself in the drive home from the post-office. Bert was satisfied of Tom's affection for Evelyn, and thinking that Fate had been sufficiently hard to Tom in the loss of his crop and in Jack's trouble, he was bound that, not at least from him, should Tom learn of the loss of his love.

Thus, with an unconscious conspiracy of reserve, yet with entire confidence in each other's sincerity, it followed naturally enough that in the long interview between Tom and Bert, neither referred to that which lay nearest to each one's heart. Tom accepted with gratitude Bert's offer to take over the full charge of Connemara Farm—the selling of the team, the hay and the oat stack which had escaped the fire, and the paying with the proceeds of such bills as the Dennis boys had run up in town during the summer. As regards the farm itself, the title-deeds were still in their father's name, but Bert promised, either for himself or Jim Hardie, that the land should be seeded on shares in the following spring—beyond that, their plans for the future did not go.

'Who knows,' said Bert, trying to speak cheerfully, 'who knows, by then the war may be over and you will be coming back in time for a good harvest yourself.'

'Ay, or under the sod with a Boer bullet in my ribs—well, it's awfully good of you, Bert, to take so much trouble, and I hope it will be a bumper crop, even if I'm not here to share it—oh, by the way—there's the old mare —I suppose I'd better sell her with the team—she's getting up in years, but I might sell her to the mailman—Oh, confound it, no, the old girl has deserved better than that of me—I say, Bert—just keep the old mare for my sake—if I come back I'll take her again—and if not—why, she will do for your sister—or Miss Raye—to tote round with—she's quiet and safe.'

'Sure, Tom, I'll be glad to—and bring her to meet you home again, and now I must be off, or it will be late before I'm home, and you know how the mater worries—good-bye, Tom, I may be down with Jim Hardie on Wednesday to see you off, but if not, good-bye.'

'Good-bye, Bert; give my love to them at the Dingle—your mother and your—and the girls,' and Tom's voice shook a little as he made the change, 'good-bye at any rate till Wednesday.'

They both knew perfectly well that it was a final parting, but the fiction of Wednesday saved the situation and suppressed any evidence of the emotion that stirred so deeply in their hearts.

CHAPTER XXIII

TAD JORDAN'S TRUST

When one is five-and-twenty and Irish it is hard to keep up for long a high level of pessimism and self-abnegation, and when Wednesday came Tom Dennis was half-surprised and half-ashamed to find the blank door of despair of future happiness which he had slammed to, so to speak, on the night of the fire, and double-locked on the news of Jack's disaster, was beginning, by the mere lapse of time and circumstances, to be slowly opening again and letting in on the path of the future certain, as yet wavering but promising, rays of hope. The line dividing the sublime from the ridiculous is at all times very fine, and Tom above all things hated to think he had made himself ridiculous by a rather too tragical display of emotion to Bert Enderby and his brother Jack. The fire was, in truth, as he said to himself, 'a nasty jar,' but he knew perfectly well now that it alone would not have killed his hopes of winning Evelyn for his wife, nor even have delayed for long the declaration of his love—why should it? If she did not return his affection the sooner he knew of it the better, and if she did, what a poor thing it would be to let the matter of a few hundred bushels of wheat come between them and the happiness of facing the future together. He had certainly made an ass of himself about losing the crop, but this African business was quite another story—he had got to go—he had probably talked a lot of rot about the disgrace of Jack's imprisonment, after all the disgrace of a gaol is in what brings you there—but he had got to go—were Jack to go alone and ill befall him—that way lay shame in the eyes of all whom he loved—and of all who loved him. He had got to go, but hope was not to be lightly daunted now—what was this war in Africa after all—England had been caught unprepared, but the Empire was stirring, and in a few months these miserable Boers would be whipped into submission—why, by spring it might all be over and he back again and driving the old mare up the Dingle lane and meeting Evelyn by the gate maybe, and the wooing that had waited so long would be all the sweeter for the toil and peril between. (It's worth a king's ransom to be five-and-twenty and Irish when the devil is trying to paint the future all black.) What bally rot he had talked to Bert about a Boer bullet in his ribs—he'd be doing some shooting himself about then—and his old uncle at home had, so he said, half a dozen Crimean bullets tucked away in his anatomy and never a bit the worse but a twinge now and then and a bit limp in one leg.

By Wednesday Tom was still going to Africa sure enough—but he was coming back.

The morning Tom spent in writing a long letter home to his father, telling of his arrangements with Bert Enderby, and endeavouring by a brighter tone to relieve the rather lurid and despairing picture he had given in his letter a week earlier, telling of the fire and of the hopelessness of attempting to keep on the farm. Of Jack's trouble in town no mention had been made—they might hear all that story some later day, now it would only add to the old folk's worry and anxiety at their going to the war—and the call to Canada for help would be sufficient justification for their going in their father's eyes.

The afternoon was to be devoted to a final tramp with Tad to kill the few hours remaining till Jack should be released and they made their start for Brandon.

Tad had honestly and truly quite a high opinion of his father—in strictly church matters and in the orthodox way of cutting potato sets or planting peas, Dad was quite infallible, but Tad could not but recognise that Dad had his limitations on some very vital points—as regards the time to be spent on homework, the sacredness of public holidays from chores, and the safety of bathing in the treacherous Little Saskatchewan without parental supervision—but on the whole, Dad was fairly satisfactory by comparison with some fellows' fathers. His suggestion that Tad should stay home as a companion for Tom during these last few days had more than confirmed Tad in his general good opinion of his father—as a father—as a 'sport,' of course—but one must not expect everything.

On the earlier afternoons Tom and Tad had followed the many-winding course of the river, hoping to pick up a stray duck or two, but such ducks as the sharp, frosty nights had not started on their journey to the south for the winter, were exceedingly wild and wary, and Tom and Tad had brought home little but weary limbs, wet feet and a huge appetite when they returned to the rectory at night. This last afternoon was to be devoted to surer, if less honourable game—to the shooting of rabbits in Cowan's Bush, two miles down the river, and soon after dinner the two set out, Tad carrying a rolled-up grain-sack as game bag, and Tom, the rector's old, double-barrel, keeper's gun. While still on the public road they walked along briskly, for Tom was sensitively unwilling to run across any one he knew, but when they turned on to the old trail following the course of the river to Cowan's farm they slackened their speed, Tom lit his pipe and Tad settled down to a good talk about the war. With such a good-humoured and congenial listener as Tom Dennis, Tad found the prospective shooting of 'fat Dutchmen' by the former almost as attractive as the prospective shooting of bush rabbits by himself. And Tad was a born conversationalist—as dogmatic as Doctor Johnson—and demanding nothing but receptivity on the part of his companion. He had picked up from the English papers at the rectory a knowledge of the geography of Natal, the Orange Free State, and the Transvaal, which would have won him high honours on an examination paper, though he would have scorned to acquire it for any such unworthy purpose, while his knowledge of where various English generals were placed and of what units were under their command, was probably superior to that of the average intelligence officer at the front. The boy's enthusiasm fairly won Tom out of himself and stirred him to a real interest in the future of England and the war, which had been sadly dulled these last few weeks by his interest in Evelyn Raye and Connemara Farm. It made him resolve that since Africa needs must lie between him and the only future worth having, that he would rouse himself and face Africa with a resolution that if—no, when—he came back he should not be ashamed of the part he played there. By the time he reached the woods, by the aid of Tad's imagination the war was over, Tom and Jack were at least non-coms, even if one of them had not won a commission, and Tom found himself promising to bring back for Tad a variety of mementoes of the war—a Boer shell, unexploded for preference, some assegais for the walls of Tad's bedroom, a Kruger sovereign, an assortment of South African stamps—'and,' Tad concluded his list, 'if you could bring Dad some Dutch bulbs that would lick anything of their kind in town—why, he'd be more tickled than if he was made bishop.'

In their previous tramps along the river Tom had always carried the gun —a blue-winged teal rising from under the bank twenty yards ahead not leaving the time necessary for Tad's deliberate aiming—and Tad was quite content with the reflected honour of carrying such ducks as Tom might shoot, but to-day was to be Tad's field-day. The road through Cowan's Bush was little more than a deep-cut cart track winding along the sloping side of hills, which, on the one side fell away to swampy willow beds by the river, and on the other rose steeply, covered with young poplar trees and bushy undergrowth, to the high land of open prairie above. The plan of operations which Tom suggested, while it seemed to Tad the extreme of self-denial on Tom's part, fell in with the latter's humour far more than the personal slaying of the poor, white-tailed little creatures who had their homes among the stumps on the hillside, or the heavy clumps of willows by the river. Tad took over the gun with scarcely concealed eagerness, though with rather a sense of greediness in depriving Tom of what must be a keen delight to every properly constituted person; he also accepted with an air of modest attention the careful directions which Tom gave him as to

116

not leaving the gun cocked while going through the bush, keeping the muzzle raised up and well in front of him and covering the trigger guard with his right hand while going through scrub. Of course, they were very unnecessary, but no doubt Tom felt bound to do it out of deference to Dad's feelings. Tad was to be free to skirt the woods on either hand of the road, and Tom would await him at a point some half mile further on where the trail bent down to an opening on the river bank.

In a few minutes Tad was scrambling up the hillside, now covered thick with fallen autumn leaves, and Tom, refilling his pipe as he went, took his way leisurely along the trail. Here in the woods not a breath of wind was stirring—the sound of Tad's tramping through the crisp, dry leaves, with now and then the cracking of a dead and fallen bough beneath his feet, soon died away, and the quiet peacefulness of his surroundings turned Tom's thoughts from all the storm and stress of these latter days to the quiet Sunday afternoons at the Dingle when Evelyn and he had sat beneath the trees in the little poplar bluff, or strolled down the lane to meet Bert bringing home the cows from the meadows. It was two weeks ago since Evelyn's hand lay in his as he asked if he might bring her the first news of the threshing—asked, and—yes, surely, he received his answer in the trembling pressure that had set his heart beating and sent his hopes as high as heaven. And now—soon there would be half a continent and the trackless wastes of the Atlantic between them—and that gentle pressure the only answer to an unasked question. Poor Tom,—he felt that it would be easier to face a certain hell than to endure through the dark and threatening future the torture of such a slender and unsubstantial hope. It was hard enough to go—but to go and leave no one behind who even knew all the love and passion in his heart. If he could, without disloyalty to his manhood, only leave one behind who knew—one who in simple sincerity would hide or reveal the story of his love to Evelyn if he should die in that far-off land— hide or reveal as time should show whether knowledge or ignorance of his love made for the peace and happiness of her future. The old story of the disconsolate lover whispering the story of his passion to the leaves and flowers when a hard fate forbade that it should be told in the loved one's ears is no idle myth or foolish fancy of a maudlin poet. If Evelyn's love for him were nothing but frank friendliness springing from a bright and sympathetic disposition—if it were only such that the news of his death would win maybe a few tears and place his memory among the half-sad and half-happy associations of the past, why should he seek to compromise her conscience, if, in the time to come she should love another, by the suspicion that she had been in some subtle sense disloyal to himself? But if her love for him were as his love for her—the very heart and centre of her being— how cruel to leave her to mourn his death in the uncertainty, torturing to a true woman, lest she have opened the sacred door ere the god of love sought admission.

Sometimes hastening his steps, sometimes loitering, swayed by the quickly changing tenor of his thoughts, Tom had reached the appointed meeting-place and thrown himself down on the sward by the river's bank to await Tad's coming, and now the boy came in sight around a bend in the trail, the gun in one hand and the game sack thrown over his shoulder. From time to time Tom had been half-conscious of the report of the gun— sometimes sounding sharply as not far from the trail, and at others echoing dully far up the hillside. From Tad's sagging walk no less than from his beaming face as he drew near, it was very manifest that he, at least, had re- alised his ambitions, and Tom was preparing to throw himself as best he might into the enthusiasm that befitted the occasion, when the quick thought came in a flash, 'Why not tell the kid? By George—I believe he'd understand me better than any one else—I could talk to him without feel- ing such an ass as I would to Bert or Mr. Jordan, and if it comes to his telling Evelyn—she wouldn't mind him like any one grown up, and if not, the little beggar can be as tight as a steel trap in keeping his mouth shut—at any rate, I'll drop a hint and see how he takes it.'

'Well, Tad, what luck? I could see by your face a hundred yards away that it was not too bad—lots of rabbits?'

'Oh, just splendid. I felt real mean that you weren't with me—seven rabbits—and say, Mr. Dennis, there's a partridge at the bottom of the bag.'

'Why, I thought partridge were taboo here——'

'Well, we're not supposed to shoot them,' replied Tad, laying a little stress on the 'shoot,' as not feeling sure if that was the implication of the unknown word 'taboo.' 'Mr. Cowan does not mind the rabbits, but his boys get ratty if any one shoots the partridges—but the little beggar brought it on himself—just flew up in a tree and looked as if he thought I couldn't hit him—anyway, I've tucked him in a corner at the bottom of the bag in case we meet the boys, and we needn't say anything unless they ask a straight question. I didn't hunt for him anyway,' added Tad apologetically, evi- dently easing his conscience by throwing the moral onus on the unlucky bird, 'and I only used eight shells for the seven rabbits—a shot apiece ex- cept for one chap that hopped just as I fired and I broke his hind leg and had to give him a second to stop his squealing—he squealed horrid, and for a minute I wished I hadn't hit him at all—it made me feel sick—still, if he had sat still he'd have got the first shot in his head and that would have been the end of it.'

'Well, I guess the partridge is not a very serious matter,' replied Tom. 'You'd better sit down for a while and cool off and then we'll stroll home, and I'll carry your bag for a bit.'

'Oh, I'm not a bit tired,' said Tad eagerly, 'I'll carry the bag—I've had all the fun, and it must have been pretty slow for you.'

'Oh, I've been all right, Tad, I didn't feel like shooting to-day—I've been feeling a bit like I used to do at home on the last day of the holidays before I left Connemara to go to school in Dublin—a sort of saying good-bye to home feeling, Tad, but you've never left home?'

'I wish jolly well I was big enough to be going with you——'

'But wouldn't you feel sorry to leave Minnedosa and your Dad—and your mother, Tad?'

'Oh, of course, you know, a fellow would not like that sort of thing,' replied Tad uneasily, 'but,' he added conclusively to such an unpleasant line of thought, 'you're away from home anyway—and you'll be no farther off in Africa than you are here, and it's a lot bigger thing to be shooting Boers in Africa than rabbits in Manitoba.'

'Still, I'm awfully sorry to go, Tad, now the time's come. I hate saying good-bye to you and your Dad——'

'Dad's awfully sorry you're going, too, and so am I—I guess I'll fix the rabbits so that they won't be so heavy to carry,' and Tad rose hastily, emptied the rabbits out on the grass and took out his jack-knife—this way of talking was embarrassing.

'And there's some one else that I'm sorrier still to leave,' went on Tom, relieved that Tad's preoccupation with the rabbits kept the boy's eyes away from his own. 'There's Jim Hardie and the Enderbys——'

'Oh, yes, they are an awfully decent sort,' commented Tad, without looking up from his gruesome task, 'Bert is a regular brick and Daisy is more fun than a sideshow.'

'And there is Miss Raye, too,' added Tom slowly and watching as much as he could see of Tad's face.

'Isn't she splendid,' burst out Tad, becoming suddenly enthusiastic, dropping the rabbit on which he had been just operating and wiping his gory hands on the lining of his rough jacket. 'When she was at our place in the holidays we had all kinds of a time—she can make English puddings—Stiff Dicks and Spotted Dogs, that knock the spots off even mother's lemon pies—and she'd turn down the crackest player over at the tennis club to have a single with me—just a kid like me—and for tramping down by the river, she was better than a boy and didn't mind tearing her petticoats and things—why, no more than I do—why, she came down here with me fishing one day, and we sat down and had our lunch, just where we are sitting now—but,' and Tad came back suddenly and without any warning to the original question, 'she's not your sister or mine—I wish she was, only sisters are not like that.'

119

'Tad,' and Tom's change was as swift as his own, 'Tad, I love Miss Raye better than any one else in the world.'

As he expressed it to himself afterwards—'this was a down and outer' to Tad, he flushed to the roots of his hair, for a moment he looked Tom blankly in the face and then sought refuge in putting his rabbits back in the bag. 'She's an awfully fine girl, Mr. Dennis,' he stammered, 'I hope you will both be very happy in your wedded life,' he went on, clutching in his desperation at a turn of words he had often heard his father use at the conclusion of marriage services at which he was sometimes present, when mother was out of the way, and some stray couple had come unprovided with the necessary witnesses.'

'But I'm not very happy, Tad, for you see I've never told her—I meant to have done so when we had threshed, but now the crop's gone——'

'She's not the sort of girl to care a red cent about that,' said Tad decisively, 'if she cares for you like that—she'd take you if you hadn't a sh——'

'I know, Tad, but I've got to go to Africa now, and it would not be a square deal to ask her and then, perhaps, go and get knocked on the head, or come back with only one arm, or the Lord knows what—no, Tad, but I couldn't go without some one here knowing—someone I could trust to tell her if I don't come back—and if she cares—cares a whole lot, you know— to tell her that I died loving her with the last beat of my heart—and if she does not care like that—if she seems able to live on and be happy, and perhaps to learn to love some one else—why, then, that one that I leave behind and trust with my secret—he must just forget that I ever told him, and just remember only that Tom Dennis trusted him.'

'I understand, Mr. Dennis,' and there were tears in Tad's honest eyes and a sob in his voice, 'I understand, Mr. Tom, I'm only a kid—but you can bank on me.'

'And, Tad—if I don't come back—and if she should care very, very much, give her this ring,' and Tom slipped off a plain gold ring that he always wore on his little finger, 'and tell her how and where it was given to you—and if she does not care in that way, why, Tad, you will keep it in memory of our happy times together, and to remind you that when you were only a boy you had a poor unlucky beggar of an Irishman for your friend.'

Ten days later the *Sardinian* was slowly steaming down the St. Lawrence, bearing her contingent of a thousand good men and true—the eager response of the fair Dominion to her mother's call, and amid all the prayers wafted to heaven from the stately mansions of old Quebec, from the lonely homesteads on the Western prairies—amid all the prayers from mothers, sweethearts and wives for those on board the good ship, were

120

none more pathetic in their pleading than those from that little room in the Dingle where Evelyn Raye committed the one she loved so well to the care and protection of Heaven.

CHAPTER XXIV

POLITICS AND CRIBBAGE

The exuberate outburst of loyalty which accompanied the departure of the Canadian Volunteers for Africa gradually simmered down, and by the time the gushing reports of the Eastern papers had been reproduced in the Western dailies and re-reproduced with local touches by the weekly organs of the little Manitoba towns, the worthy settlers of the Minnedosa country were looking round for a fresh stimulant to relieve the monotony of the coming winter season. Nor had they to look long, for the local Government of the province dissolved the Legislature, possibly trusting to their patriotic enthusiasm in helping to raise the African contingent turning the thoughts of their opponents from criticising too closely their stewardship of purely provincial affairs. But let their motives pass; even Solomon found four things that were too hard for him to understand, and he was never on the inside of Western politics, or surely he would have frankly admitted that there was a fifth—the way of a provincial government with its constituency.

We are not concerned with any of the very vital issues which, so the opposing candidates said, were involved in the election in the Minnedosa riding. Each of them claimed a monopoly of Loyalty, Patriotism, Integrity, and of every moral virtue which the grammarians spell with a capital, each of them was satisfied that the return of his opponent would, in some undefined way, affect the stability of the Empire. It is sufficient to say that by January when all the pother was over—to the outward eye, at least, things seemed very much the same as they were before—the throne was still standing, the recently opposing candidates had resumed their old-time friendly relations in their little card club in town, and despite the recent extreme political heat, King Frost had his usual firm winter grip of the land.

Incidentally, the election had produced results at the Dingle more interesting and possibly more far-reaching than those of a distinctly political character.

The threshing being safely over and the fall ploughing done, Mr. Enderby and Bert threw themselves with great zeal into the contest and were away from home two or three evenings a week, either attending committee meetings in town or semi-political gatherings in neighbouring school-houses, where, under the guise of box socials or concerts to bolster up the finances of one or other of the churches in the settlement, an opportunity was given to the rival candidates to meet the electors and to woo the suffrages of their wives and daughters. To these gatherings Mr. Enderby insisted that either Miss Enderby or Daisy should accompany him, Mrs. Enderby being held excused on the score of delicate health, as it would never do to give a handle to the unscrupulous Grits by any appearance of English exclusiveness.

The entirely honest simplicity of mind which enabled Mr. Enderby to believe that Western Conservatism was the legitimate heir of the old English Tory party of his youth, made him fall an easy and unconscious victim to the not entirely innocent fashion in which Daisy turned his enthusiasm to the furthering of certain little plans of her own. With much plausibility she reasoned that as one of them must stay home with their mother, she had better be the one to forego the pleasures of the socials—she admitted with a self-depreciating humility that she could not be trusted not to give offence by some hasty and too caustic criticism of a neighbour's singing or cookery, while Marion was sure to be so sensible and in every way an acceptable sacrifice to the Canadian spirit of social equality. Really, Mr. Enderby thought to himself, he must have been unfair in sometimes fancying that Daisy was a trifle selfish and inclined to impose on her elder sister in the work about the house and so forth, and he made up his mind not to forget this little incident when he came to get her a new dress at Christmas time. Marion fell in with the arrangement with a due reluctance, though possibly in her own mind she did not accept the sisterly self-denial at quite its face value. Her habit of thought was too precise and correct for her to admit to herself that her acceptance of it had anything to do with Dugald M'Leod's announcement to Bert on the preceding Sunday, that he rather thought he would vote Conservative this time, as they seemed disposed to spend more Government money on the country roads and bridges—at any rate he would go and hear what they had to say for themselves. Dugald having always been reputed a Grit, Mr. Enderby and Bert looked on this as a very handsome concession—and when the fateful day came Dugald duly voted Conservative. That on the evening of the day on which the party victory was celebrated by a supremely bountiful supper in the Lakeside school Dugald should, under the influence of loyal choruses and lemon pies and coffee, have been notched up to such a high pitch of courage that he proposed to Marion and was accepted as he drove her home by moonlight—that, in Mr. Enderby's eyes, was only a happy coincidence of circumstances due to the kindness of unassisted providence, and his congratulations to the blushing Canuck on having found political salvation and a wife at the same time were entirely sincere and free of all afterthought.

Mrs. Enderby alone was not entirely satisfied with Dugald's new and assured footing in the family circle—but there were alleviations even amid her regrets—had not her husband's influence and Dr. Casey's powerful speeches brought Dugald from the Radical wilderness into the Conservative fold; now, if Mr. Jordan would only use his opportunities, when Dugald accompanied Marion to the English Church, for demonstrating, as could so easily be done, the advantages of Episcopacy over every other form of Church government, Mrs. Enderby felt that in time she might be reconciled to the shadows which hung around Dugald's ancestry. It was not a point which seemed to interest Dugald himself at all. All she had been able to gather from certain seemingly very casual questions, was that his father kept a corner store, and his uncle, on his mother's side, was a blacksmith in 'our town' in Ontario—these admissions were not very promising, but when he added that 'most of the folks in our parts had farms which were part of a land grant to soldiers disbanded after the old wars,' she felt there were at least possibilities of better things—soldiers have officers, and officers by every canon are gentlemen—and his wooing of Marion might be the survival of unsuspected affinities of birth and breeding. If in later times she did occasionally in confidential moments speak of him to Daisy as 'poor' Dugald, the epithet was not held to imply anything of personal reproach—it was only the sympathetic expression of resignation to a decree of fate.

Having pleased her father and so tactfully made smooth the difficult path of Dugald M'Leod, Daisy was not the girl to refuse any compensations for her lonely evenings at home with her mother and Evelyn which chance should bring in her way. She could not be expected to foresee that Evelyn, in her capacity of schoolma'am, and so the common property of the settlement, would be drawn into the socials and concerts—still less that Chris Raye would take to coming up to the Dingle two or three evenings a week to see his sister. Yet, so it turned out, and, as Daisy explained to her mother, when the latter expressed her mild surprise that Chris cared to come up and still stayed on after finding Evelyn and Bert away, it was very natural.

'You see, mother, Jim Hardie is away at the meetings and there is only Mrs. Hardie and her noisy boys and the baby down there. In all the rush of the fall work, of course, he was too busy to come up or feel lonesome, but now the poor boy hasn't a soul to talk to—I don't mind a bit talking to him about his wild flower specimens and the butterflies and beetles he collected in the summer—really it is quite interesting, and he forgets to be so painfully shy when there is only just ourselves here—I might teach him to play cribbage, and then the three of us could have a game, and you would enjoy it too, mother.'

124

'Well, I'm sure I do not mind,' Mrs. Enderby replied mildly, 'only I think you had better leave me out of the game—for I do get so confused with the counting and never can remember the difference between "his nob" and "his heels"—and, indeed, they both sound rather vulgar—and he is quite a nice boy and never uses the dreadful slang that is so trying, and indeed, Daisy, it would be a great comfort if you would break yourself of the way you have sometimes of expressing yourself. Your dear grandfather——'

'So I will, mother,' interrupted Daisy hastily, 'I'll not "eat" or "bet" a single thing that is not distinctly edible or meant to be wagered in quite a correct way—and then when Evelyn is able to stay home more I'm sure she will be pleased to think we have been kind to him.'

'Well, I'm sure I would be very glad to do anything to please Miss Raye—for she's a sweet, kind girl, and,' went on Mrs. Enderby quite innocently, 'I often feel quite thankful that your father decided to take her in, and that Bert does not seem to mind driving her to school or calling for her if it is a rough day—only he's such a dear, unselfish fellow, he would not say a word, however inconvenient it might be.'

'Oh, I don't think you need waste any sympathy on Bert—why, mother, do you mean to say that you cannot see he's been dead gone on Evelyn ever since she came, and that the only thing that kept him out of the running was because he did not think he had a show while Tom Dennis was round—why, I could have shaken Bert a dozen times to see the weak way he allowed Tom to sidetrack him, but it was none of my funeral, and I like Tom too—but, mother dear, you are too innocent for anything.'

'Well, I hope, my dear, I am too "innocent,"' replied Mrs. Enderby, much disturbed and evidently hurt by the pitying tone of Daisy's last words, 'I hope, my dear, I am too "innocent," if by that you imply that I do not grasp the meaning of the extraordinary terms you use in speaking of your brother's kindness to Miss Raye—but if you wish to imply that I am lacking in perceptiveness, I wish to say that your Aunt Penelope, my dear father's maiden sister, often remarked, when I stayed with her at Bath, that my powers of observation were quite beyond the ordinary——'

'Of course, mother dear, I didn't mean to be rude—but you are so unsuspicious——'

'Well, we will say no more about it, and I do not mind admitting, if that is what you mean by those expressions, which I shall not repeat, that I did think that Tom Dennis was rather marked in his attentions, and I did wonder whether your father ought to do anything about it.'

'Why, good heavens, mother, why should Dad put his spoke in—the Dennis boys, and Bert too, for the matter of that, are old enough to look after themselves.'

'Yes, my dear, of course, but in the case of Mr. Tom Dennis there are other considerations which I hope I am not too "innocent" to understand,' and Mrs. Enderby's sarcasm had the mildness of a misunderstood sheep. 'You must remember the Dennis boys were entrusted to your father's care when they came out—and you may not know,' again mildly sarcastic, 'that their father's elder brother is an earl—only Irish, of course—but still a very old title—and he is a bachelor—and when he dies—and he has to go to Carlsbad every winter for his liver, poor man—why, Tom's father will take the title, and Tom is the eldest son——'

'Why, mother, and Tom would be an earl some day—and I never knew.'

'Well, the Dennis boys never spoke of it themselves, and your father and I thought the neighbours might think we were proud of their being here —but there is no harm in your knowing—I only hope the poor boys will not come to harm in Africa—those dreadful Boers seem so republican, and would never show a bit more consideration to an earl's son than a just common soldier.'

'Well, mother, I don't see that that would make any difference if he were in love with Evelyn, she's just as good as Tom Dennis any day, and now he is away, if Bert could win her he would be a very lucky fellow.'

'Still, a peer is a peer, Daisy, and I may be allowed to understand that Tom's marrying a country school-teacher, however estimable a young woman she might be, would be a shock to his mother, and she might feel that your father ought to have spoken to Tom.'

'Well, I'm very glad Dad didn't, for Tom is not the sort to put up with an outsider chipping in—but since that seems to be at an end, for I don't believe Tom said a word to her before he left, why, if I were Bert I would buck up and have a shot at her myself. I'm sorry, mother, but I didn't mean to put it that way—I mean I should dearly love to have Evelyn for a sister, and surely you would not mind her being a school-teacher—she's quite a lady.'

'Well, you see, it would be different with us—not that I ever dreamt of such a thing, and I am sure it never entered your father's mind; but if she made Bert happy we quite understand how little what one does counts in the colonies, and, as you say, Evelyn is quite a lady, and I noticed the other day in one of her father's old books there was quite a fine coat of arms with a full sun for a crest, and the motto at the bottom—'Rayonnent les rayes'—sounds quite Norman; I am not quite sure what it means—though I had a French governess at school—still it would be a comfort to myself if there should anything come of what you fancy.'

'Well, mother, we shall see what we shall see, only don't let Evelyn or Bert fancy you have such a thought in your head, for she is a deep, quiet sort of a girl, and even I cannot make a guess at how things stand—only if I can manage to give Bert a look-in—why, I'm going to do it——. Now, mother, dear, you had better toddle off to bed, and I'll wait up till our lovers of all sorts get home from the meeting, and I'll have hopes of Bert if it turns out that Dad drives home with Jim Hardie and Bert brings Evelyn home in the cutter with Tom Dennis's old mare—that would be fine for Bert—but a bit rough on poor Tom if he only knew what use was being made of old Biddy in his absence.'

CHAPTER XXV

GRIEVANCES OF A CHORE BOY

The month of January was, in Daisy's picturesque language, 'a peach of a month,' not that a word suggestive of ruddy bloom and south walls is really very apt for the best of Manitoba Januaries, but she was looking beyond mere climatic conditions, to which in her sturdy health she was largely indifferent, to the kindly fashion in which Fortune seemed to be furthering her own particular aims. Of course it was very cold, but the sleighing was good, and there were things doing which made sleighing worth while. First, the Tennis Club and then the Bachelors in town gave dances, for which a general invitation for the family and friends was sent to the Dingle, and though Mrs. Enderby demurred a little on the score of there being no adequate chaperon, she allowed herself to be overruled, and each time a party of four was made up of Bert and Evelyn, and Chris and Daisy. These dances involved some very pleasant preliminary evenings at the Dingle—for Daisy undertook to teach Chris the mysteries of the two-step and the Highland Schottische, and though he possessed a full measure of awkwardness and shyness he was fast arriving at the stage when the pleasure of pleasing Daisy was superior to all other considerations.

Usually it had been necessary to propitiate Marion before making any plans which disarranged the ordinary routine of the household, but under the influence of her own wooing and winning Marion proved wonderfully complaisant, and Daisy was quick to discover that her badinage about Marion's 'Canuck,' which formerly was a great matter of offence, was secretly now rather a source of gratification to her sister.

Probably the only one of the household who had any real grievance against the new order of things at the Dingle was Sam, the Barnardo boy—a chore boy without a grievance would not be a chore boy, so that was to be expected—but even his grievance rested on rather shadowy grounds, and found little sympathy from his fellow Stepneyite at Jim Hardie's. 'Don't you get all you can eat three times a day, and a warm bed——' expostulated the latter, 'and a boss that doesn't sling you any lip, or raise Cain if you are a bit late in the morning—what are you grousing at?'

'Who's talking about the boss or the blooming grub,' retorted Sam, 'though Daisy, she burnt the bread twice last week, and Miss Enderby—

128

Marion I calls her—always sets a little jug of cream for her ma, and skim milk is good enough for the rest of us—it's not the vittles I'm talking about but the blooming carryings on this last month, and where do I come in, I should like to know? If all the folks are home I might as well not be there for all anybody thinks of *me*—it's pretty lively—isn't it—oh, of course—there's Bert and the schoolmarm playing their cribbage in one corner, and Daisy and that English guy from your place messing about with their weeds and grubs in another, the "old man" pretending to read the paper with a snore once in a while on the sofey, while the "old lady" darns stockings with one eye open to see as Daisy behaves herself—I suppose that's what chaps like you and me came to Canada for—eh, what? And if it's not that it's worse—there's Daisy—she clears all the things away and it's "Dad, won't you play us a tune?" and the old man takes down his fiddle and they dance—that English guy must be put through his paces before Daisy shows him off in town—and nobody asks me if I can dance—not much—Why don't I go and sit in the kitchen? I did one night—and ran into Marion cuddling her sandy-headed Canuck with the lamp turned down, and pretending to be washing the supper things as she'd took out two hours before—What did she say?—she up and says as sharp as you please—"You can take this lamp and go to bed, Sam, and you must be up early in the morning, as your master," this with great contempt and bitterness, "your master is going to town." But the old lady takes the cake—why, one night last week, when everybody was out except the boss, she sat looking at me quite a while as I was a-dosing by the stove, and at last she up and says "Don't you think you should improve your mind, Sam, by a little serious reading so as to have something to think about at your work—would you like me to teach you the Church Catechism?" I was that took aback I didn't know what to say, but I managed to get out as my eyes were sore from the snow—and she took it quite serious-like, and, will you believe me, she went and put a lot of greasy stuff on them and me had to sit and take it as if I was thankful for it, and sit the rest of the night with a 'ankercher round my head like a washerwoman—she's the limit for simpleness, but I do admit she means well—does the old lady.'

The 'peachiness' which so appealed to Daisy and the 'carryings on' which had scandalised Sam, both passed away with the coming of February, and the farm work which, with the exception of necessary chores, had been largely quiescent during the cold, short days, again became more exacting, both at the Dingle and at Jim Hardie's. Jim and Chris Raye were on the road from early dawn till after dark four or five days in the week, either bringing home wood from the bush or drawing hay from Jim's hay meadows in Sweden, while Bert Enderby was kept busy drawing grain to town to procure the necessary money for paying off the bills for the housekeeping and notes for farm machinery, which were becoming more and more insistent with each week's mail. Indeed the bundle of letters and papers from old Dawson's became rather an object of dread than of pleasant antic-ipation, and Daisy, who was not very orthodox in her views, often declared her belief that bills rather than filthy lucre were the root of all evil—did they not keep her father fussing about the house at unseasonable hours, they moved her mother to unprofitable reminiscences of the happy days when her papa met all such things with a cheque at Christmas, while Mar-ion, unduly careful to Daisy's thinking at all times, became possessed with a zeal for small and vexatious economies, evidently under the impression (Daisy's view again) that she could liquidate a nine months' grocery bill by putting only one egg in a batter pudding.

And the English letters and papers, in their way, were even more de-pressing than the duns of the Minnedosa tradespeople, for they told of nothing but disaster upon disaster in the Boer war. Ladysmith was in the blackest hour of her heroic resistance, and as hope followed hope so did failure step upon the heels of failure, as Buller's relief columns were thrown back again and again from the blood-sodden banks of the Tugela.

Of the Dennis boys and the Canadian contingent but little news had reached the Dingle. In the beginning of February Bert had a short note from Tom Dennis, written just as they were entraining for De Aar and the front. They had had a rough and comfortless passage but both were well— that and a promise to write more fully when they reached camp, was all it contained beyond a cutting from a Cape Town paper telling of their recep-tion on landing in South Africa.

The climax to Daisy's disgust, with things in general and Boers and bills in particular, was reached one Thursday evening toward the end of the month. Though it was nearly nine o'clock, Bert and his father were still up at the granary bagging the load of oats which the former was to take to town in the morning, and Mrs. Enderby and Evelyn were sitting by the stove sewing, while Marion and Daisy were laying the table for the early breakfast the next morning which Bert's visits to town involved.

'I shall be truly thankful when all this going to town and getting up in the dark is over,' said Daisy, as she placed some cold pork and marmalade and butter on the table and covered them with an open newspaper. 'It al-ways suggests the flight of the Israelites out of Egypt—everybody half asleep and cranky, and Bert comes in to his breakfast from the stable, if not with his loins girded and his staff in his hand, at least with an old scarf round his coon coat and his fur cap on his head, and in a great rush to get away—I don't suppose they had any cold pork, or possibly marmalade— but at any rate they got out of the land of bondage—and we have all the discomforts of it and have to stay in it. Well, I suppose we may as well go

130

to bed now, Marion, or Bert will be tapping at my door—"six o'clock, Daisy"—before I get to sleep—are you coming, Evelyn?'

'Oh, I will wait till Mr. Bert comes in. I may not see him in the morning, and I want to ask him to leave a little valise for me at the Dawsons as he goes by—I forgot you were in the kitchen when I was telling your mother—I am going to stay with Miss Dawson for a few days and go to school from there.'

'Stay with Miss Dawson—Mary Ann Dawson—for a few days—why what in the name of all that's crazy are you going to old Dawson's for?'

'Daisy, dear, do be more courteous in your way of speaking,' interrupted Mrs. Enderby, 'I'm sure it is very kind of Evelyn to go, and quite proper for her, too, as a clergyman's daughter, when old Mrs. Dawson is so ill, and poor Mary Ann has no one to help her in nursing her mother.'

'I promised Miss Dawson when I was at the office yesterday,' said Evelyn quietly, 'she looked so wretched and worn out, for she has been having hardly any rest at nights, and very little I expect in the daytime, for Mr. Dawson does not seem to even look after the cows and things, and people are in and out a good deal for their mail. So I said I would go up after school to-morrow and stay till——'

'Oh, I know it is not any good saying anything,' broke in Daisy rather impatiently, 'only it's not going to be very gay here while you are away and you may be there till spring if you are going to wait till the old lady hands in her—no, mother, I won't say it—till she takes her departure for the Elysian Fields—though that hardly fits in with her horror of muddy boots, but Doctor Casey said the other day he was tired of people asking him if she was dead yet, as if it was his fault that she wasn't.'

'I'm sure,' interrupted Mrs. Enderby mildly, and quite innocent of any double entendre, 'that no one blames the doctor for her lingering so long— he says it is just the tenacity of the Irish peasant constitution—the same thing that makes them so slow in paying their rents in the Old Country— though I don't quite see what the doctor meant by that—only I hope that they will keep the house warm, for Bert said after supper that there were rings round the moon, and that he expected that we should have a change to colder weather, and you might take Daisy's thick dressing-gown in case.'

'Oh, I'm sure I shall be quite comfortable,' said Evelyn cheerfully, 'and if Mr. Bert is up for the mail I'll send you word how I am getting along, and in any case I'll be down to church a week on Sunday.'

'Well, good-night, mother; good-night, Evelyn, I suppose what must be must be, and you and mother are both as irresponsible for your parson's daughter instinct for pastoral visitation as old Mrs. Dawson for her slowness in dying—you and I, Marion, are just ordinary farmer's daughters and had best get to bed. By the way, Evelyn, I'll remind Bert if he shows any sign of forgetting the mail-day,' with which Parthian dart Daisy followed her sister upstairs to their own room.

'Now, what do you make of that, Merry?' asked Daisy as she closed the door and set down the little hand-lamp on the dressing-table.

'What do I make of what?' replied Marion rather sharply, 'I do wish you would not make that kind of remark to Evelyn—I'm sure she does not like it.'

'Oh, nonsense, she must know very well that Bert is dead gone.'

'Why need you use such vulgar terms, besides I don't believe such a thing enters her head.'

'Well, suppose it doesn't, there's no harm in putting it there—what's this idea of hers in going to the Dawson's?'

'What idea should there be except to help Mary Ann and be kind to the old lady—what crazy notion have you got in your head now, child?'

'Oh, of course, I'm crazy—that's what people are always told if they keep their eyes open while other folks have theirs shut—I suppose you haven't noticed that Evelyn is in a state of restless excitement every mail-day till Bert comes in with it—and of course, you never noticed last week when Bert opened the paper and exclaimed "Why, the Canadian boys may go into action any day"—you didn't see how white she went?'

'Of course we were all excited—you know it quite upset mother, and she could talk of nothing but the Dennises all evening. I did think there might be something between Evelyn and Tom Dennis last Fall, but that must have ended when he left, and she has never breathed a word about him all winter.'

'She's not of the breathing kind,' remarked Daisy, 'but any news there is to come will be at the post-office before it comes here—I don't say she wouldn't have gone in any case, for she's awfully good-natured and self-sacrificing and that kind of thing—but all the same, I fancy she won't be sorry to get the first glance at the papers, and this nursing business will help to put in the time till news does come.'

'Indeed, it would be dreadful if anything did happen to the poor boys, when we've all known them so long, but I think you have been letting your imagination run away with you, and it's not quite nice to watch Evelyn in that way.'

'Very well, snub me if you like, Marion, I'm used to it—I hope Dugald won't find it rather trying when his turn comes' and Daisy retired into silence and her own thoughts.

132

CHAPTER XXVI

A DISAPPOINTING FUNERAL

The cold spell which Bert had foretold came in the following night with snowstorm and bluster of clouds and wind, which by the middle of the next week had been subdued by a steadily falling temperature to a clear sky and a biting breath of air from the north-west. It was not a wind that whistled openly across the prairie and swayed the bare branches of the poplar bluffs behind old Dawson's house, but an insidious draught that crept along the ground, baring the hillsides and filling in the sheltered hollows with fine particles of frozen snow, particles as icy and crisp as the driven sand of the desert. There was no touch of warmth or kindliness or sympathy in the iron-hard earth under its crystal canopy—there was no touch in the steel-blue vault of heaven, where the moon rode high in a clear light of untouched and untempted virgin purity. Even the rare sounds that broke the silence of the silent night were themselves full of suggestion of animate or inanimate pain. Ever and anon from the frozen river nearly half a mile away would come a report, clear and sharp as a rifle-shot, as the ice-bound stream, that in summer babbled of wild roses and the loves of the kingfishers, sought relief from the intolerable strain of the Frost King's rule. From far up the valley came an answering protest—at first low and wailing, then rising by degrees to a blood-curdling howl—a coyote gripped by intensity of suffering, appealed in despair against the agony of existence.

Within the old log house even a more relentless foe than winter had, after long and varying conflict, come to close grips with old Mrs. Dawson. When Evelyn came in from school in the late afternoon Mary Ann's tear-stained face left no need of question.

'Yes, Miss Raye, mother's had a change, and I don't need no doctor to tell me what it means—I've been in other folks' troubles too often not to know.'

'She seemed sleeping so quietly when I left,' said Evelyn gently, 'I hoped she was going to have a good day and not be troubled with her cough.'

'I tried to think so too, and made believe to myself as it might be a good sign, though I knew all the time it was foolishness, for a person as has been wracked like poor mother has, cannot stop coughing all at once and it

133

mean any good—and no more it did. I knew by my hand on her forehead and the flush on her face as the fever was rising and by noon she got terrible restless and kind of wakened up.'

'Did she know you and was she able to speak?' asked Evelyn.

'Not to say know me,' replied Mary Ann, 'sometimes she would seem to for a minute and then wander off again—and she would talk—quite fast for a bit and then as if whispering to herself—but it was all foolishness, poor dear, and she didn't know what she was saying—it was all about her old home in Ontario and father when he was young, and my little brother Jack as died when he was a baby, and she tried to put her arm round my neck when I stooped over to listen and called me her little Molly—and she's not called me that these thirty years gone—and it's been more than I can bear,' and poor Mary Ann's voice broke in a sob. 'I gave her some of the doctor's stuff a while ago, and she's been quieter since, but her breathing is terrible irregular—father he is with her now—but here I am leaving you standing in your wraps and the bit warm supper I've ready for you getting cold—I'm that moiled I don't know what I'm doing.'

Evelyn suffered Mary Ann to help her off with her jacket and muffler, for her own fingers were stiff with the cold, and then sat down to the soup which Mary Ann had poured out when she saw Evelyn coming through the yard to the house. Though the frost was keen without and she had had a cold walk up from the school, Evelyn had little appetite in such an atmosphere of sorrow, still to please Mary Ann and to satisfy her sense of hospitality, she ate the soup and made some pretence with the cold meat and toast which Mary Ann pressed upon her.

'Now, Miss Dawson, you must let me sit with your mother while you lie down and get some rest—I'm sure you are worn out, and your father too.'

'Well, if you will take father's place for a while till I tidy up and he gets some more wood in—but I'm not going to leave mother's side to-night—I'm afraid of her resting so quiet and still, and I'd never forgive myself if—if anything happened and I was not there.'

Old Dawson made no difficulty about resigning his place by his dying wife's bedside, though Evelyn could hear various self-pitying complaints about the condition of his back and the darned drifts of snow round the wood-pile when he reached the other room. In a little while, however, the sound of dishes being put away ceased, the last armful of firewood was dropped with a noisy clatter by the box stove and Mary Ann came into her mother's room.

'Father is going to lie down on the lounge and will keep the fire in maybe for an hour or two if he does not fall asleep, and sure, Miss Raye, you had better go and get some sleep yourself, and I'll call you if—if I'm needing you—you've been up half the nights ever since you came.'

'Oh no, I'm not a bit sleepy, let me sit with you—it will be so sad and still for you here alone.'

'Well, I'm not denying you're a comfort to me, and I'm sure poor mother would take it so too if she could know.'

So through the long silent hours the two women sat, Evelyn at the foot and Mary Ann at the side of the bed. From time to time, with gentle carefulness, Mary Ann would replace a sheet or coverlet tossed back by some restless movement of her mother's arm, or wipe away the cold dew gathering on the now pallid brow. At midnight Mary Ann moved quietly into the living-room to make up the fire, for old Dawson had long since fallen asleep, and after an absence of a few minutes came back to Evelyn's side with a whispered urgency that Evelyn should go and have a cup of hot tea and a bit of cake which she had set out for her. It was kinder to go than to protest, but Evelyn was scarcely seated by the table ere a hushed but startled cry brought her back—the dreaded change had come. At a sound from her mother's lips Mary Ann had turned up the lamp, and in its full light for a few brief moments Evelyn saw old Mrs. Dawson's face as no one in the settlement, who only knew her as an old woman, had ever seen it. The lines and furrows of the past and its sorrows seemed smoothed away, it was the face that leaned over a child's crib in the Ottawa Valley long years ago— and the smile and the whisper of a mother's love—'Mother's here, Jackie, my own, mother's here.' Swift as it came, the change passed, the years, though not the lines, came back to the quiet, wearied face, the love-light faded from the tired eyes, a few long trembling breaths and the fluttering heart forgot to beat again.

The daily round of toil and hardship in a woman's life on the Western prairies often brings a power of self-control, which is far removed from the callousness to feeling which the more emotional dwellers in cities judge it to be. After a brief desolating outburst of passionate weeping, the heritage of her Irish blood, Mary Ann composed herself to the pious fulfilment of her last cares for her mother with all the skill of her experience in such sad offices, gathered in her nursing among her neighbours, and with the nicest exactness of obedience to what she believed her mother would have wished. And her mother's wishes were not a matter of conjecture, for years before all that would be needed at such a time had been carefully stored away, from the decent black silk gown to the lace-frilled handkerchief she had worn first as a bride; and at times of house-cleaning and the like the old lady was wont to bring them out for airing and to hunt for possible moths—for it would have honestly grieved her much to think that her reputation for cleanliness and good housewifery should be compromised by a moth hole or speck of mildew exposed to the eyes of the critical and curious at her own burying.

The funeral followed on the second day after old Mrs. Dawson's death, and old Dawson, who had moped about the house in a disconsolate fashion for the past few weeks—a state more the result of a general feeling of discomfort and of the absence of his wife's guiding will in the daily farm life than of any livelier emotion, woke up, if not to a sense of his loss, at any rate to a sense of what was due to himself in the matter of a funeral in the family. A lavish order for the most florid style of funeral cards was sent down to the printer in Minnedosa, with directions for one to be posted up in every store in town, he himself distributed them among all callers for mail at the office and such of his neighbours' wives as the news of the death brought on visits of condolence to Mary Ann, while a packet was taken down to the school by Evelyn—at his request—for the children to take home to their parents. And after all the funeral did not come up to old Dawson's expectations, and indeed left a sense of soreness which rankled in his mind long after all softer emotions had faded away.

In the first place, the undertaker in town at the last moment refused, on the ground of the deepness of the trails, to send the gorgeous new hearse which he had just got up from the East, and in place thereof sent a set of very ordinary bob-sleighs from the livery stable—and even at that only one of the horses was black, and the other an entirely inappropriate grey. To make matters worse, old Dawson had cheapened a little on the grade of the coffin, just a plain, cloth-covered black in place of the polished oak with very showy silver finishings, relying on the new hearse, never yet seen in the settlement, as his *pièce de résistance*, and as more in the public eye on the drive to the cemetery. The old man felt again that the bitter coldness of the day itself was a part of the conspiracy of things in general against his receiving his due measure of importance. The deputation from his lodge in town was of the slimmest proportions in numbers and did not include any of the more highly titled worshipful or knightly members—it is true they sent a wreath of flowers of emblematic form and decked properly with knots and bows of ribbon of the orthodox colours. What probably touched old Dawson the closest on the 'Orange' side of his feelings was the thoughtfulness of one especial old crony, who, unable to come from his own infirmities, had yet the true brotherly thoughtfulness to send up under the safe cover of the undertaker a generous-sized flask of Old Rye. It was a small thing in itself, but old Dawson thought it showed a good heart, and indeed it probably did have a share in producing the very becoming emotion which the bereaved husband manifested at the more touching portions of the minister's funeral address.

136

Of the more purely English portion of the settlement he did not expect much—their slackness in attending such functions was a matter of common repute among their Canadian neighbours, but he did think when the funeral procession reached the town line and he looked back to count the following sleighs and to check off in his own mind the families represented, he did think that Mr. Enderby and Bert might have come in a rig of their own instead of coming in Jim Hardie's bob-sleighs. The two or three settlers whose wives had come with them to the service at the house out of sympathy for Mary Ann, only accompanied the procession for a short distance, then turned off to their own farms. The bitter cold, the approach of evening, and the duties of the home, made it unreasonable for women to make the four mile journey to the cemetery, and it was not expected that Mary Ann would accompany her father to her mother's grave—even local custom, so exacting in many little things, did not require it in the middle of winter, but when the time for starting came it was found that poor Mary Ann's heart was set on this last sacrifice of love—if only it were possible, but it was mail-day and some one must be there when the mailman came to receive his bag and to sign his way-bill. Evelyn, who had promised to stay at the Dawson's, at any rate till Sunday, willingly offered to remain—it would not be for so very long—she was not in the least nervous at being left alone, and Mary Ann gratefully accepted her offer and took her place by the minister's side in his cutter.

CHAPTER XXVII

CANADA'S SACRIFICE

Evelyn stood at the window and watched the mournful procession till the last sleigh had turned on to the town line, and then busied herself putting the house in its usual order, for the very limited number of chairs available had been supplemented with planks placed on boxes to provide seats for as many as could crowd into the office living-room where the funeral service was held.

That done, she washed up the cups and saucers, hot coffee and cake having been handed round to those who had had the long drive from Minnedosa, and though she felt that Mary Ann would deprecate her 'mussing herself' with the housework, still it was a relief to herself to keep occupied till they returned, or till the mailman came.

Her ready offer to come and stay with Mary Ann was the natural outcome of her own character and of the influence of her father's companionship when she went with him among his parishioners in the little village at home. Just as she was a child with the children in their games at school, just as she would go with Jim Hardie to see his calves or his little pigs, or take a sympathetic interest in Mrs. Hardie's worries about the ailments of her children or the delinquencies of the chore boy, so when she found Mary Ann Dawson worn and weary with the care of her sick mother, it was a readiness quite without thought of any self-sacrifice that led her to come so willingly to her help. Daisy had done Evelyn no more than justice in admitting her readiness for 'that sort of thing,' yet there was more truth than Evelyn herself perhaps would have admitted in Daisy's other conjectures, and there had been since Tom's leaving a certain eagerness in the way in which Evelyn threw herself into whatever was interesting to the other members of the Dingle household that sprung from a tender anxiety for Tom's safety, an anxiety the harder to bear because through the cruelty of circumstances the love that prompted it must be concealed. That love itself had in some subtle way changed its character as time passed—there were singing birds in her heart that night as she walked back to the Dingle with her brother after poor Tom had told his tale in refraining from telling it—though she only whispered it to herself he was her own true lover. As the story of his loss at the farm and of his brother's disgrace come, and of how

138

he met it—he was more than her lover—he was her hero—offering himself to the call of his country and to his loyalty to his promise to his mother. If the hero came safely back from the perils of war she would find the true lover again, she never doubted that—but till that time came the spirit in which she waited gave an eagerness of anxiety to serve and please others which had not escaped Daisy's sharp eyes, though it rested on emotions deeper and more womanly than came as yet within Daisy's rather narrow outlook on life.

Evelyn had put away the last of the clean dishes, put a fresh supply of wood in the stove and lit the lamp, for though it was only four o'clock it was already growing dusk, when she was startled by the sound of sleigh bells outside, followed in a few minutes by a loud knock at the door. The door opened before she reached it and a young man entered with a rough canvas bag over his shoulder, which he threw on the floor.

'I guess this is Dawson's post-office, Miss? I've brought the mail—is the postmaster round?'

'Yes, this is the post-office,' answered Evelyn, 'but Mr. Dawson is away, he has gone to the cemetery, his wife is being buried to-day, but ——'

'Oh, I didn't know as there was trouble in the house—I'm sorry I came in so rough like, Miss, if you are one of the family; you see, the regular mailman is laid up and I'm just making the trip for him, and I don't know the folks here.'

'Oh, no, I'm not one of the family,' answered Evelyn, 'but I am staying with Miss Dawson for some days, and I promised to look after the mail if it came before they were back—I have the key here.'

'Well, Miss, I guess that's all right, and if you will give me the key I can fix it up.'

Evelyn handed him the key and he unlocked the padlock of the mail-bag and tumbled its contents on to the floor, and proceeded to sort out the various packets into two heaps—putting the one on the table and the other back into the bag.

'Now, Miss, I reckon that's all as is for here—the rest in the bag goes on to "Sweden"—this here,' laying a printed form on the table, 'is the way-bill, and if you'll sign that and put it in the bag, why, I'll lock it and you can have the key back—I suppose there's nothing to take up north from here—the old man in town said there might be a parcel or so.'

'Oh, no, thank you,' said Evelyn, 'Miss Dawson said there was only the packet of letters you have put in the bag, but she hoped you would be kind enough to take back some things to town on your return to-morrow that have been left by one of the settlers.'

'Of course, Miss, I'll not forget in the morning, and now I guess I'd best be hitting the trail again—for it's heavy going and it'll be late before I make "Sweden"—so long, Miss, and I hope the folks here are not feeling too bad.' He was rather a rough-spoken and abrupt young man, but he did not wish to be thought lacking in proper feeling, and he found Evelyn's gentle, refined courtesy a little rebuking and embarrassing. Evelyn opened the outer door for him and closed it after him, so that he might put on his heavy driving mitts before going out into the bitter cold, and then turned back to the heap of mail on the table.

There were two or three packages of letters neatly tied up, a big bundle of magazines and papers of various kinds, obviously English, and two large packages of papers of uniform size. Mary Ann had told her not to trouble about the mail, but to just leave it till she came back; if any one called they could wait or call again—'in course,' she added, 'if you like to look through the letters you can see if there's any for yourself or the Dingle folks.' Evelyn put the packages of letters in the office pigeon holes without untying their strings—it was not there that her anxiety lay and she would have felt a certain distaste for turning over letters not intended for herself —but what was hidden away by the wrapper of the bundle labelled '*Winnipeg Free Press*,' or its companion bundle '*The Winnipeg Telegram*?' The last paper that had come to the Dingle had bid them prepare for news, thrilling, startling news of the Canadian boys at the front—news that might be so glorious for the national spirit, but so cruel and crushing for the individual heart, and now perhaps that news was come, separated only from her knowledge by that thin sheet of wrappage—dare she tear it away and know the truth? Twice she took a knife from the table to cut the stout cord around the bundle of the *Free Press*, and twice she laid it down again irresolute; then came the thought—'they will soon be back again from the cemetery, and perhaps, too, Mr. Hardie or Bert coming in for their mail—if there is aught to hear it would be harder with them present than to face it now alone—and perhaps, after all, there is no news or good news.'

With a quick decision lest her courage should waver again Evelyn cut the cord and quickly tore off the outer wrapper, and taking the first paper that came let her gaze sweep rapidly over the big headlines on the front page—'Ladysmith'—'Buller'—'The Tugela'—nothing terrible then of the Canadians or Lord Roberts and Cronje or it would be here, and she went back more calmly to the top of the sheet and read the various telegrams slowly. Her finger was already slipped between the leaves to open the next page to see what of less interest there might be, when her eye caught a little paragraph—'For news of the Canadian Contingent and their losses see page six.' With trembling, fumbling hands that seemed suddenly numbed and deadened Evelyn slowly turned the corners of the pages over till she came to six, and then desperately opened the paper wide—Ah, here were big headlines again—'Canadian Sacrifice for the Empire—Losses in First Canadian Contingent. Killed 19, Wounded 60. Four Westerners killed—Nine Wounded,' and below two pitiless columns of names.

For a brief moment the whole page went black before her eyes, and then slowly from the formless blur of capital letters and figures stood out as though it were the only printing on the page—'Four Westerners Killed —Thomas M. Dennis—Thomas M. Dennis,' and she repeated the name half aloud in the unaccented, emotionless tones of a child talking in its sleep—then with a sharp cry of realisation—'Oh, God—not my Tom—not my own boy—not my love'—then God in His mercy gave her tears.

CHAPTER XXVIII

A TIME OF DECISIONS

A thrill of pride and sorrow flashed through the wide Dominion when the tidings of loss and victory at Modder River reached Canada, a thrill of higher pride and deeper sorrow when they were followed in a few days by the news of the still more glorious victory at Paardeberg and the surrender of Cronje and his army. The record of the heroism of those who died was graven deep on the annals of the young nation of the West, but with the passing of time the sharper sense of general sorrow for those who had given their lives for the Empire was merged in the pride and anxiety with which the fortunes of the first Canadian Contingent and its successors were followed to the long, dragging conclusion of the war.

The news of the death of Tom Dennis and of the wounding of his brother Jack, for Jack's name was among the nine Westerners wounded, made a profound impression in the Minnedosa country, it brought the price of victory home, and full honour was done to them at every gathering, social, political or religious, that was held for a month afterwards in the community, but naturally, it was at the Dingle, at Jim Hardie's, and among the neighbours around Connemara Farm, that the personal sense of loss was keenest and lasted longest. And all showed their feeling in their own way—old Berg, as he looked across the waste of snow that lay between his own home and where the log house and buildings of Connemara Farm stood in all the dreariness of an abandoned homestead, confided to his 'old woman' a little plan he had talked over early in the winter with Big John Cameron and some of the threshing gang, of ploughing and seeding Connemara Farm by a 'bee' in the spring—'the one poor lad is gone now and maybe will never know, but if his brother comes back in the Fall it will be some easier than coming home to a place with naught but weeds on it.'

Many a time as Jim Hardie lay on his load of hay or tramped behind his team on the trail up from Sweden his thoughts went back to his trips with Tom Dennis the previous winter along the same road—or still more often to that glorious summer's day when Tom had taken the schoolmarm up to Amanda's wedding. Jim Hardie's thoughts were always kindly—often strangely tinted with religious or sentimental feeling, though, whether

142

grave or gay, they seldom succeeded in any articulate expression beyond, 'It's too bad—too bad.'

Evelyn dreaded the return to the Dingle on the Sunday after the ill-news came—still, hard as it was, it was the easier of bearing from the unrestrained outburst of weeping with which Daisy welcomed her back—for Daisy had honestly loved Tom as a true comrade and helper after her own heart in her various schemes to keep the 'all work and no play' spirit of the West from a too undisputed ascendancy. Indeed, all at the Dingle were too truly grieved at the fatal tidings to have at the time any thought of prying beneath the brave composure which came to Evelyn, when, on the day following the memorial service which Mr. Jordan held on the Sunday and which was practically attended by all the nearby settlers, she returned to her duties at the school and, outwardly at least, life resumed its monotonous routine.

Still, as the weeks passed on, Evelyn could not help feeling as if in some way she were the object of a conspiracy of kindness on the part of the family at the Dingle to make life, if not brighter, at least less obviously sad for her. There were more frequent days when Bert would call round for her at the school to drive her home on the plea that it was too stormy, or the trails too full for her to walk home alone. The war ceased to be spoken of at meal times as the one subject of conversation, and while there was no obvious hiding away of the English illustrated papers with their terrible pictures of the Modder fight and Cronje's surrender, Evelyn was left to discover them for herself, when she was alone, among the pile of Old Country papers and magazines on Mr. Enderby's special little table.

As March passed into April Evelyn was called from the silent indulgence in her own sorrow into which she was in danger of falling to a more wholesome and active life by the necessity of facing a future, which, if it were dark for herself, was full of hope and happiness for others.

Dugald M'Leod, so wavering and diffident in the early days of his courtship, now revealed unsuspected reserves of resolution and ardour in urging Marion to consent to an early marriage. At the time of his acceptance, Marion had, with due maidenly coyness, declared that she could not think of a shorter engagement than a year, and the time was left vaguely defined as 'sometime in the Fall.' But the trouble was that as the snow melted away and the warm days came, the Fall seemed farther away to Dugald than it had at the beginning of the winter before. It would be an injustice to his name to say that with the spring he turned lightly to thoughts of love; but if one says Scottishly lightly, it would not be unfair, for he pleaded not only the homeless forlornness of his bachelor life, but the untidy wastefulness of his English housekeeper and her irregular success in the making of porridge. Marion was secretly very pleased with his eagerness and forgave him the prosaic porridge, but she would not hear of leaving home, for her mother's sake, till all the rush of farm work and spring cleaning was over at the Dingle. Finally, the young folks—love is always young—left the choosing of the happy day to Mrs. Enderby, and though Marion knew that that was only another way of leaving the decision with Daisy, she was not uneasy as to the outcome; for while Daisy could not be trusted to fall in with Marion's view as regards the farm work and the spring cleaning she could be trusted not to defer unduly any promise of excitement and festivity for herself.

Spring was bringing the necessity of other decisions beyond the naming of Marion's wedding-day. Evelyn's year's engagement at the school would soon be up, and already she had received a cordial request from the trustees to remain as teacher for another year, coupled with the offer of a higher salary. Left to follow the promptings of her own heart alone Evelyn would have given up the school and offered herself as a nurse to the field hospital that was following the new contingent to South Africa, but with Evelyn, her heart followed her duty, and she was pledged to her brother, and Chris's plans, too, were very unsettled. It had been understood from his first coming to the West that after a year at Rosebank Chris should take up a homestead in one of the new provinces, and that Evelyn should live with him and keep house. Chris had taken very kindly to the new life, and for a long time talked of little else to Bert and Jim Hardie than of what he hoped to do when he had a place of his own, but as the winter passed so did his keenness for homesteading—at least in Saskatchewan or Alberta. He took to suggesting tentatively that perhaps, after all, he was hardly fitted for grappling with the rougher conditions of the Edmonton or Saskatoon country—it might be wiser to buy an improved farm in Manitoba—Jim Hardie knew of two or three good places not far from Rosebank, or he might take up a homestead in Sweden—a lot of those Swede fellows were doing well with cattle and selling cordwood and it would not require so much money to start with as a prairie farm. All of which struck Jim Hardie as being wonderfully thoughtful and modest in a young Englishman, for they were usually so cocksure of their capacity to do anything that any one else could do, and Jim never suspected ulterior motives. The people at the Dingle, with the exception of Mrs. Enderby, were hardly so unsophisticated. Marion said she thought it would be very nice for Daisy if Evelyn remained, if not at the Dingle, at least in the settlement—Marion knew there was a wrong side to Daisy's usual amiability—besides, Daisy had been very nice lately, and 'nice' means a good deal between sisters. Bert, in his rather slow deliberate way, remarked that 'it was probably the wisest thing for Chris to do, he was pretty green yet, and' (incidentally) 'the mater would not miss

Marion so much if Miss Raye'—under Daisy's full, open stare, Bert hesitated and grew red.

'We quite understand, Bert; really as a family our mutual consideration is quite delightful—now, if you will tell Evelyn how we have decided her future—why, I'll try and impress,' rather sharply, 'Chris with a due sense of his greenness.'

'Don't be crazy, Daisy,' said Bert impatiently, 'of course, it's no business of ours—you always will put things——'

'As they are, my dear,' retorted Daisy mockingly, 'it's sad, being so young, that I have no illusions either as regards your or Marion's ideas—I represent the candour of the family—but don't be uneasy, Bert, I'll be as secretive for once as Evelyn herself, and leave you to hoe your own row.'

While it was Chris's indecision that was responsible for the scraps of conversation reported above and for Evelyn's uncertainty as to her own future, it was Chris himself who, after all, found the solution of all their uncertainties. At least, Chris always claimed he found it, and Daisy never contradicted him—which is strong evidence in favour of his claim when one remembers Daisy's candour. If—why be distrustful?—though Chris found the solution he was more than willing that Daisy should impart it to the rest of the Dingle circle, for he was one of those shy, reserved young fellows whose courage only comes in fits and starts, and leaves them afraid to claim the fruits of victory after winning it. If you gave Chris an inch he was as likely as not to be so flustered that he would hand it back again. Daisy was not like that—being candid, she often said she liked 'all that was coming to her'—and it usually came—if not, she fetched it.

In the West, among the farmers, most things relating to the heart—and a few relating to the next week's work—are settled on Sunday. Chris's solution, however, came on a Saturday—he was new to the ways of the country—besides, he did not know it was coming till it was there—Daisy is to be blamed if she did—at any rate, she fell in with local proprieties by not saying a word about it till the next day.

Now, although Daisy did not in the least mind the shock of a surprise for herself, she was more thoughtful for her mother, and took some little trouble to arrange for a quiet, undisturbed opportunity for a long talk with her on the Sunday afternoon. It so happened that it was what Daisy called their 'off Sunday for religion,' but as it was a lovely, sunny day, Bert readily fell in with Daisy's suggestion at dinner-time that he should drive Evelyn to Mr. Jordan's afternoon service in the next settlement, eight miles away. Though Evelyn would rather have escaped for a walk through the woods by herself or down to Jim Hardie's to see her brother, she could not decline without seeming ungracious, when Daisy assured her that Chris had said the night before that he had some stable work to do, neglected in the rush of seeding, and that he would not be able to tidy up till supper-time, when he would come to the Dingle. For the rest Daisy had no anxiety —Dad's 'off' Sunday habits were well established, and Marion and Dugald could now be quite trusted to eliminate themselves for the afternoon.

Mrs. Enderby and Daisy went out on to the verandah to see Bert and Evelyn start off in the buckboard, and stood watching them till they drove out of the lane on to the town line, and Mrs. Enderby turned round to re-enter the house.

'Don't go in yet, mother,' said Daisy, 'it is lovely and warm out here, and I've brought a cushion for the old chair and a wrap for your shoulders.'

'I ought to write to your Aunt Mary this afternoon, you know I always write to her on the Sunday we have no church.'

'Well, you can date it to-day, mother, and finish it some other time, and she will never know the difference—be a dear, mother; you see I am left alone.'

'Well, for a little while, perhaps, I can stay and keep you company,' replied Mrs. Enderby, sitting down and drawing the wrap round her shoulders. 'I'm afraid it's going to be very quiet for us all when Marion is gone, and if Evelyn and her brother leave, too—I was thinking of that as I watched them driving away, and I did wonder—but it is foolish to fancy such things.'

'Did wonder what, mother?' asked Daisy.

'Well, I did wonder whether possibly your brother seeing so much of Evelyn as he has done this winter—and she such a dear girl—but, of course, he's always so thoughtful and kind to everybody and never has a thought outside the farm work unless it is at election time—but still, when I saw him putting the rug round her knees and putting up the umbrella to keep off the wind at the back—I couldn't help thinking of the high dog-cart your father had when he was a young man and before we were married. With the skirts girls wear now I am sure they never could get into one, but perhaps they make them lower.'

'Oh, girls have more courage now, mother, than they had then—besides what's the use of clocks on your stockings—but did you mean you were wondering if Bert was gone on Evelyn?'

'You know, Daisy, I would not use such a word for the world—but perhaps that expresses my thoughts.'

'Why, mother dear, of course he is gone—hopelessly, helplessly gone —it's been sticking out of him all over for the last three months—but what Evelyn may say—that's another story.'

'I'm sure no girl need wish for a worthier lover,' said Mrs. Enderby bridling a little, 'a mother never had a better son, and if it's family—why, there was an Enderby among the barons who signed Magna Charta, and if

the copy in papa's old history was correct he was a shockingly bad writer
—indeed, Bert himself writes a very poor hand.'

'Oh, it's not that kind of thing,' interrupted Daisy, 'that will be the difficulty, but you know, mother, Marion and I sometimes thought she cared for
poor Tom Dennis—but she's so quiet about everything that we never really
knew, and there was no good worrying you.'

'Well, I'm sure I'm very sorry for her and for Tom, too, poor fellow, if
it was so. I knew she grieved for him, but so did we all—but I think you
and Marion must be mistaken, for I never noticed anything between them
last summer—and I'm very observant,' added Mrs. Enderby complacently.

'Well, perhaps you are right,' admitted Daisy, who did not wish to press
the point just then, 'and, of course, mother, we should all be delighted if
Bert were successful——'

'Oh, surely, dear, your father and I would welcome her like a daughter
—but it would be very disappointing to her brother after all his plans.'

'Of course, mother, it would if he were to go away homesteading—but
he is thinking of buying a farm here or homesteading up in the bush.'

'Well, that would be very nice for us all if what you suggest about Bert
should come true, but the poor boy would be dreadfully lonesome if he
stayed on his farm, and you know the dreadful way some of the English
boys get into of going to town and not going to church—of course, he
could come over here on Sundays, and we might bake his bread—unless,
indeed—but that's a great risk—no, I'm afraid that would not do——'

'What is a great risk, mother? Surely you are not afraid of Chris taking
to drink or anything of that kind—I'm sure——'

'Of course not, my dear, I'm surprised at your suggesting it—such a
well brought up young man and a clergyman's son—I was thinking of his
getting a housekeeper—but you know poor Dugald's experience and how
he feels it, and he used to a bachelor's life so long.'

'Oh, I'm afraid Dugald isn't quite disinterested in his plaintiveness
about the way the groceries go and Mrs. Tomkins's bad baking—but,
mother,' and Daisy who was sitting on a cushion by her mother's side, took
her mother's hand in her own. 'Mother, did you never wonder why Chris
comes up here so often?'

'Why, no, Daisy, why should I? I'm sure it's very natural, with his sister here and he so anxious to learn about farming from your father and Bert
—besides, down at Rosebank, while the Hardies are very worthy people,
there are three children and the baby—besides, Mr. Hardie has no conversation, and Mrs. Hardie only the other day said she had never had a baby
with such difficulty in teething, you see it is getting the bottom ones first
and that always makes it worse—and I was telling her I had just the same
experience with your brother, and your poor father hardly got a night's

sleep till Mr. Jordan brought up some powders they always used at the rectory—I think it was Stedman's—I know the box was very particular about its being one or two "e's," though I never could see what difference that could make to the baby—but it must be very trying to a young man like Mr. Chris, who has not the feelings of a father——'

'Of course, mother, and I'm sure Mrs. Hardie would be very grateful, but,' and Daisy made a plunge, for the time was slipping away, 'but last night when Evelyn and Bert and I were walking back part of the way to Rosebank with Chris, Chris found another way out of his difficulties—and —he hopes you and father will like it.'

'I'm sure it's very nice of him to value our opinion,' replied Mrs. Enderby with much approval, 'young men nowadays seem——'

'Yes, mother, I know; but you see he was talking of going away, and of the nice times we've had this winter and of there being no one to take an interest in his plants and beetles and things, and I suppose I was sympathising with him a little, and the others had walked on ahead—and all at once he somehow took my hand and asked me if I wouldn't go——'

'But, surely, child, he is not going to keep a museum, and it would be quite improper if he were——'

'No, no, mother dear, he asked me to marry him—and I said "Yes." '

'Marry him! How can you startle me in such a way,' and Mrs. Enderby searched in the bosom of her blouse with a trembling hand for her handkerchief. 'I'm sure it's very unkind of him to put such thoughts in your head—such a child as you are——'

'I'm a year older than you were, mother, when you married——'

'Oh, but that was quite different, and your father had such a masterful way in those days, and I had always let him decide things ever since we were children together.'

'Well, I guess that was a mistake, mother, but you've been very happy, and of course, it could not be for a long time—and we'll be guided by what you and Dad think best——'

'Well, I'm sure I do not know what your father will say—and there's Marion and your brother,' replied her mother doubtfully, though evidently growing more favourable to the new and startling proposal as she regained her composure, and her imagination came into play again. 'Of course, if Mr. Chris stays, Evelyn will stay, and if Bert's heart is set upon her, as you girls think, it might help him——'

'I'm sure it would, mother; Chris and I talked it over last night, and Chris said he was sure Evelyn would come round in the end, even if she had cared for Tom Dennis, if she found that his happiness depended on her taking my place here so that Chris and I might have a home of our own, and Chris thinks so much of Bert that he said he was sure Evelyn couldn't

148

help growing to like him—not perhaps like I like Chris,' with a blush, 'but well enough to marry him—and you see Bert is so much older and would not expect so much.'

'I am not so sure of that,' said her mother doubtfully; 'your father expects just as much fussing as ever he did, and will not stay in the house half an hour if I am out.'

'Well, that's very nice, too, mother, and thank you ever so much for being so good to me, and I'm sure Chris will thank you too when he comes up—and you'll be nice to him, mother, and give him a kiss—the poor fellow is frightened out of his boots at the idea of asking Dad, and if you tell Dad first it would make it so much easier all round—because Dad always thinks what you think in things of that kind.'

'Well, dear, you must not think I've consented till I ask your father, but I'll speak to him when he wakes up—he and I were to settle the day for Marion's wedding this afternoon so that she could tell Dugald before he went home, but everything seems to be happening at once.'

'Now Chris is not going away, and if Evelyn stays on, and I'm sure she will, it will be easier for you to spare Marion. If they were to be married at the end of June, why, they could have their little honeymoon before haying, and Evelyn would be having her holidays and would be here with us, and Bert and Chris would not be everlastingly working, and we could have a lovely time—now, run along in, mother, and tell Dad, and I will go and meet Dugald and Marion and make them happy—the last Wednesday in June for their wedding-day—splendid.'

It had been a long and strenuous engagement, but Daisy's heart was rejoicing as she went to meet the more sedate lovers, whom she could see coming along the path through the wheat field beyond the stables. She had won all along the line, and was honestly proud of the way in which she had steered clear—or almost clear—of the slang which always had such a disturbing effect on her mother's nerves, and, while her mother's consent was a little hesitating she felt quite easy that it had been won in fact, and it was a simple truth that she uttered to herself in a consoling relapse from her precision of speech—'the one that gets the mater on his side has got the whole blooming show.'

CHAPTER XXIX

GREAT NEWS FOR MARY ANN

In very ancient times, an Eastern naturalist, of high biblical repute for his wisdom, with that wonderful gift for connoting apparently disconnected details, which seems, oddly enough, to be confined to men of science and women of a sentimental temperament (Charles Darwin might be cited on the one side and Mary Ann Dawson on the other among the moderns), has remarked with surprise on the wonderful part played by birds in the dissemination of secret intelligence. Had that great savant lived in the West to-day he would have been still more surprised, perhaps, by the way in which, in this regard, modern civilisation has learned to supply the deficiencies of nature with so great a measure of success that probably people know each other's business with more detail and less exactitude of truth than in the time of Solomon.

There are few small birds on the prairie except the blackbirds, and such small birds as there are seem chiefly occupied in looking after the survival of the fittest from the numerous hawks, while the blackbirds, with a true Western spirit are entirely preoccupied with the crops, and, providing they can find an oat field fairly near to a slough or a river, are callously willing for their human neighbours to indulge in all the secretiveness they desire. But where Nature fails, Western civilisation steps in; the cities have the daily press, the little country towns their weekly local paper, and the rural settlements the post-office and the chore boy. Civilisation has this advantage, too, over science—while the Eastern naturalist made no pretence to explain the *modus operandi* of his bird—that of the chore boy and Mary Ann (as symbolising the rural post-office) follows logical psychological lines. The advent of the post card and the open-ended circular letter had been looked on by Mary Ann and her mother as a step in quite the right direction, and added appreciatively to the interest of the mail-day, but at the same time it only made more offensively obvious the unworthy suspiciousness of others, who not only supplemented the mucilage proper to the envelope by the plentiful application of gum to the last crevice, but even added (mostly English people, these) the flagrant insult of wax and a seal. In time, probably, such people will understand better the breadth of Western people's interest in their neighbours' family affairs, and also that to make a thing difficult is, in the West, to ensure its being overcome. These crude devices were usually allowed to succeed, but they sometimes provoked unworthy suspicions of entirely moral young Englishmen in the settlement—suspicions in the case of old Mrs. Dawson running on the lines of previous insolvency and unpaid tailors' bills—Mary Ann never went beyond breach of promise, or at the worst, bigamy.

Of course, some allowance should be made for the insularity of those born and bred in the 'Old Country,' but it is disappointing to those who are eager to hurry up the assimilation of races, to find the old national defects cropping up in the next generation. In the case of Mr. Enderby, with his easy, kindly way, little allowance was required, and long since the Canadian portion of the settlement had tacitly agreed to wink at Mrs. Enderby's bad headaches which annually prevented her appearing at meal times when the threshers came to the Dingle. Bert passed muster as a regular Canadian, but the girls would sometimes 'throw back' to the old Leicestershire squire point of view in the most disconcerting way. Oddly enough, Sam, the Barnardo chore boy, himself a Britisher born and bred, was the chief sufferer from these freaks of type survival, and probably his most cruel disillusionment with the Wild West of his imagination was when he discovered that he had a 'proper place' (so Marion called it), and was expected to keep it. Usually, he looked for sympathy in his grievances—sometimes, as we have seen, in vain—to his brother chore boy at Rosebank, but latterly he had dropped into the way when he was sent to the post-office of confiding them to Mary Ann.

Now, Mary Ann not only took the interest in her neighbours' doings proper to her sex and her vocation as assistant postmaster, but from the added loneliness of her life since her mother's death and from her love and gratitude to Evelyn, which were very real, she had grown to look upon herself as intended by Providence to further—in some way as yet not very clear—the bringing together of Bert and Evelyn. We are told by the moralists that the goodness or badness of an action lies in the intention with which it is done, and it is to be hoped it is so, for while Mary Ann's intentions were very good and a credit to her heart, they did in the end, as we shall see, lead her into a course of conduct, which without being too severe, one must call questionable, and to which some, with a very high standard for other people's behaviour, would even apply a harsher term.

Now, Mrs. Enderby's letter to Aunt Mary was not finished till the Wednesday, and though it would not leave the Dawson post-office till the Friday, it was desirable that there should be no longer gap than was necessary between the suppositional Sunday of its writing and the official date of its posting stamped on the envelope, so on the Wednesday evening, Sam, the chore boy, was dispatched with it under strict injunction from

Marion not to loiter by the way or stop gossiping at the office. Both commands were familiar to Sam, even to staleness, but though they were familiar they never ceased to stir in his mind a feeling of resentment—were they not a part of Marion's avowed purpose of keeping him in his place? He usually asserted what he called 'a fellow's rights' by disregarding both with a fine impartiality, but to-night he positively hastened to obey the former of them that he might have the greater latitude of disobedience for the latter. He felt that he had such a varied assortment of Dingle tidings to impart to Mary Ann that he would not only 'get even with that Marion,' a thing very desirable in itself, but that he would also establish on a still firmer footing his already friendly relations with Mary Ann, which meant at the least a big piece of cake, and possibly pie.

He was fortunate enough to find Mary Ann alone and comparatively at leisure for a woman on a Western farm—cutting potato sets for old Dawson to plant on the morrow. She was seated on an old chair in front of the house door, a bag of potatoes on the one side and a pail on the other to receive the sets as they were cut. It was an uninteresting, if not laborious, occupation, and Mary Ann greeted Sam as a welcome break in its monotony.

'Good evening, Sam, I thought you must be coming up to the office when I saw you on the town line. I've been wondering two or three times to-day how it was there was no one up from your place, there's generally a letter on the Monday, or Tuesday at the latest, after no church Sunday, for your boss's sister in the Old Country.'

'Well, I guess this is it,' replied Sam, reading the address of the letter in his hand laboriously, 'Miss Mary Enderby, Sea View Cottage, Hastings, England.'

'That's it right enough—lay it on the doorstep—for my hands are mucky, and I'll take it in when I've finished the pertaters, and sit you down on the step and rest yourself a bit. It seems a pretty thick letter now it has come—two stamps on it and all,' went on Mary Ann casually. 'I wonder what some folks finds to write about—but they say the old lady has a bit of a temper as well as a tidy bit of money, and I guess Mrs. Enderby has to make up some kind of a story whether or no for the girls' sake till she drops off.'

'She didn't have to make up no story this week,' replied Sam with much meaning. 'There's been story enough of itself to fill more letters ner one.'

'Well, to be sure now, not that it matters to me—but I hope as nothing is wrong up to your place?'

'Oh, I don't know as you would call it "wrong," ' admitted Sam grudgingly, 'but such goings-on with Daisy and that Chris chap at Hardie's as never was.'

'Do say,' ejaculated Mary Ann; 'I did wonder if anything would come of his being up there so much all winter—but he seemed such a shy young man that I never thought that he'd have the heart to ask her, but some of those shy ones are the boldest in the end.'

'Yes, and some young women have the nerve of two—she just cornered him till he had to—why, I know how the whole blooming thing was done—asking and all—I'm no simple guy if that Chris chap is.'

'You never mean to say as how him or Daisy told you that—because I shouldn't believe you—and,' in a fine tone reproof,' it's very wrong for a lad like you to go and make up things about folks.'

'Tell me! not much!' and Sam's voice fairly quivered with sarcasm. 'If I only knew what they told me, I shouldn't know when I had a belly ache—and if they'd up and tell me more I shouldn't have to find out in a kind of a——' Sam wriggled and hesitated—'in a sort of a kind of a way—as some folks as don't know how I'm used would call——' and Sam hesitated again, he had never felt the English tongue so defective. Mary Ann helped him out.

'Sort of being curious you mean, Sam, and, in course, I don't hold with young folks prying, but I'm sure you meant no harm and you needn't mind telling me—you see, with being such an old neighbour and keeping the office—why, they'd expect me to hear and every one knows I'm not one to make trouble by telling.'

'I'm sure you wouldn't, Miss Dawson,' replied Sam, grateful for her charitable construction and proceeding with his story with renewed confidence. 'You see, it happened like this. On the last Sunday as was everybody had gone off after dinner except Daisy and the old lady and me, and Daisy she says to me as I was a kind of keeping out of the way in the kitchen till Marion and her young man had gone for a walk, for she always has some kind of a chore for me if she sees me idle for a bit, Daisy says to me as pleasant as you please, "I'm sure you must be tired, Sam, after all the harrowing you've done this week, you may take the English papers up to your room and it won't matter if you drop asleep, I'll call you before supper." Well, I thanked her and got the papers as have the war pictures and I went upstairs and took off my boots and lay down, and all sudden-like I started a-wondering why Daisy was so keen about my getting a rest—she fusses over her mother and her dad but she don't worry about me—it's "Sam, here, and Sam, there, and Sam, hurry up," with her all the week, and then I minded how she kind of crowded the schoolmarm into going off for a drive with Bert, and told Marion she needn't mind helping with the dishes—and I got fly to her having some little game of her own. So I up and opened my door quiet like and crept down the stairs and listened—there wasn't a one in the parlour but I could hear Daisy and her ma out on the verandah, and I—well, I, kind of a——' again Sam's vocabulary failed and again Mary Ann came to the rescue.

'You mean you couldn't kind of help hearing what they were a-saying ——'

'Yes, that's it, Miss Dawson, for Daisy, she was talking quite in her natural way and not a bit as if she minded of any one hearing, and they were talking of Bert and the schoolmarm as well—and in course, the schoolmarm isn't one of the family and I've as much right to know about her as any one else.'

'Of course, Sam,' admitted Mary Ann, 'and Miss Raye is a dear friend of my own, and I'm sure would confide in me before any of those folks there if she knew how anxious I am for her to be happy—still, I wouldn't let you repeat what you heard if I was only curious like some folks as don't have any feeling for other people's troubles—and you was saying, Sam?'

By the end of the next half hour Mary Ann was in possession of all the leading points of Daisy's conversation with her mother—in fact, Sam's version, allowing for a few idiosyncrasies of grammar and style, was almost verbally accurate, and he wound up with a reassertion of his moral position—'If folks treat a fellow as if he wasn't of no account, and snap him up till he's skeered to open his mouth—why they've no one but theirselves to blame if he keeps his ears and eyes open a little extra.'

'And, in course, Miss Daisy never suspicioned you were there?' asked Mary Ann.

'Why, I was that fast asleep, will you believe me, that she had to call me twice to come down to supper,' and Sam leered with a keen sense of his own cunning.

'Well, I don't know as I blame you overmuch,' went on Mary Ann, 'but Daisy would be terribly vexed if she knew as you'd happened to overhear her, and if you ask me, you'll not say a word about what you heard—or maybe it will get you into trouble and you might lose your place—in course, there's no harm in telling me, but other folks might get talking if they knew.'

'Oh, I'm not afraid of them catching me,' replied Sam with great confidence, 'besides, Daisy, she made no secret of her lovering and walked that Chris chap off into the kitchen after supper to help her wash up the dishes, just as bold as you please, and the boss and Mrs. Enderby talked about it quite openly after they had gone out—though, of course, no one thought it worth while to actually tell me.'

'Still, it would never do for youse to be repeating what Daisy and her ma said about Mr. Bert and Miss Raye—I wouldn't be in your shoes if it came to Mr. Bert's ears.'

'Who's going to repeat it?' retorted Sam with some warmth, not liking the undertone of reproof that had come into Mary Ann's voice. 'I'd never have said a word of their goings on only you seemed to like to know.'

'Of course, Sam, I should never have let you run on so, only Miss Raye is a great friend of mine, and it's only right I should take an interest in things as concern her, and I'm sure, Sam, you'll never breathe a word of it to a soul else—and now I guess you'd better be getting back, or they'll be wondering what keeps you so long—I daresay you could manage a piece of pie and a doughnut or two after your walk? A small piece, did you say? Well, we must not make it too small for a big growing lad like you, as will be a young man before we know, and thinking of courting the girls for yourself.'

Sam stammered and blushed, much flattered by such a suggestion of coming manliness, and was soon on his way back to the Dingle, a couple of doughnuts in his pockets and munching a large section of raisin pie. On the whole, he was quite satisfied with his visit, the material recognition of his appetite harmonising well with his recovered sense of his own importance in society from Mary Ann's delicate allusion to his own eligibility as a lover himself.

CHAPTER XXX

A LETTER FROM AFRICA

Mary Ann went about her usual work on the day following Sam's visit with a greater cheerfulness and sense of general content than she had known for a long time. Her morning was fully occupied between milking the cows, feeding the calves and pigs, an hour with the poultry and young chickens, and then dinner to get ready for old Dawson and the hired man at noon. In the afternoon the weekly churning and butter-making did not allow of much time for connected thought on subjects outside of themselves, but from time to time, over her churning, Mary Ann would let her mind run on scraps here and there of Sam's conversation of the evening before, and they promised well for when she should have time to sit down and think out the whole situation, and its probable bearing on her own part in Evelyn's and Bert's future. That, of course, was her *pièce de résistance*, the roast and the pudding of her feast of mingled fact and fiction, the rest of Sam's betrayal serving merely for side dishes. On general principles it was satisfactory to know the date of Marion's and Dugald M'Leod's wedding before any one else in the settlement—even before the minister—and after the butter had started to come and during the more deliberate turns of the barrel churn while it was gathering, she sketched out the probable course of that happy event—Daisy, of course, would be bridesmaid and Bert best man—or maybe Chris Raye, now he was to be one of the family. Would Marion Enderby wear white or coloured? That was a nice question, involving as it did a claim to youth or admission of age on the part of the bride which would expose her to criticism whichever way she decided. Mary Ann was in an unusually kind mood, and had just decided in favour of white as quite suitable when the increasingly heavy thud of the butter called her back to realities. After running off the whey, putting in some cold, fresh water and giving the churn a few turns to make the butter gather, she put it on the butter-board and then followed the salting and working—a process too strenuous to allow of any thought or breath for aught else, but when Mary Ann came to the making of the pound prints she picked up the thread of her thoughts at another point—so Daisy had managed to catch a young man after all! Well, maybe it was as well—although Daisy was a little too sharp and ready with her tongue she could work if

156

she liked, and then she knew the ways of the country, and Mr. Chris, though he was a nice, well-mannered young man, was terrible green. The old folks at the Dingle too would be pleased to see Mr. Bert settling down and would be real glad to have a nice young lady like Evelyn to home, with their own daughters living near by. Yes, on the whole, Mary Ann decided, when the time came for her to announce it publicly, that Daisy's engagement should be put before the settlement in a favourable light, and her self-denying ordinance to give no hint of it at present would be more than compensated for by being able to say—'in course, I've known about it this long while, and the day fixed and all, even before the minister, but I don't meddle with other folks' affairs.'

At last the butter-making was finished, the various utensils washed and put away in the dairy, the house tidied up and her own working gown exchanged for a clean, highly starched print dress suitable for the warm day, and for the hour or two's leisure before the mailman came, followed by the usual dropping in of neighbours to see if there were any letters or papers. For a few minutes Mary Ann sat down in the old rocker, a little back from the open front door, out of the sun and still to have the benefit of the fresh outer air, and deliberated how she should spend the leisure time—for leisure with Mary Ann was only a comparative term, and this afternoon it meant such occupation for her hands as would not interfere with the easy freedom of her thoughts. The alternatives of making over an old Sunday dress for second best or of knitting some mitts for the summer Fair only presented themselves to her mind to be rejected—both useful and necessary in their place, but not in harmony with her humour to-day. At last the light of inspiration, followed by a complacent smile, brightened up her rather heavy features and she rose quickly and went into the adjoining room, which she had made her own since her mother's death. In a few minutes she returned and laid upon the table a large parcel covered with a piece of clean sheeting, which, on the removal of many pins, revealed several blocks or squares of patchwork, of an intricate pattern, together with a number of rolls of materials of many sizes and colours. Mary Ann drew up a chair to the table and sat down to gloat over her treasure. 'To think,' she said half aloud, 'to think as I never thought of that afore—and me too sad when I've seen it lying there in the drawer ever to take it out—much less to have the heart to finish it—and mother would be real glad if she knew—it's just the very thing, and my feelings will be in every stitch I put in.' The unfinished quilt had a history of its own, the materials had been gathering a long time and represented most of the new frocks which had been worn in the settlement for the past four or five years. The actual piecing together of the many-shaped scraps into squares—(for it was to be a crazy quilt—the type which allows most scope for the imagination and ingenuity of the

157

artist) had only been commenced some year or so before, when, under the influence of an appeal at her place of worship, Mary Ann had determined to make an offering of her treasures and of her labour to the Indian mission cause of her denomination. She had worked at it with great zeal, at first, in the face of some discouragement from her mother, to whom such Indians as the old lady had met with did not appeal, their persons did not suggest the use of soap and water and their attire was obviously innocent of a weekly wash—besides, a quilt, in her mind, presupposed a bedstead and a floor—things hardly probable of finding among the wandering dwellers in teepees. Still, Mary Ann might have persevered to the end, for she was not without a gift of obstinacy, if only she had remained true to her first flush of missionary sacrifice, but, alas! for human nature, as the quilt grew in intricacy and beauty under her hands, she was betrayed by the creature of her own devising. While still outwardly proof to her mother's arguments, her pious purpose was by degrees sapped away by thoughts which came to her own mind as she stitched away at her task—after all, would even the most enlightened squaw appreciate as it should be appreciated the elaborate 'craziness' of the quilt—much less could she enter into the associations that were linked with some of the pieces in the squares—that lovely bit of delaine, for instance, in the centre with twined hearts in silk herring-boning, from the dress Susan Brown had made in town for her wedding with Jake Smith, and then Jake went off and married Maria M'Kail the day before the wedding—what would that piece mean to an Indian? It would be nothing to a squaw but so much protection against a frosty night. It ended in Mary Ann seeing the reasonableness of her mother's views and leaving the future proprietorship of the quilt an open question, its place in the mission bale being taken by some coarse, woollen knitted mitts—a mingled triumph of commonsense and the wiles of the tempter. The unfinished quilt was put away when her mother fell sick and she had never had the heart to take it out since till the happy inspiration came to her to-day to finish it and make of it an offering to Evelyn for her wedding with Bert Enderby. It is no use objecting that, even with Sam the chore boy's reinforcements of news, that Mary Ann had no sufficient grounds for believing with such confidence that the wedding would take place—with all the additional prosaicness of their sex very responsible farmers in the West quite often reap, harvest and sell and spend the money of a crop of twenty-five bushels of wheat to the acre on the strength of a favourable seed-time or the early coming of the June rains. If poor Mary Ann had been obliged to confine her thoughts and hopes to actualities, her life—like yours or mine—would have been a dull business.

So deeply engrossed was she with her task and her providing for Bert and Evelyn's future happiness that, though not usually nervous, she uttered a startled 'Sakes alive!' when there was a sharp knock at the door and the mailman entered with his bag. For once he was not a welcome visitor, and took his departure as soon as the formalities of his business were over. Sometimes he would linger for half an hour or so discussing local politics with old Dawson if he were about the house, or chatting with Mary Ann about the doings in town, but being a married man he was skilled in the reading of the feminine barometer and never out-stayed his welcome. With another half hour or so that particular square on which Mary Ann was engaged when he came would have been finished, and it was with a decided feeling of offence against the innocent mailman that she folded up her work and replaced it in her room, and came back to sort out the mail before any one else came to the office.

It was with a very unusual lack of interest that Mary Ann set about her task. The big bundles of weekly papers were laid on one side, and after changing the date of the office rubber-stamp and giving it two or three trial dabs on a piece of wastepaper to see that it gave a clear impression, she sat down at the desk and cut the string with which the package of letters was tied, and arranged them conveniently to her hand for stamping.

So preoccupied were her thoughts that she proceeded with her task mechanically, not even taking the trouble to read the addresses, much less to conjecture on the probable contents of the various letters. Once indeed, she paused at an envelope with a black border—Mrs. Enderby, The Dingle— but passed it on with the rest, after mentally deciding that the border of black was too narrow to announce the demise of Aunt Mary or any near relative of the family. She had reached the last one, and was already preparing to rise from her chair as she gave it an extra vigorous stamp to mark the conclusion of her work, when her eye caught some letters written in bold, dashing style in the bottom left-hand corner of the large, square envelope, so boldly and clearly formed that their import struck home to her brain like a stab—T. M. D.—and she quickly read the rest of the writing before her—Miss Evelyn Raye, The Dingle—and the name of the office and so forth.

T. M. D.—Thomas M. Dennis, not for one moment did they admit of any other possible meaning. Not once, but a score and more of times had she seen them on letters which Tom himself had posted with his own hand —they had been the object, not only of remark but of censure on the part of old Dawson, who looked on them as a possible infringement of the rules of the mail service, which said the address only should be written on the front of a letter, and the old man was only partially satisfied with Tom's chaffing explanation that he did it to lessen the shock to his friends of his writing at all.

But while T. M. D. inevitably meant Thomas M. Dennis, Mary Ann's mind refused to acquiesce in the apparent consequence that Tom was still living. T. M. D. meant Thomas M. Dennis, admitted—but Thomas M. Dennis was dead, the *Winnipeg Free Press* said so, the Minnedosa paper said so and added a lot of complimentary things about him which it never would have said if he were living—why, and Mary Ann's spirits revived for a moment under the fresh item of evidence—why, the English Church minister had held a memorial service and preached a funeral sermon—in fact, just as good as buried him—'though, in course, they hadn't the corpse.' The more Mary Ann thought about it, the more surprised she became; she brought out from her room the copy of the paper which had first brought the news of Tom's death—there it was, marked by her own hand with a black ink cross against his name, and the date of the paper, February twenty-second, and here on the letter was March twentieth, and the name of some heathen place in Africa. Slowly it began to come home to her that Tom was alive—and if alive, what then? The lack of consideration which had allowed him to survive the newspapers, and even the minister's sermon, might admit of his coming back and upsetting all her plans when everything, as she had said to herself that very afternoon, 'was going so beautiful.'

At this point Mary Ann heard the sound of a rig driving up to the door, and hastily thrusting the offending letter into her pocket, she hurried to face the world with what courage and composure she could—at least the letter's coming should be her own secret till she could see the future in a clearer light.

More than one settler remarked to a neighbour, as they left the office that evening, on the unusual crustiness of Mary Ann's manner and the sharpness of her tongue. The hired man, an East End Londoner, whose inexperience of farm work was usually atoned for in her eyes by the extreme smallness of his wages and his willingness to help round the house, was glad as soon as he had had his supper and done the chores to retire to his own room. He was a young man of a cheerful disposition and musical tastes, and was wont to receive kindly encouragement from Mary Ann in his efforts to extract from a concertina with a defective key-board the accompaniment to his singing of 'The Old Folks at Home,' 'Skylark,' 'Won't you Come Home, Bill Bailey?' and other classical lyrics, which he sang with a sentimentality which made up, to Mary Ann's mind, for any strictly musical defects. To-night he had scarcely achieved a rather staccato prelude to 'Mother Kissed Me in My Dreams,'—usually a most popular number of his repertoire—when he was crushed by the unequivocating question from Mary Ann as to whether he thought that 'folks as has been worritted all day by cooking victuals for them as eats more than they earn, wants to

160

be kept out of their beds by such like catawaulings.' He retired, hurt, but still hopeful of a more favourable domestic atmosphere on the morrow, and was soon asleep and dreaming.

There remained old Dawson. The burning of coal-oil in the summer-time was against the established rule of the house, but since her mother's death Mary Ann had relaxed somewhat the strictness of the old lady's discipline and usually allowed her father to sit up for an hour or so on mail nights for a second after-supper pipe and to read *The Sentinel*—a sound organ which combined politics and Protestantism in nicely balanced proportions, suited to old Dawson's principles and mental capacity. But there was no dispensation to-night—a second question, as pointed as that to which the hired man had succumbed, sent the old man grumbling upstairs—'them as was always a-talking of a lame back had best rest it when they could,' and did he think as 'them as did the men folks' work outside, as well as their own inside, could do without their night's rest?'

At last, Mary Ann was alone and free to face her problem, which, being now secure of ample time and due privacy, she did with great deliberation. After making such preparations for the morrow's early breakfast as were possible over night, she lit the lamp and carried it into her own room and closed the door. The letter was taken from her pocket and placed on the little table, and she then proceeded to remove her print dress, whose starchy neck frill had been adding to her acute sense of irritation during the evening, and replaced the more restraining portions of her attire with an old woollen shawl and sat down to think out the whole situation afresh. For the present she was not concerned with the letter itself, she must go farther back and work up to it by degrees; she felt now, in her recovered composure, that at the first realising of what that T. M. D. stood for, she had shied at the letter as a young and nervous horse will shy at some strange and unexpected object which is suddenly revealed on making a sharp turn in the road. She felt that she was too old and too experienced to shy, and that perhaps now, when she was able to approach it more cautiously the letter might reveal a less disturbing appearance. She followed in her mind the whole course of events for the past year, as far as they affected the lives of Evelyn, Tom Dennis, and Bert Enderby, and in the main outlines it is marvellous how well informed she was and how near the truth she came in her deductions—the baffling point was the depth and nature of Evelyn's feeling for Tom Dennis, and that, in the end, brought her back to the letter, but this time in a slower and more tentative way—she was not going to shy again. The letter was from Tom, and Tom was alive—but—and she put the question to herself slowly, for she was determined not to accept a new idea too hastily—was it a love-letter? She had taken that for granted; now, holding her imagination well in hand she allowed her mind to formulate some alternatives—might it be only a friendly letter, explaining how it was that the false news of his death had been circulated—might it not be sent to Evelyn so that it might not startle Mrs. Enderby, who might open it if addressed to Mr. Enderby or Bert, or was it sent to Evelyn that she might tell the school children and so spread the news in the settlement—or might there have been some understanding between Tom and Evelyn and now he was writing to say he had changed his mind and was not coming back to Canada? One by one Mary Ann suffered these suggestions to enter her mind, only to reject them, but out of them arose a new thought, the slowness of the coming of which can only be explained by the mysterious constitution of the female mind—and the thought was this—that, after all, the simplest way of knowing, instead of guessing as to what the contents of the letter may be, is to open it and read it.

It is only fair to Mary Ann to say that the bluntness with which the question suggested itself honestly shocked her and brought a darker shade beneath her usual sallow and dull complexion. She laid down again the letter which she had taken from the table a minute before and hastily rose and turned the wooden button which was intended to secure the door from inopportune opening. It is to be feared that at the same time she turned the button of her mind which shut out the voice of conscience. The turning of the button was the crossing of her Rubicon. Mary Ann had never actually opened a letter entrusted to the office before—it is true, when vexed by obvious suspicions in the shape of gum and sealing wax that she had often vaunted to her mother of her ability to overcome them if she so desired—it may be that once or twice when letters had come open by themselves or by the carelessness of the senders—that she had taken an incidental glance at their contents—'for surely folks who took so little pains with their fastening would not mind a body knowing what was inside.' Mary Ann would not have opened any abstract letter for a hundred dollars cash down—as a matter of honesty—not to open Tom's letter was an impossibility—as a matter of temperament.

With her, to resolve was to act, and in a few minutes the spirit-lamp used in her mother's sickness was lighted, the little kettle steaming and the three sheets of cheap paper covered by the bold writing of Tom Dennis's hand were lying open on her lap. It was an odd freak of human nature that, having yielded to temptation she entered on the consummation of her ill-deed with a sense of resentment against Tom as the instigator of her fall.

CHAPTER XXXI

AN UNLUCKY POSTSCRIPT

Though Mary Ann was now fully determined to read Tom's letter it did not follow that she should do it at once. On the contrary, she first made a little tour of the other room, saw that the bolt was drawn in the outer door, listened at the foot of the stairs—her father's snore was in its usual key—and, returning to her room, turned the button and drew closer the curtain which screened the window. She hesitated for a moment as to whether she should kneel down and say her prayers, but hastily decided in the negative, foreseeing difficulties—better leave them till afterwards since she was relying on the contents of the letter justifying her reading of it—spiritual ethics become very involved when once they have been allowed to slip a cog. Finally she sat down, and again taking up Tom's letter she read it steadily through to the end, and as Daisy Enderby often said that what Mary Ann knew, everybody knew, which, by the way, was not always the case, there can be no impropriety in our sharing her knowledge.

'BLOEMFONTEIN, SOUTH AFRICA,
March 20th.
'MY DEAR MISS RAYE,—You know the mingled disaster and disgrace which led my brother Jack and myself to volunteer for South Africa. I think you know the words that were in my heart and almost on my lips when we parted in Jim Hardie's lane. I left Minnedosa firmly determined that if I survived the year's service I would return to Canada and tell you plainly that from the day I first saw you and drove you up to the Dingle, there had been only one aim and hope in my life—to win you for my wife. Hard as it was to leave you without a word of explanation—of farewell— yet I felt that it would be cruel to you and harder still to myself, to tell you of my love and then leave you, if you loved me, pledged to an unlucky fellow who before the year was up might be lying under the veldt, or so broken and maimed by the fortunes of war as to be unable to win for you even the hard living of a Manitoba homestead. And if you loved me not, the rough road of duty which my word to my mother laid upon me, would

be a road that my Irish nature—up to-day and down to-morrow —would never have the steady courage to follow to an end beyond which lay no hope. At the last day my determination to leave you in silence so far failed me that I entrusted my secret to young Tad Jordan—forgive me if I ought not to have done so— to leave you without telling my love was hard—to leave you and mayhap to die and you never to know that I loved you seemed to separate you from me not only in time but eternity. In telling Tad I thought I had provided for your knowing or not knowing of my love if I did not return—leaving the boy—for he is a good boy and true as steel—to do as he thought kindest to you, and now by a strange turn of fate I am telling you my own story; after all it is difficult to tell.

'For two months when this reaches you, you will have believed that I was dead, and I cannot hope honestly that you have not grieved for me—and for a month I have been in the base hospital at Belmont with nothing worse to bear than the mending of my left wrist, shattered by a spent bullet—but poor Jack is dead and lying in a bluff on the Modder River with some score of other brave fellows who fell in the last rush on the eighteenth of February. He was shot through the heart not ten yards from me, and when I reached his side he was dead, without a word or sign. I kissed him and left him there, and hastened to follow my comrades who had disappeared in the gathering gloom of the twilight —filled, I suppose, with some wild passion to avenge his loss. I was stumbling along when a ball struck my wrist, and I must have hit a rock with my head as I fell, for I knew nothing till I found myself lying in the field hospital with my left arm strapped up and a bandage round my head. In two days I was sent back to the base, for though my wound was not dangerous, I was useless in the field. Thank Heaven I wrote to my mother the day I reached Belmont, and at home at least they know the truth by now.

'But I have not told you how the unhappy mixing up of our identity happened—it was our own fault—poor Jack's and mine. The last time we had our tunics off, we were always in the same tent when we had a tent, Jack, in dressing, put on my tunic and left me his—what fitted me fitted him. I called out to him his mistake as he was leaving the tent, and he replied laughing in his easy way—'We're both Dennises anyway, what's the odds?' It was my tunic through which the bullet found its way to his heart —would God it had been my heart too, if you do not love me—

forgive me, Evelyn—and it was my identification card that was turned in to the sergeant major of A Company by those who buried poor Jack, and his card that was in my tunic when they made the return of the wounded from the field hospital. That we had changed tunics and that a terrible mistake had been made never entered my head from the moment we did it till I stepped off the train at Bloemfontein this morning. It was only one of the scores of times we had worn one another's things since we were boys. The first man I met was the orderly sergeant of my own company, and when I hailed him and laid my hand on his shoulder the moment he turned round and saw me he shrank back as if he had seen a ghost—'Why, Dennis, man, we thought you handed in your checks a month ago on the Modder.'

' "No," I said, "it was my brother, Jack. I'm just back from the base hospital."

' "Well, it's Jack's name that is carried on the muster roll as 'absent in hospital,' and your name was struck off the day after the identification cards were handed in by the burial fatigue after the fight at Modder River."

'The identification cards! In a flash it all came back to me. Our confounded Irish go-as-you-please and all the unhappiness it must have brought. My mother will have mourned for me, and by now my letter will have reached her and her heart will be broken at the loss of Jack, she will have suffered for both. Jack was her own boy, though she was too true to us all for any one of us ever to have a thought of jealousy. What happiness can my escape from death bring her at such a cost?

'Out of all the miseries and uncertainties of to-day I have by to-night come at least to a clear purpose. The war, as far as fighting on my part is concerned, is over; the doctor tells me that though I can do camp or orderly-room duty, I shall not be able to carry a rifle for three or four months, and our year's service ends in September. The serious fighting will probably be finished long before then. If I were free to return to the firing line I would stay and take my luck with the rest of the boys till the end came, but there will be plenty to do the hanging around headquarters here without Tom Dennis. Our own doctor will send in my application for discharge if I am not fit for active service by the first of July, and then it will be the first boat for Ireland, or the first boat for Canada, there to claim the bride of my heart and carry her away to my own land and my own people. It is you, Evelyn, that must say which it shall be. If you love me, forgive the rough bluntness of my wooing, and do not fear but there shall be a warm welcome and a daughter's place awaiting you in the old Connemara home. I know if you love me you will let my duty shape our future, and my duty lies with the old land now—before I had to make the hard choice—this time honour and love may go the one path. A letter from our mother soon after we reached Africa told us that our father's elder brother—the old bachelor uncle I've told you of, and who seemed as if he might live for years—had had a paralytic stroke, and could, at the most, but linger for a few weeks, and his death will change everything at home. My father will succeed to his title and all the tangle and worries of an Irish landlord; as the eldest boy, my place will be at home, and doubly so since poor Jack is gone. I'm writing home to-night if ever I get this finished—I never was properly broken to letter-writing and make a horrible mess of it. I'm going to tell them just how it is with me, mother won't be surprised, I expect she has guessed long ago from my home letters last summer.

'If you give yourself to my keeping, Evelyn, never doubt of the warmth of your welcome there; my father often said in the old days when my mother teased him about the idiosyncrasies of the men of our family—that there were at least two things that a Dennis could be trusted to do wisely—the buying of a horse and the choosing of a wife.

'If you love me—ah, it all comes back to that, and between the yes and the no of it I must kill the time till my answer comes, and whether it be yes or no, this it will be, the simple, honest truth, and if I have given my love in vain, at least I have done an honour to myself in the giving of it.—Yours ever, TOM DENNIS.'

If only Tom had ended his letter when it was finished Mary Ann might have said her prayers and gone to bed, if not with a sound conscience, still with a conscience very decently patched, but his Irishman's luck had not reached its turning-point. After he had folded up his letter and put it in the envelope, as he turned it over and pressed it smooth to address it, he was struck by the way in which his writing showed through the thin, cheap envelope. 'Dash it,' he had said to himself, 'that will never do,' and taking the letter out again he had added the following explanatory postscript before wrapping it carefully in a blank sheet of paper.

'*P.S.*—I hope the extra sheet of paper won't make it overweight, but my heavy fist was too obvious through the envelope. Of course, I know the outside address will inevitably proclaim my identity to Mary Ann Dawson—poor Mary Ann, I don't grudge her that much satisfaction, but if I had sent it as it was the gimlet eyes of the old lady would have read the letter itself, and I was not writing to the whole settlement.'

Unlucky Tom! Mary Ann began to read the letter fully intending that it should never reach Evelyn—if it were likely to keep her from accepting Bert Enderby. By the end of the first sheet Bert was forgotten and she pitying Jack Dennis, when she came to Tom's pleading for himself she was wiping her eyes, and by the time she reached the end she could see Tom coming back in his regimentals, with his arm in a sling, to claim his bride, a touching scene on the platform as he landed from the train, and herself not very far in the background as a kind of confidential friend and guardian angel of the handsome pair of young lovers. The postscript came like an icy shower-bath to her sentiment—'Poor Mary Ann'—she might have forgiven that, but at the offensive phrase—'the gimlet eyes of the old lady,' her heart shut against Tom Dennis with a snap. 'The shame of it, and poor mother not more than three months in her grave,' she said indignantly to herself. 'It's not myself that is going to let Miss Evelyn read his sneering remarks of a person's mother. So you'll wait till the first of July for your answer, my fine young fellow. I'm thinking you'll wait a bit longer, and maybe when you hear your sweetheart has took some one as has none of your smart ways you'll wish you'd left "Poor Mary Ann" and her mother alone—so you will.'

Mary Ann still had tears to wipe, but they had taken an acid turn and ended with a sniff. But though Evelyn was not to have the letter it was still to be disposed of. Mary Ann smoothed out the last sheet, which at the moment of reading she had crushed in her hand, she read again the postscript; it confirmed the righteousness of her wrath and the unchangeableness of her resolution—but what should she do with it? She thought at first of burning it, but that would be rather difficult in her room, and she did not like to risk going out to the stove in case she were heard moving about and her father came fussing to see what was amiss. She had, besides, a shrinking from actually destroying it. She and her mother had been in the habit for years of taking a good deal of credit for the care with which they handled the mail, letters might be lost in Winnipeg or put in the wrong mailbag by a flighty young lady clerk in Minnedosa, but 'folks knew that when they once reached Dawson's office they were as safe as the bank.' No, she finally made up her mind it never should be said that a letter was destroyed there—only it should not be delivered—she would take care of it and see how things turned out. It would be time enough to give up the letter when it was asked for.

It ended in the letter being put back in its envelope, which was refastened with the aid of a little gum, a little judicious smearing of the whole by a damp and not too cleanly hand gave it quite a natural appearance, with such a general look of grubbiness as might be taken to be the natural result of its long journey from Africa, and it was placed among a varied assortment of old letters and funeral cards which Mary Ann kept in a little box at the bottom of her drawer.

The compromise of keeping the letter instead of burning it was so far reassuring to Mary Ann's conscience, that vexed and wearied as she was by the conflicting emotions through which she had passed, she still found herself able to say her prayers—but she blew out the lamp first—an unconscious confession that her conscience was not quite lulled to insensibility under the anæsthetic of her filial piety.

CHAPTER XXXII

MR. JORDAN PROVES DIFFICULT

It was the evening of the last Wednesday in June—Marion Enderby's wedding-day—and Mr. Jordan was jogging quietly homeward down the town line. It had been a perfect day for a wedding—'a scrumptious peach of a day,' so Daisy had described it, and everything had gone off very happily, and again, to quote Daisy, 'the whole show had been a howling success.' Yet in spite of all the parson was in rather a gloomy humour, and apt to be a little peevish if Vixen, his mare, showed a skittish disposition to shy at perfectly familiar stumps or boulders by the side of the trail. But then the day had turned out better for Vixen than her anticipations, while with her master it was quite the reverse. When she was hitched up in the Rectory yard at nine in the morning and kept going at too smart a pace for comfort under the hot June sun for the full twelve miles up to the Dingle church, she had come to the conclusion that there must be two Sundays in this week, and Vixen had no use for Sundays; her master was always in a fidget, and as often as not she had no proper time to digest her noonday oats before he would be hurrying her along to his afternoon service. In fact, all the way up Vixen had been disposed to be a little sulky, but when, the wedding over, she was driven to the Dingle and put in a cool stall by the side of her old friend, Tom Dennis's mare, with a big bundle of sweet new hay before her in the manger, she recovered her good humour; doubly so when she heard Bert say to Sam, the chore boy, 'You can take the harness off Mr. Jordan's mare and give her some oats when she has cooled down, she won't be wanted till evening.' Vixen was very fond of her master except on Sundays, and her playful jumps and starts at imaginary perils as she took her way home at a pace of her own choosing, was just her way of showing her appreciation of the decent way an animal was treated at the Dingle. It was too bad that Mr. Jordan jerked the lines and growled—of course, a perfectly proper growl—when a more than usually vigorous start to one side cramped the buggy and brought it up on to two wheels—but then the parson was not full of oats and contentment. That his vexations were rather undefined only vexed Mr. Jordan the more; he was rather fond of saying that he never worried about the difficulty of getting over a stile until he came to it, a piece of philosophy which his wife utterly repudiated as a mark of his English shiftlessness, when, as was usually the case, the stile was the meeting of a note at the bank or paying an insurance premium that would fall due in a month's or so time.

But though the parson would not vex his spirit in the dog-days by the problem of how he should pay his butcher, for instance, next Christmas, he had a fine talent for worrying himself to himself about things that affected the well-being of his church or the happiness of the scattered members of his flock. He was not, in his heart, content with the marriage of Dugald M'Leod and Marion Enderby, and at the same time he had an uneasy feeling that he ought to be. He liked and respected Dugald M'Leod—his farming, his solvency and his moral character were beyond reproach. For some time before and during his engagement he had attended the English church services with far more regularity than many of the young Englishmen in the settlement, and his attentiveness to the sermon was always quite noticeable. More than once Mrs. Enderby had expressed privately her hope to Mr. Jordan that 'dear Dugald' would by and by join the church and be confirmed. She even went so far on one occasion as to suggest to the parson that he should find an opportunity to discuss it with Dugald. He had never done so, partly because he thought proselytizing rather poor religion and very ill manners, and partly because he was satisfied that any such efforts would be ultimately a failure—as he said to his wife—'you can't wipe Calvinism off a Scotchman like dust off a table, it's in the fibre of the stock. Dugald has been coming to All Saints' with Marion while he's been courting, I suspect with very much the apology of Naaman when he went into the House of Rimmon, and he'll continue to come on and off as long as Marion can come with him, but as soon as there is a baby in the house and he goes to church alone that will be the end of it; Marion is not stiff like Daisy, and she'll go with him in the long run. I've no taste for trying to change his predestination, and when a man is named Dugald M'Leod you can take it for granted he's predestined to die a Presbyterian.'

This little thorn in the parson's flesh was purely on Church lines, a second was more personal. When Tad had brought out his father's black robes' bag to the buggy in the morning he had asked in an incidental sort of way, 'I suppose there won't be anything coming my way, Dad, out of the wedding fee?'

'I'm afraid not, Tad,' he had answered. 'I expect it will be the regulation five dollars, and your mother must have that for boots for the two little kiddies.'

'Still,' Tad had urged, 'even a tight wad might spring a ten when he's getting married—and I've three dollars I made digging seneca root, and there's a dandy racquet at Stirling's for eight.'

'Well, if he does, you shall have five, Tad, but I wouldn't build on it too much.'

It had proved to be the regulation five, and there would be no racquet for Tad yet awhile, and his father hated to disappoint him. These, after all, were only his lighter vexations as he drove along, providing a sort of background of mental depression for more serious problems. Though he loved dearly the confidence which led all sorts of people to bring their troubles to him, he often grumbled in a self-pitying way at being made, as he said, 'a dumping ground for other folks' trials,' as if he had none of his own, and there had been another such dumping that day on the part of Mrs. Enderby.

The wedding had been a very simple, family affair. After what Daisy insisted on calling the 'elegant *déjeuner*,' Dugald and his bride drove to town to take the train for Winnipeg for a week's honeymoon, and Daisy had invited three or four young men on the previous Sunday to come over for tennis and afternoon tea. Mr. Enderby, finding the time rather heavy on his hands as being neither a Sunday nor a working day, compromised by replacing his frock coat of the wedding by a loose jacket and taking Sam to help him look for a cow which had not come home for a couple of days, and was suspected of hiding in the bush with a newborn calf. This left the field clear for Mrs. Enderby's dumping. Mr. Jordan, though he would have gladly struck for home, where he had a big potato patch which needed hoeing, felt that it would be ungracious to insist on leaving in face of Mrs. Enderby's earnest invitation that he should stay at least for the early tea and a little talk with herself about the parish. He knew Mrs. Enderby well enough to know that her usual phrase 'about the parish' was often largely figurative. It might mean that he was to be urged to make a fresh effort to shepherd Dugald into the Anglican fold, a subject which might fairly be called parochial, but the last conference ushered in thus was to tell him of Daisy's engagement to Chris Raye and to ask his opinion on the propriety of announcing it in the social columns of the Winnipeg papers. However trivial it might be in reality, he knew that he would be expected to treat it with the seriousness which it was sure to possess in her eyes, so he followed her to the rustic seat in the shade of the bluff and sat down to listen with a decent air of interest and sympathy.

But this afternoon Mrs. Enderby evidently found 'the parish' a little difficult of direct approach. Starting off with saying how much Marion would be missed at home in the management of the house, she branched off into so many apparently disconnected topics that Mr. Jordan was completely mystified as to what particular point of the parish or the Dingle economy he was to be consulted about. Now, it seemed to be the difficulty there would be in keeping Sam, the chore boy, in his place after Marion was gone; now, the remissness of Mrs. Hardie in not seeing that her little

171

boys learnt the collect for Sunday-school; this led, by no very obvious route to the question of the propriety of Chris Raye driving Daisy down to the tennis tournament in town, involving in some obscure way the deciding as to whether, since Chris was an orphan, Mr. Enderby should write to Chris's uncle and guardian before Mrs. Enderby had received a letter of congratulation from Chris's maiden aunt from whom he had expectations. Just as the parson was trying to co-ordinate some vague reminiscences of the procedure in the case of the engagement of a sister of his own some twenty years before, Mrs. Enderby suddenly broke new ground with the point blank question, 'Don't you think Miss Raye would make an admirable wife for Bert?' So this was after all the real object of the little talk about the parish.

Much pleased with herself for what she considered the diplomatic way in which she had led up to the subject so near to her heart, Mrs. Enderby became more intelligible, and by the end of the next half hour Mr. Jordan was possessed of the situation with some measure of definiteness. He had been sure for some time past that, sooner or later, Bert would propose to Evelyn, but he was rather surprised to learn that he had done so a month before, and had been refused. It was evident, however, that Mrs. Enderby did not take the refusal very seriously, and was quite satisfied that in the end Bert's suit would be successful—it was quite usual for girls to show a certain reserve in such matters, but she could hardly understand any girl refusing a young man like Bert, so eminently desirable in every way as a husband. Mr. Jordan, of course, would not mention it to any one, as it was quite a secret; no one had the least idea of it beyond Marion, who naturally would tell her husband now, and Daisy, who had asked Chris to use his influence in Bert's favour. Possibly Evelyn might confide in Mr. Jordan, and in that case Mrs. Enderby felt sure he would say a good word for her dear boy—and so on, and so on.

The parson was as sympathetic as he could be; he liked Bert and all the Dingle people very much, but at the same time he could not help a certain feeling of relief when he heard Bert was not accepted; it confirmed his own opinion of the depth of Evelyn's character, and in his heart he was better pleased that she should remain single for the sake of Tom Dennis than find consolation in even such a very nice fellow as Bert.

But though Mr. Jordan was prepared to be sympathetic, he had little taste for the more active cooperation which Mrs. Enderby evidently expected at his hands, and as she elaborated in her own way the steps that were to change Evelyn's first refusal into a final acceptance, he could not help feeling a contempt for a wooer who was content to win on such terms, mingled with a pity for Evelyn, who was evidently, under all due forms of kindness and affection, to be crowded into a marriage in which there should be everything except the only thing that counts. He had absolutely, in his heart, not an atom of respect for a man who was content to accept less than all in asking for a woman's love—he simply could not understand any man feeling the slightest pleasure in securing the prize for a race in which he had come in second because the one who came in first had been for any reason disqualified. So much for Bert. As for using some kind of clerical influence to persuade Evelyn that it was her duty to sacrifice her own feelings to promoting what Bert thought was his happiness, and what seemed to be a desirable adjustment of the family affairs of the Enderbys and Chris Raye—that touched the parson on another side. Though it was not specifically stated in the obligations of the ministry, there was one which he had always held as equally binding though it was expressed in less theological terms, and that was the obligation of a man to 'play the game' in whatever shape it might present itself. Not even in his own mind did Mr. Jordan brand Mrs. Enderby as designing or unscrupulous in her schemes to win over Evelyn to Bert's suit, he remembered that she was Bert's mother and her ethics were a mother's first and last, but no less firmly did he decline to take any active part in their forwarding. Though it was in vain to tell Mrs. Enderby so, he knew that if left to herself Evelyn would sacrifice for others all that a woman should sacrifice—when that point was reached was for herself to decide, and though he gladly agreed to invite Evelyn to the Rectory for a visit to relieve a situation which was evidently a little embarrassing at the Dingle, he simply would not attempt in any way to influence Evelyn's decision. With this much Mrs. Enderby had to be content, though there was certainly an undertone of grievance, when, in telling Daisy of her failure afterwards, she added that she had never before found Mr. Jordan so difficult.

While talking with Mrs. Enderby Mr. Jordan had gone no further in his own mind than a determination to remain neutral, but there had been an appeal in Evelyn's eyes when she accepted his invitation for her to come down for a week or two at the Rectory, which had touched him on a softer spot than all Mrs. Enderby's anxieties for her poor, dear boy—it was the appeal of a hunted animal when it finds an unexpected, and possibly hostile obstacle between itself and its last refuge. It vexed and worried him at intervals all the way home, it probably gained Vixen a cut or two of the whip beyond the due of her own skittishness, but that it won a final victory may be inferred from a half audible grumble to himself as he got out of the buggy in his own yard, 'I'll be—bothered—if the poor girl shall be hounded—let who will be put out—and now I suppose I've got to disappoint the kid about his racquet—when Dugald gets the doctor instead of the parson, he'll find it doesn't come quite so cheap.'

CHAPTER XXXIII

TAD IS ON THE INSIDE TRACK

Mr. Jordan was just beginning to unhitch Vixen when Tad appeared at the yard gate.

'Hello, Dad, so you're back; anything doing?'

'No, my boy, I'm afraid not, you'll have to make my old racquet do for a while, but I'll see what we can do after the tournament; perhaps I can get you a good second-hand one, and I may be able to help you out with a dollar or two. I'm sorry, but I warned you not to expect too much.'

'Oh, it's all right, Dad,' and Tad busied himself with the straps on the other side of the mare that his disappointment might not be too evident. 'I knew it was an off chance—why, when I was at the Dingle last Fall Dugald wouldn't take a half day off his work for the chicken shooting—not even the first day of the season, mind you, and the Dingle Barnardo boy told me at Easter that he never even went courting Miss Enderby unless it was a Sunday or a wet day—I wish he'd got Daisy instead of her sister, there would be something doing when she wanted a new dress.'

'I guess it's best as it is, Tad, and you can put the mare away while I go in and get some supper, for afternoon tea is not very satisfying—where's mother and everybody?'

'Oh, mother and the girls are over at the tennis courts, but mother left the supper things on the table in case you wanted any—and oh, Dad, there is a letter for you on your study table, from the old country, with a swell crest on it—mother thinks it's from the Dennis's father in Ireland.'

'All right, Tad, I'll find it; you may as well fix up Vixen for the night before you come in, she's not too warm to have a pail of water and she does not need any more oats, she's too gay as it is,' and Mr. Jordan walked off to the house and into his study. He picked up the letters lying on the table, two or three obviously bills and the other—yes, it was from Tom Dennis's father from the Connemara post-mark. The parson did not open it at once, but took it with him into the dining-room and laid it down unopened while he cut himself some cold meat and brought in the teapot from the kitchen stove—he would read it while he had his supper. He felt no curiosity about it, though he had vaguely wondered at its being so thick and heavy when he first picked it up, and he did not expect it would be very cheerful reading. He had written to Mr. Dennis a letter of condolence when the news came of Tom's death, and this, of course, was the answer. He left the letter lying while he ate his cold meat, and then spreading himself some bread and butter and pouring out a second cup of tea, he pushed his chair half back from the table and took up the letter—it certainly was unusually bulky—probably he was wanted to settle up the affairs of the boys' farm; it was not likely Jack would ever come back to the West—as well not, for he was not fitted for it—but the parson sighed as he cut the envelope open and drew out its contents, so many Old Country boys had come into his life and dropped out again—too often with failure and disaster of some kind, but this was the saddest ending of them all.

As he opened out the letter a second smaller envelope fell out, and as he read its superscription all his reminiscent sadness vanished—'Entrusted to Mr. Jordan for Miss Evelyn Raye, from Tom's mother'—matters must have gone further then with Tom and Evelyn than he had ever dreamt of, and the poor girl had been facing her life at the Dingle all these months with a broken heart and not a soul to help her—and there were three closely written sheets for himself in a firmer, stronger hand.

Mr. Jordan unconsciously squared his shoulders and pulled himself together mentally as he opened them and pressed out the creases of their folding that he might read them the better, but he had not gone beyond the first few lines when his self-controlled deliberation gave way to a startled cry—at first wondering and unbelieving—'Tom alive!' and then repeated in a slower and deeper tone as the conviction came home—'Tom Dennis is alive——' and then without a pause hardly to take breath he read the long letter through to the end. The parson was not usually given to the display of his emotions, but it came at the end of a long and worried day, the letter of the poor father himself swayed backwards and forwards between his joy at Tom's escape and his sorrow for poor Jack, so that as he ended his reading Mr. Jordan felt smothered by his conflicting feelings. He rose hastily from the table and threw open the window—there seemed no air in the room. By force of habit he put his hand in his pocket and drew out his pouch and pipe, and filled the latter and lighted it though his fingers trembled so that he could hardly hold the match. For some minutes he paced backwards and forwards, up and down the room, pausing now for a moment to straighten a picture that was hanging a little out of the square on the wall, now to pick up one of the children's toys lying untidily on the floor. By degrees he recovered his composure and came back again to the table and sat down and re-read the letter, more slowly and deliberately this time. It was in its facts the same strange story that Tom had written in his letter to Evelyn—which was still lying in Mary Ann's bottom drawer—but as he re-read it there were questions arose in Mr. Jordan's mind which had not impressed him on

175

his first reading. 'Why had Evelyn never received Tom's letter?—Was it some mishap in the mail service, or——' but he could not carry that question further now, he would stop at what was certain, and it was certain the letter had never reached her hands—but what did Tom's father mean by saying, 'I understand from my son's letter that he entrusted the secret of his attachment to your son, Tad; excuse me if I have got the name wrong, and that perhaps he can throw a little light on a situation which is still to us, rather uncertain and distressing.' Mr. Jordan read the sentence a second and a third time, becoming more puzzled each time. How in the world could Tad know anything about it? The probabilities of there having been an understanding between Tom and Evelyn had been discussed in the boy's presence more than once, and he had never given a sign of being in possession of any secret—surely the boy would have told his mother. For a moment Mr. Jordan was vexed to think that Tad had learned so well the lesson of being silent about what his parents talked of in the family circle; however, he could soon find out the truth, and going to the window he called out loudly, 'Tad, I want you, right away.'

'All right, Dad, I'm coming, as soon as I've run the buggy in the shed.'

'Never mind the buggy, I want you now.'

A minute afterwards Tad hurried into the room.

'Why, what's the matter, Dad, you're not sick?' for he was quick to see that his father was much disturbed.

'Oh, no, Tad, but I've had a very surprising letter, and it has upset me a good deal—it's about Tom Dennis.'

'I guessed it was when I saw the post-mark—mother had half a mind not to give it to you till the morning, she knew you would be tired, and it would be sure to be kind of miserable like——'

'Well, it's not quite that, Tad, but there has been a great mistake made about—about the two Dennis boys.'

'Why, what mistake, Dad—they're not both dead?'

'No, no, but in the list in the paper—it was poor Jack who was killed and Tom is alive and well.'

'Tom alive!' and for a moment Tad was speechless. 'Tom alive! Really alive—is that true?—Oh, isn't that great! Why—why—everything will come right again—and aren't you glad, Dad, I feel as if I could shout.'

'Hush, hush, boy, remember his brother is dead, and his father and mother have had all their grieving twice over—and, Tad, there is a great deal in the letter about Tom and Miss Raye, I cannot half understand it, and his father says you can explain it all——'

'Oh, that's all right, Dad, you need not worry about that—of course, I've been on the inside track——'

'Why, what do you mean by the "inside track"?' asked Mr. Jordan impatiently, 'inside track of what?'

'Of this love business and all that kind of thing,' replied Tad rather awkwardly. 'It seems all rather tommy-rot since he's alive and can come and do his own courting—but there was a ring I was to give her, and a sort of a softish kind of message if Tom got killed and she seemed to feel too bad about it, but if she seemed to worry along all right I was to keep the ring and say nothing—just keep mum, you know, Dad.'

'Well, of all the commissions to entrust to a mere child like you! It's Tom Dennis all over—but where's the ring, and why did you never say a word to Miss Raye or your mother?'

'The ring is in my pants' pocket—I wear it sometimes when I'm by myself—Tom said it was for me if I didn't give it to Miss Raye, and I've been beastly uncomfortable about it. I very nearly told her when I was up at the Dingle at Easter, but she seemed so rummy when I tried to talk to her about Tom, and said I was a cruel boy when I asked her if she wasn't sorrier it was Tom that was killed instead of Jack, and the next minute she started off laughing about some bally joke of Daisy's, and there was Mr. Bert sniffing around her all the time and she as nice to him as you please—and I just thought she didn't deserve to know that—that Mr. Tom was like that—you bet I'll never bank on another girl.'

'Well, Tad, I suppose you did what you thought best, but I'm sure you were wrong in thinking Miss Raye did not care——'

'Why didn't she say so, then?' interrupted Tad rather resentfully.

'You'll grow wiser in some things when you grow older, my boy,' replied his father. 'In the meantime, since you know so much you may as well know the rest. As soon as Tom discovered the dreadful mistake about the report of his death, he wrote to Miss Raye and told his own story, and if he hears by the first of July that she loves him,' Mr. Jordan found his telling of a love story to his own small boy increasingly embarrassing, 'why, he will come straight out here on sick leave and marry her and take her back with him to Ireland, and if she doesn't write and accept him, why, he will go home to his father and mother and that will be the end of it—do you see?'

'But his letter to her, Dad?'

'Why, that she never got, and, poor girl, she doesn't even know he's alive, and altogether it is rather a jumble—and I don't know what to do for the best.'

'Oh, if that's it, Dad, you leave it to me. The holidays begin on Friday, and it wouldn't matter if I missed school to-morrow, and I could get a lift up north with the mailman and I could go to the Dingle and tell Miss Raye and give her the ring—that is if you're sure she hasn't gone back on Mr. Tom.'

'Oh, I'm certain enough about that, but the rest of it is not so simple. You see, Bert Enderby has asked Evelyn to marry him, and though she said "No," at the time, his mother and sister think that she could be won over in time to change her mind.'

'Still, when I tell him that Mr. Tom is alive there will be no kick coming from Mr. Bert—he's only been like a kind of substitute in a football match when one of the star players gets knocked out for a bit; when the star gets his wind he comes back into the game and the other fellow just drops out, and nobody worries about him.'

'But Mrs. Enderby will worry, and it's very awkward after a talk I had with her to-day, that I should have to take an active part in hastening a probably inevitable disappointment for all the people at the Dingle. Mrs. Enderby will try to be glad Tom's alive, and she will be nice to Miss Raye, but in the bottom of her mind she will have a grievance against me, and things will never be quite the same again. I wish I had had this letter before I went up this morning—it would have made rather a strenuous time but it would be all over by now. As it is, I promised to call for Miss Raye at the school on Friday on my way back from a visit to Mrs. Bigley—it's the last day's teaching and Miss Raye is coming down here for a visit—but I cannot call for her without letting them know about Tom first.'

'Suppose, Dad,' suggested Tad, 'that you write to Jim Hardie and tell him all about it, and ask him to tell Mr. Enderby on Friday night, and then it will get to Mrs. Enderby in a kind of round about way, and you need not be mixed up in it at all, and you can tell Miss Raye as you drive home.'

'You are very ingenious, Tad,' and a smile flickered for a moment on his father's anxious face, 'but if there's a nasty thing to be done, it may as well be done first as last, and I hate roundabout ways. I shall go to the Dingle myself on Friday; Bert and Tom were great friends and Bert ought to be a man about it, and if his mother chooses to think I've treated them badly, why, well, she must, and I must put up with it—and I suppose I can call at the school afterwards and tell——'

'I'd like to do that part of the telling,' interrupted Tad, 'You see, that was properly my job, only Miss Raye side-tracked me just when I got started—how's a fellow to know which is the right end of the stick when a girl acts up like that?'

'You needn't apologise, Tad, for your inexperience,' replied his father with a little amusement at the puzzled earnestness of Tad's question, 'the diagnosing of a woman's affections still finds me only a neophyte.'

'Well, I am not a never fight—if that's what you mean, Dad, and I don't want to do that other thing to anybody, but I shouldn't like Mr. Tom to think I'd not kept my promise.'

'Well, seriously, Tad, I believe it would be much better for you to call for Miss Raye—easier for both her and for yourself, but I don't see——' and there was a long pause during which Tad, who had sat down some time before, forked over his tousled hair with both hands in the search of inspiration. At last it came—

'Say, Dad——' and another pause. 'Say, Dad, you know the Enderby girls often use Mr. Tom's mare and buckboard for toting around, and Miss Raye sometimes drives her to school—well—suppose you drop a note to Miss Raye to-morrow and ask the mailman to leave it at the Dingle as he goes by, and you can ask her to take the buckboard to school on Friday and say you will drop me off somewhere as you go to Mrs. Bigley's, and that I will drive her down as you find you have another visit to make—that would be all right, Dad.'

Tad hastened to add as his father looked doubtful, 'It would be true—at least true enough—and if you go to the Dingle you have another visit, and it would ease things up at the Dingle for Miss Raye not to go back after they know about Tom.'

Tad's suggestion did not offer much easing up to the parson for his own visit to the Dingle, but after talking over with his wife far into the night the whole wonderful story of Tom's escape with its complication of anxiety to himself, it seemed the most promising solution of a problem so full of possibilities of both joy and sorrow to those whom fortune had brought within the circle of its activities.

CHAPTER XXXIV

THE BEGINNING OF TAD'S 'LAY-OUT'

Since no better way out of his difficulties offered, Mr. Jordan on the following morning wrote a brief note to Evelyn saying that if she would take the old mare and buckboard to school on the Friday that Tad should call for her in the afternoon and drive her down to town, since he found that he would not be able to come himself as arranged. This note, with twenty-five cents for his trouble, Tad took over early to the mailman, with many injunctions that it was to be handed personally to some member of the Dingle household. In the absence of any specific orders to the contrary Tad thought it best to return home and report the fulfilment of his errand, by which time it was too late for him to be in time for school, and his father was too preoccupied to dispute Tad's suggestion that he might as well have the day off to prepare for the next day's trip—though, except to Tad, it was not very obvious that any preparation was necessary.

For himself, Mr. Jordan found the day drag heavily on his hands; he still had one of his Sunday sermons to prepare, but after trying for an hour to concentrate his thoughts on some suitable topic for his discourse, he gave it up in despair and betook himself to the hoeing of his potatoes for the rest of the morning, and in the afternoon he wandered off down the valley and through Cowan's bush—a favourite refuge when he wished to escape from other people's troubles or his own—and to-day he felt that he had plenty of both. A meeting of the town school board, of which he was a member, brought him at last to bedtime, still feeling, as he told his wife, rather like a Guy Fawkes conspirator, waiting for the moment to apply his match to the gunpowder.

There was no need to call Tad on the Friday morning, for when his father came down for breakfast he found that Vixen had been fed an hour before and was already harnessed. Tad himself had put on his Sunday suit for the occasion and was superintending the putting up by his mother of a very plentiful lunch for himself, for it had been decided that when his father turned off the town line to go to Mrs. Bigley's, that Tad should have a little picnic by himself till it was time for him to walk the mile or so to the school-house for Evelyn—a first suggestion that he should call at one or other of the nearby settlers for dinner having been discarded as likely to expose him to awkward questions as to why he had come up to the settle-ment. Tad had no doubts as to his own ability, in his own words 'to put one over' on any too curious inquirer, but his father objected to any strain being put on the boy's strict veracity—not being accustomed himself to the breadth of view of the school-boy maxim—'Ask me no questions, and I'll tell you no lies.'

It was still quite early when they started, and Mr. Jordan drove himself till they had passed through the town and over the railway crossing, when he handed the reins to Tad with what the latter considered very unnecessary injunctions as to keeping them tight in case of Vixen's shying. Usually when he found himself alone with his father Tad was prepared to do most of the talking and was satisfied with an occasional acquiescence in his views, or answer to his questions, but he found Dad this morning so en-tirely irresponsive that at last even he relapsed into silence and his own thoughts. Thanks to Vixen's liberty to set the rate of their travelling it was as leisurely as she thought would escape a jerk of the reins or a touch of the whip, she walked up all the hills with a decent appearance of making an ef-fort and sidled down them as if afraid of her knees, with an occasional smart trot on the level to give an impression of willingness. However slowly she might go it was fast enough for her master, for the task before him only seemed the more unpleasant the nearer it came, and beyond his distaste for his own part came many misgivings as to the wisdom of allow-ing Tad to share his responsibilities. More than once he thought of going first to the school-house to see Evelyn before going to the Dingle—well, he would suggest the idea to Tad—they were within a half mile of where he was to turn off the town line and it must be settled one way or the other.

'I suppose, Tad, you wouldn't like me to go down to the school-house now, before I go to Mrs. Bigley's; perhaps, you know, it would be——'

'Oh, no, Dad,' and if his father hesitated, Tad was quite decisive, 'why, of course, that's my job.'

'Still, it won't do for you to go blurting it out suddenly—it would be a great shock——'

'Of course, I sha'n't blurt it out, Dad—why, I've been figuring it out all the way up and got it down fine—I've got a regular lay-out for the whole show.'

'That's all very well in your mind, my boy, but very often what you call a "regular lay-out" does not work when the time comes—and Miss Raye's mind may go swift to a conclusion before you get started—and I'm afraid of the consequences.'

'Oh, that's because you're used to what you call "breaking bad news,"' said Tad shrewdly, 'good news won't hurt. Of course, she may give a squeal or cry a bit, but she'll be so jolly glad Mr. Tom's alive that she'll soon get over it—and if there is anything of that sort it would be a lot nastier if we were both there than only one—and she won't mind a kid like me.'

'Well, perhaps you are right, Tad, and we will leave it so; in any case you had better tell Miss Raye before you hitch up to leave the schoolhouse, and there's Mrs. Brady's close by if you need any help of any kind —I wish it was all over.'

'Oh, we shall be all right, Dad, and you'll find us as gay as larks when you get home—and here's the turn in your road—Whoa, Vixen.'

Tad handed his father the reins and jumped out—'Wait a minute, Dad, while I get my lunch out at the back—that's all right—I'll mooch around for wild strawberries for a bit and then go and have my dinner down by the creek, and put in the time till the afternoon—good-bye.'

'Good-bye, Tad, take your time driving in to-night, and mind the crossing at the railway—good-bye.'

'Dad's a good sort,' thought Tad, as he stood in the road and watched the buggy till it disappeared behind a bluff in a turn of the trail, 'he's a good sort, but he's the limit to fidget about a fellow's driving—I suppose he can't help it,' with which kindly allowance for his father's weakness Tad slung his schoolbag containing his luncheon over his shoulder, and getting over the snake fence into the field adjoining the road, took his way to a little cluster of trees by the creek, where he had before determined to have his dinner, and to think out finally his plans for his part of the show, which plans were not quite so devoid of difficulties as he had allowed his father to believe.

When Mr. Jordan had put on one side as irrelevant his half-expressed wonder as to what had become of Tom's letter to Evelyn, that was the end of it as far as he was concerned; he had enough evident difficulties to encounter without bringing in further ones by conjecture, but his remark had set Tad thinking—not so much as to what might have become of the letter as of what it might contain of interest to himself. He did not suppose that the letter itself mattered so very much to Evelyn now—Tom was alive and would be coming back himself soon—that would be the big thing for her— but since Mr. Tom had evidently told his father about that conversation down by the river in Cowan's bush and about the ring, it might very well be—so Tad thought—that Tom's letter to Evelyn would have something to say of his promise to bring home some African curiosities for Tad; probably since Mr. Jack was dead and he had been wounded himself Mr. Tom would not care to bring back the live Boer shell, but the assegais would be all right; or some Dutch coins, they would be very much easier to keep as the nucleus of his collection of coins than the occasional pieces of foreign silver which found their way into the collection plate, as not probably negotiable at the candy store—and of course, there would be some stamps, if unused he would be ahead of any of the other fellows at school.

The longer he thought about it, the more Tad felt that the missing letter must be found—it was all very well for Dad to put it on one side, and, of course, Dad would not go and ask old Dawson any good straight questions —Dad hated to be nasty, even to an old crank like that, but since Dad had not actually forbidden him there was no reason why he should not go to the office up north and do a little nosing around for himself. Surely Mr. Jordan's misgivings, as he left Tad standing by the side of the road, would have been largely increased if he had dreamt of what his son included in the vague term 'a regular lay-out for the whole show.'

A cursory examination of such wild strawberry plants as he found among the grass round the willow scrub satisfied Tad that the berries were too small and too unripe to be worth the trouble of picking, so though he judged by the sun that it was not yet noon, he decided to eat his lunch— that could be stretched out for an hour or so by reading the sporting sheet of the *Free Press* in which it was wrapped, and then by following the roundabout course of the creek to where it passed at the back of old Dawson's buildings, he would get rid of the time till the men would be out in the fields again, and he would be nearly sure to find Mary Ann alone. Everything seemed to favour his plans, for, when an hour or two later he came out of a bluff through which the creek ran and in sight of the post-office, he had the satisfaction of seeing old Dawson and the hired man drive off in a wagon with a wide-spreading hay-rack on it, evidently on their way to the hay meadows, and so the course was clear. Tad watched the wagon till it went out of sight down the trail, and then leaving the creek he struck across the open piece of prairie so as to reach the road between the town line and the house. He endeavoured to make his approach in as casual a manner as possible, in case Mary Ann was looking from the windows, and stopped now and again to pick a flower or two, or to look for suppositional strawberries by the wayside, but when he came to the open gateway, leading through the garden and potato patch to the house, there was nothing for it but to take his courage in both hands and go straight up to the door—his last thought as he knocked on it with his knuckles being—'Hang it all, she's only a woman and can't eat me, and anyway, they don't keep a dog.'

A second knock, and a sharp voice called out—'Come in, sure you're in a hurry.'

It did not sound very promising, but as Tad opened the door and entered the voice changed to a much more friendly tone, 'Why, if it isn't the minister's son—come right in—I thought it was one of the neighbour's children—they come worriting after their mail and can't wait for a body to dry their hands—I'm just mixing the butter down—and how's your Pa and the folks to home—I suppose you're staying up to the Dingle again for your holidays?'

'Oh no, Miss Dawson, not yet, though I am to come up a little later when the wild raspberries are ripe. I just came up with Dad—he's gone to see Mrs. Bigley——'

'Ah, I heard at meeting on Sunday as how she was very low; by your Pa coming up I guess they don't think she's going to last long—and her with three little tots and a husband that never comes home from town, not to say sober—and you'll be waiting round for your Pa to pick you up on his way back—but sure alive! I'm forgetting, and you won't have had your dinner.'

'Oh yes, thank you, I've just had my lunch down by the creek——'

'Well, a hearty boy like you can always do with a bit of pie or cake extra, and I'll get you a drink of fresh buttermilk.'

'Oh no, thank you, Miss Dawson, I had a big lunch and I have a lot left in my bag; I couldn't eat a bit more,' and Tad spoke with a hasty decisiveness, for this preferred kindly hospitality threatened to disorganise his contemplated 'lay-out.'

'Well, if you say so, I'll just go on with my mixing, and you can rest a while and maybe have a piece before your Pa calls for you.'

'Oh, I'm not going back with Dad,' Tad felt he must make a plunge. 'I'm going to call at the school for Miss Raye and to drive her down to town with Mr. Tom Dennis's mare and the buckboard that's been at the Dingle all winter and——'

'Well, that will be fine for you all—there isn't a nicer-mannered nor to say kinder-hearted young lady in this country—and the folks say the way she gets the children on in their learning is just wonderful. There's Mrs. M'Tavish was telling me only last week as how her little Pete—and if there's an idle little rapscallion in the district he's it—can just figger like a ——' Mary Ann's momentary mental search for a worthy comparison let Tad into the conversation with a rush.'

'And I've got great news for her—just great,' and in spite of Tad's effort to keep cool there must have been a thrill in his voice, for Mary Ann stopped suddenly in her work and looked at him sharply.

'Why, what does the boy mean? If there's any bad news for her your Pa has never left a child like you to go and tell her—it would be a shame—so it would.'

'I did not say it was bad news,' protested Tad, 'it's good news—just splendid—there's been a letter come to Dad—you're not going to be sick, Miss Dawson?' for at the word 'letter' Mary Ann went suddenly as near white as her complexion allowed, and clutched at the side of the table.

'Oh, it's nothing—nothing at all—I have a dizzy spell at times these hot days, when I stoop over my work—but you was saying "your Pa," ' and Mary Ann resumed her work, this time with her back to Tad.

'Dad had a letter on Wednesday from the father of the Dennis boys, who used to be up here and went to the war—it was Mr. Jack that was killed and his brother is all well and alive.'

'Sure, now, and that is great news—father, he'll be real pleased—he always liked that Tom one best—he was more friendly like when he came for his mail.' Though Mary Ann's voice was fairly steady there was a dull tone in it. 'But why need you go telling the schoolma'am, poor thing, it will only worrit her and it's not likely as the young man will ever come back to this country.'

'Oh yes, but he will—and I guess it won't be very long first, for he's to get sick leave—you see he was wounded—and Dad thinks he may be back in six weeks from now.'

Poor Mary Ann felt as if the solid earth were crumbling under her feet, but she was not one to yield without a struggle. 'Well, if I were your Pa I wouldn't go for to tell Miss Raye as he was a-coming back before you know for sure—maybe he will be for going home first—in course, I couldn't help hearing what folks said about his being took with the schoolma'am last summer—folks know so much about their neighbours round hereabout—and I'm sure no one would be gladder nor I should for her to be happy—still, after you've gone and told everybody, if he didn't come back it would be terrible hard on her, folks would be saying——'

'Oh, you bet, he'll come back,' the suggestion of faithlessness on Tom's part robbed Tad of his last compunction. 'You bet your—your bottom dollar.' Tad blushed at his narrow escape from an indelicacy. 'He'll come like a shot when he gets the tip, and Dad is going to cable to-night if everything is all right.'

'Your Pa seems to be very busy all at once,' said Mary Ann acidly. 'I think a minister like him might be better employed looking after folks as is alive than trying to bring back them as the papers says is dead—and himself as good as preaching their funeral sermon—I call it less than decent.'

'I don't care what you call decent,' retorted Tad, with an angry flush at the reflection on his father. 'I guess Mr. Tom won't call it "decent" when he finds Miss Raye never got his letter, and he'll get as busy as Dad when he gets back.'

'What's the boy talking about with his "letter"?' and Mary Ann appealed scornfully with outspread open hands to some imaginary third person. 'If folks send letters from forrin, heathen lands, where everybody is a-fightin', they've only themselves to blame if they get lost, without casting their slurs on decent folks as never lost a one in twenty years; you ask the postmaster in town and see what he'll tell you.'

'I did ask the postmaster in town,' Tad's temper was running away with his manners, 'and he remembers the letter quite well, for he says the letter was so fat that he weighed it twice over to see if it was overweight, and then let it slide because if he put the overcharge on it your father as likely as not would not send the five cents down.'

The evidences of Mary Ann being 'sick' this time were so evident and alarming that Tad's anger evaporated as quickly as it had arisen, for she stumbled rather than walked to her father's old arm chair by the stove and threw her apron over her head.

'It's a cruel boy as you are, to come telling a lonely woman as she's a thief,' she sobbed. 'My poor mother would turn in her grave if she knew as she'd worn herself into her grave keeping the floor clean after a lot of idle young fellows as never wiped their feet, be it never so muddy outside, and her that careful she wouldn't mislay even an almanac for kidney pills if so be as it had a name on it—only to be called a thief after all—it's cruel hard, so it is.'

Tad had anticipated some possible emotion on the part of Evelyn in his lay-out, but of a distinctly pleasurable nature, though possibly embarrassing; this collapse of Mary Ann was altogether beyond his calculations.

'But, Miss Dawson,' he stammered, 'nobody says you are a—nobody thinks anybody has—I didn't even say—not for sure, that I knew Miss Raye hadn't got the letter—but that I thought she hadn't, and I'd ask her so that I could get the stamp for my collection—and the postmaster just said that perhaps it hadn't been called for or perhaps got in the wrong box—he *did* say that the post-office people in the country were a kind of—a—amateurs, you know, and not regulars like their clerks in town.'

Mary Ann's sobs were subsiding and she was doing some hard, if rather spasmodic, thinking behind her apron.

'Well, perhaps you didn't mean to speak so hard—and you a minister's son—and indeed your Pa did call up after mother's funeral and was as kind as could be, and said a prayer just as if we had been his own folks.'

'Oh, I'm sure Dad never thought a thing about it,' said Tad, much relieved to get on easier going, 'and all that the postmaster said was that perhaps it had got a—kind of delayed—you know.'

'It is just possible,' and Mary Ann's voice implied a very remote contingency as she wiped her eyes on her apron and rose from her chair, 'it's just possible if it came on that day when father sorted the mail, because I hadn't cleaned myself after the butter-making, and that boy from the Dingle was fussing to get their letters before I could go over them myself—and father's reading of print, let alone writing, isn't to be trusted, even when he's got his glasses on—I'm not saying but what he might make a mistake, and if it will make you easier like I don't mind looking over the boxes.'

'I'm sure if you would it would be awfully kind of you,' said Tad gratefully, 'and I don't mind waiting while you finish the butter and can have a good look.'

The butter finished, Mary Ann retired to her room—to wash her hands, she said, and after a delay of a few minutes reappeared.

'Here's a picture book as you can be a-looking at while I go over the boxes,' she said, handing Tad a copy of the *Graphic*. 'It's for Miss Raye and came only yesterday, and I'm sure she would not mind your opening it, and you can take it along to her.'

This, perhaps, hardly matched with her claim to exactness in following office regulations, but it was not desirable that Tad should follow her too closely in her search for the missing letter, and Tad was entirely unsuspicious. He had done little more than slip it out of its cover and straighten out the stiff leaves to look the better at the pictures when Mary Ann gave a startled cry—when not too flustered Mary Ann had considerable talent—rather warped and developed along wrong lines.

'Sure to mercy! and if here is not a letter for Miss Raye,' and she turned quickly round from the office desk, 'from Africa and all, and with the letters T. M. D. in the corner, just as I often mind seeing on Mr. Tom's letters to his Ma—now, isn't that real wonderful?' and she looked Tad steadily in the eye.

Tad was almost too pleased to speak. 'Why, that's great, Miss Dawson, I'm jolly glad I came, I'll take it right along to Miss Raye—she won't be glad—oh, not at all!'

'And you'll tell her how sorry I am father made such a slip—be sure I'll never leave him to sort the mail again, and you'll be certain and let Miss Raye know how it happened—to think as it's been lying here among some old bills of father's as had nothing to do with the office at all—and the poor dear never to know.'

'Oh yes, I'll tell her exactly,' promised Tad eagerly and in all good faith as he took the letter, 'and I'll tell the postmaster in town that she's got it all right—and she'll be so pleased with the good news I've got that I'm sure she won't blame you a bit, and besides, it wasn't your fault, was it, Miss Dawson?'

'Well, I hope she'll forgive me—us all, I mean, and give her my love and tell her as there's never a one as hopes she will be happy more true than Mary Ann Dawson—now, maybe you'd best be going or school will be out—good-bye.'

It had been a Waterloo for all Mary Ann's plans, but thanks to the open frankness of Tad's disposition, she felt she had made a good retreat from the battlefield—though she realised from a sudden weakness in her knees that if he did not go soon, that his evident trust in her good faith would bring a greater breakdown and sickness than that which had at the first proved so alarming and disconcerting to poor Tad's 'lay-out.'

CHAPTER XXXV

'GIRLS ARE THE LIMIT'

If Mary Ann was anxious that he should go, it may be taken for granted that Tad was no less willing to be gone. That his leave-taking was rather informal may be inferred from his answer to his mother's inquiry, that she hoped he had not forgotten his manners.

'Well, you see, mother, she seemed so keen on getting rid of me that I just opened the door and beat it,' which, since kindness is courtesy, should save Tad's reputation for good breeding. In truth, so afraid was the boy of a second encounter with any of the Dawson family that he continued to 'beat it' till the post office was out of sight and he was well on the crossroad leading to the school-house. Feeling sure at length that there was now no risk of meeting old Dawson or of being overtaken by Mary Ann, if she should change her mind and want the letter back, he slackened his speed, first from a run to a rapid walk, and finally turned off the track and threw himself down under a clump of willows to recover his breath and to consider how far he should follow out his morning ideas for what, in his mind, he had called the second part of the show. The first part had certainly been unpleasant beyond his anticipations, and he admitted to himself that he had been far too cocksure—but then, he had got the letter—and he took it out of his pocket and submitted it to a close examination. It was smeary and grubby looking—but then he had read that the soldiers in Africa often had hardly enough water to drink, and even Mr. Tom, who was always so clean, might not be able to spare any to wash with—or—of course, that was it— old Dawson's fingers would be sure to be dirty—they always were—but it was good and thick. While allowing for all 'that sort of thing'—even mentally Tad preferred a paraphrase for the expression of the softer emotions— surely, such a jolly, fat letter called for some things that were worth writing about. However that might be, the telling of Evelyn came between his hopes and their realisation, and Tad came back from dreams to realities. Of course, it was much pleasanter to tell good news than bad, but he had undoubtedly blurted with Mary Ann, and though he could not imagine Miss Raye going sick in the same horrid way, might there not be other manifestations for joy which would be equally, or even more alarming. If Dad had come along at that moment, it is quite certain that Tad would willingly have resigned the running of the show, and have been quite satisfied with what politicians call a position of greater freedom and less responsibility—but Dad was not likely to come along—very probably at that very moment he might be engaged in his own show at the Dingle—and the thought of its exceeding unpleasantness gave Tad a fresh courage for his own self-imposed task.

'I guess I'll just wade in and trust to luck,' he said to himself, as he got on his feet and brushed off the bits of dead grass and twigs from his clothes. 'There's one thing jolly sure, she can't cut up rough with me——' and then his mind swung to the opposite extreme of possibility—'Great Scott! She'll never get soft and kiss me and think it's Mr. Tom,' and Tad was red to the roots of his hair.

'If it were done, when 'tis done, then 'twere well it were done quickly'—a favourite saying of his father's when going on a disagreeable errand came into Tad's mind as he walked along, and he quickened his pace at its suggestion. What a lot of tommy-rot there must be in those old fellows his father was so fond of quoting and wanting him to read—probably that was a bit of Dickens or Scott or some other wise guy—if a thing was done, of course, it was done, and there was no bally 'if' about it. There was Pete M'Tavish coming out of the school door—he must hurry along.

A dozen or more boys and girls followed in Peter's wake, and as Tad entered the school-room he found Miss Raye sitting writing at her desk. She looked up as he entered—'Why, Tad, it's you, how nice of you to come for me. I'll be ready in a minute when I've finished making up my school register for the term.'

'All right, Miss Raye, I'll just have a look around for a while at the pictures and things on the wall.'

'Very well, Tad, there's nothing very wonderful, I'm afraid, just little maps and drawings of the children's doing,' and Miss Raye resumed her writing.

'Nothing very wonderful,' as Miss Raye said, but still, Tad found them interesting—he was somewhat of a map drawer himself, though with no taste for the more artistic use of the pencil—and he mentally contrasted the Lakeside productions with the town school standard. 'Some artists in colour, these country kids,' he criticised to himself, as he came to a row of maps of Manitoba, tacked up on the wainscoting side by side, 'pretty high blue for their lakes, and every one's got Minnedosa marked bigger than Winnipeg, and the little Saskatchewan a regular St. Lawrence, guess they haven't travelled much.' Tad had been once to Brandon and twice to Neepawa.

'Say, Miss Raye, this is no kid's map,' and he pointed to a larger map placed higher on the wall.

'Oh, that's nothing, Tad, just something I began and never kept up—I'm ready now, just as soon as I've put my books away.'

'Oh, that's nothing,' thought Tad to himself, with a second sharp glance at the map before he passed on to the next picture, and a nasty lump in his throat, 'that's nothing, but it says—"Route of the Canadian Contingent in Africa"—and it ends with a cross at Modder River, and our fellows are up at Pretoria.'

'I wonder why it is,' he went on aloud, 'that the boys draw the best maps and the girls draw the best pictures of flowers and things.'

'Just part of the inequality of the sexes, I expect, Tad,' replied Evelyn with a little laugh, 'boys for travel and girls to stay at home. Now, we'll have a little lunch that I brought on purpose, and then you may hitch up for me—for although I can take the harness off a horse I'm always a little hazy about which strap goes into which buckle in putting it on—those ones that go underneath, you know.'

'Oh yes, I know,' replied Tad with great confidence, 'but it's funny, your bringing a lunch, for I saved some of mine, too—some lettuce sandwiches and a hunk of mother's cake.'

'And I have some bread and butter and a little jar of cranberry jelly in my pail; why, we'll have quite a feast—you might bring in some fresh, cold water from the well, and I will set our little table.'

So far, everything was delightful—Evelyn seemed in the best of spirits. Tad little knew how relieved she was at the prospect of escape from the Dingle—at least it was a respite, and Tad was always ready for a meal, especially when it was free from the usual formalities of plates and knives and forks. It was not till the last sandwich was gone and Evelyn was replacing her napkin and the little jelly jar in her pail that Tad realised that he still had to make the first step in the breaking of his news—forgotten for the last half hour, it came back upon him all at once. However was he to begin?

'Say, Miss Raye, I suppose I'd better be hitching up, or would you like to rest awhile?'

'Rest a while! Why, Tad, I've been in the school-room all day—I shall be just delighted to be moving.'

'Oh, yes, of course,' said Tad awkwardly, 'only it's easier you know, to talk sitting down; well, I'll get the mare—and, oh, I brought a paper from the post-office for you.'

'For me, why, have you been up to Mr. Dawson's, Tad?'

'Yes, I just—kind of dropped in there, you know, and Miss Dawson said you wouldn't mind my opening it to look at the pictures.'

'Of course not, Tad, and you can put it in the little box under the seat of the buckboard—I suppose there were no letters for me at the office?'

191

'I think I'll put the paper and your pail and things in the rig first,' replied Tad hurriedly and running towards the door, then turning quickly as he reached it, in desperation—'I suppose you weren't expecting any—particular letter, Miss Raye?'

'Oh no, Tad; now Chris is out here, we are all here; you see we are a very small family—and there's no one to write what you call "particular" letters.'

Such a smile of unconscious sadness passed over Evelyn's face—such a touch of entire and accepted loneliness sounded in the quiet tones of her voice, that all Tad's elaborately-thought-out procedure for breaking his news carefully forsook him utterly, and left him as helpless as a rudderless boat in the whirl of Niagara.

'Oh, don't say that, Miss Raye, and don't look like—like a fellow that's hooked a whale of a jackfish and it goes and snaps the line on him. Dad had a letter on Wednesday, and there was one in it for you, and a jolly particular one, too.'

'Why, Tad, what can you mean—a letter in your father's for me?'

'Oh, that shouldn't come yet, Miss Raye, only you've got me rattled—but it was a good letter—just a splendid letter—and we are all tickled to death—and Dad's gone to tell the Enderbys—and if Mr. Bert is broke up it serves him right—but you're glad aren't you, Miss Raye—isn't it great?'

'Oh, Tad dear, do try and tell me what you mean,' and Evelyn, pale and trembling came hurriedly to him and laid her hand on the boy's shoulder. 'There's only one could send me good news, and that's impossible.'

'Nothing's impossible, Miss Raye, not when the newspapers go and make such rotten mistakes and put the names all wrong in the paper.'

'Tad, Tad, for heaven's sake, tell me.'

'Aren't I telling you?' and Tad tried to think it was just impatience at Evelyn's slowness of comprehension that was making his voice so husky and full of jerks—'and if I make a mess of telling you Dad will be as mad as a wet hen—but Mr. Tom Dennis was never dead, and he isn't dead now —and, please, Miss Raye—I—promised Dad I'd be careful and not scare you, and there you are going on worse than Miss Dawson,' which was literally and alarmingly true, for after a convulsive effort to steady herself by her hand on his shoulder, Evelyn's grasp suddenly relaxed and she slid limply to the floor. From his habit of asking questions Tad's mind was stocked with a very varied assortment of odds and ends of information as regards behaviour at births, deaths and marriages, and here was Evelyn, as he said afterwards to his mother—mixing things all up with a funeral stunt just when he was working up to a wedding march.

He had heard of people fainting before but had always been rather sceptical of it, looking on it as just a girl's trick to be made a fuss over—

192

Oh, yes, he had seen one once—that stout old lady that tumbled off the bench last Fair day after a heavy dinner in the Church tent on Show day—he remembered how Dad had sprinkled a glass of iced lemonade—the first thing handy—on her face, and then he loosened—but that was impossible for him—he'd try the other, and he hastily fetched a cup of cold water from the school pail and sprinkled a few drops gingerly on Evelyn's face. He was immensely relieved in a few minutes to see the colour returning first to her cheeks and then to her lips—she wasn't dead anyway, which was his first panicstricken thought. Her eyes opened, at first vaguely, and then, as memory came struggling back, 'I'm so sorry, Tad, for being so foolish, you were telling me——'

'I'm not going to tell you any more unless you'll promise not to go and scare a fellow——'

'But it is true, Tad? Please help me,' and Tad took her hand as she rose up, and with the help of his arm reached the chair by her desk—'But it's true that Mr. Dennis——'

'Mr. Jack was killed and Mr. Tom wounded—and he's nearly better, and he's going to get sick leave.'

'And is he going home to Ireland?' and a blush came with the question.

'Oh, yes, he's going home to Ireland——' Tad's self-confidence was evidently returning, 'but he's coming round this way—kind of longest way round the shortest way home.'

'But Tad, dear, how do you know? It's all so very wonderful—and why did you come to tell me—of course I am—sorry poor Mr. Jack is dead, and —you're sure it is true, Tad?' with a fresh flush of anxiety.

'Do you think I'd have let myself in for—for all this sort of thing if it wasn't?' protested Tad with some energy—'why, their father wrote to Dad, and they've got it all fixed up, and there's a letter for you from Mr. Tom's mother—a kind of backing Mr. Tom up, I guess, and all you've got to do is just to send Mr. Tom a cable saying—you—tumble to it, and he'll start right away.'

'Oh, but—Tad,' and Evelyn's face was a confusion of blushes and embarrassment—'Mr. Tom has not written a word to me, and even if what you say is true I couldn't——' and the roses became peonies.

'Oh, but he has written,' replied Tad eagerly, 'you won't go and be—soft again?' with a sharp look of distrust, 'He wrote, and the letter came a month ago.'

'But why, why did I not get it?—Who could be so cruel?'

'Oh, it was just old man Dawson got it mixed up with his own papers, and Miss Dawson never knew it had come till I called, and she found it, and she's awfully sorry about it; however, it's all right now, and I guess it doesn't matter—only there may be a message for me, you know—perhaps you can read it as we go along?'

'Oh, give it me now, please, Tad,' and Tom's heart would have been satisfied if he could have seen the trembling eagerness of her hands as she took the letter from Tad—'Perhaps you would not mind hitching up, and then I will be ready.'

Tad certainly did not mind hitching up, and escaped thankfully to the shed where he executed a *pas seul*, much, probably, to the astonishment of the old mare. Though full of curiosity as to the contents of the letter as affecting himself he loitered as long as he could over the harnessing and hitching up, and then sat for some minutes on the porch step. He felt, as he said afterwards, that he thought there would be less risk of any further display of feeling if he let his news and the letter 'soak in.'

Perhaps he may not have waited long enough, and there may have been too great a fullness of feeling for the completion of that process. The fact remains that when he re-entered the school-house Evelyn met him at the door, and 'before a fellow could do anything she just put her arms round my neck—yes—and kissed me twice—girls are the limit!'

Tad did not hurry the mare to town, and Dad, who had been home for a couple of hours, and who had been waiting for them anxiously, was thankful for Tad's whispered aside as he jumped out of the buggy first, 'You bet, it's all right, Dad; she's got the ring on her finger, and is as happy as a clam,' which is allowing great capacity to the clam.

It was late on the following morning when Evelyn entered the dining-room, where Tad and his father were lingering over their breakfast, and there was a happy, if shy blush on Evelyn's cheeks as, after the usual greetings, she turned to the parson. 'Would you mind, Mr. Jordan, sending a message——' and the grin on Tad's face broadened as she hesitated, 'a message, a cablegram I think they call it, to—Mr. Tom—just to say——'

'Oh, after what you told me coming down, Miss Raye, I thought that was part of my job and I sent one an hour ago.'

'Oh, but Tad, dear, whatever, whatever did you say?'

'I just said, "You're first, rest nowhere, beat it for Minnedosa. Love from Evelyn. Tad Jordan." '

The boy was evidently reckless of the results of this fresh evidence of the completeness of his lay-out, and left his father to face any embarrassment on the part of Evelyn that might follow.

CHAPTER XXXVI

AN OPEN QUESTION

Though the parson was scandalised, and Evelyn brought to the blush by the sporting form of Tad's cablegram, the boy himself was entirely unashamed, and when in the course of a few days an answer—or rather two answers, came, one to Evelyn herself and one to Tad, he felt that he had entirely the best of the argument. 'My English may be pretty rocky, Dad, but you see it did the trick. In his cable to me Mr. Tom says he is bringing me stacks—that's his own word, Dad—of curiosities, and though Miss Raye did not show me her own she looked so jolly rosy and happy that I scooted out of the room—for fear—she might do it again, you know.' In some things boys of that age are as disingenuous as their sisters a few years older.

Now that it was all over Tad was secretly rather more than proud of the success of his show—the only weak point to his mind being the rather uncomfortable terms on which he had left Miss Dawson, and even that was removed a week or two later.

Evelyn was in the hammock under the trees in the rectory garden, with a book on her lap for appearance sake, when Tad came running round the corner of the house. 'Oh, I say, Miss Raye, there's Miss Dawson in the study, and she wants to see you and she's got a big parcel and she looks kind of shaky. You won't be down on her about the letter, will you? I'm sure she was awfully sorry, and she can't help old Dawson being her father, you know.'

That Evelyn was not 'down on her' may be inferred from the fact that Mary Ann looked unmistakably happy when she left the rectory an hour or so later. She had made a full and entire confession of her lapse from the narrow path of official righteousness and regard to the regulations of the office; her peace offering of her cherished quilt had been accepted with some blushes—'she's a dear old thing, and it was delightful of her to give it to me,' Evelyn confided to Mrs. Jordan afterwards when she showed her the *chef d'œuvre* in the privacy of her own room—'but I wouldn't for worlds show it to anybody else—not till afterwards.' For Tad, Mary Ann left her love and a large package of very high-grade cookies. 'I never could have had the courage to tell you,' she admitted tearfully to Evelyn as she brought her confession to a close, 'if it had not been for the child—his eyes were that kind and trustful, and me telling him a black lie—the poor innocent—it near broke my heart after he had gone—so it did.'

Now slowly, now swiftly, the days passed away for Evelyn; sometimes to her wistful longing it seemed as though the ship that was bringing her lover to her would never reach port; at other times she would be seized with a panic of shyness as to how she should have the courage to meet him when he came.

Tad never relaxed in his devotion to his trust, though he could not forbear wondering at the intricacy of the female mind as revealed by the frequent changes in Evelyn's spirits. As usual he took his wonders to Dad.

'Miss Raye's awfully nice—for a girl—sometimes pretty near as good as a boy—and I wouldn't say a word to any one else, but she's a bit batty—yesterday she sat in the hammock all afternoon and just mooned, and this afternoon down in Cowan's bush, when we were picking cranberries she was as wild as a hawk—scrambled over the fallen logs and laughed when she tore her petticoats and raced me for more than fifty yards down the trail and nearly beat me—I guess when Mr. Tom has married her he'll wonder some days where he has got off at.'

The *Hibernian*, homeward bound, was steaming slowly down the St. Lawrence, and Tom Dennis and his wife were standing on deck, watching the sun sink behind old Quebec. The kindly shelter of a life-boat gave what Tom judged was a sufficient privacy for his arm to rest on Evelyn's waist —'You see, that arm is a bit stiff yet from the old Dutchman's bullet, and it aches if I let it just hang loose,' and Evelyn accepted the excuse as sufficient. 'Do you know, Evelyn, that though I meant to ask you if you would have me—and pretty nearly did a year ago—yet actually as a matter of fact I never did—and I suppose it's too late now?'

'Well, Tom dear, I'm afraid it is, since what you call your Irishman's luck has hampered you with a wife without the asking—still, it would only be keeping up the name of your countrymen to marry first and do your asking afterwards.'

'If you make fun of my Connemara ways I'll just kiss you where you stand, and the ship's parson is nursing the first sensation of sea-sickness right at the end of the boat—and as for marrying first and courting afterwards, why, as we say at home—there are worse things than that same.'

A few minutes' silence, and the sun, who had been blushing for some time, discreetly hid his face at a turn of the river—'How dusk it's got all at once, Tom,' and Evelyn looked up in Tom's face. 'I didn't tease you, did I, Tom?'

That's always been an open question between them—but Tom maintained that he was justified by the terms of his threat.

THE END

www.ingramcontent.com/pod-product-compliance
Lightning Source LLC
Chambersburg PA
CBHW011718240626
47153CB00009B/2902